HUNTED PRINCESS

CURSED THRONE

BOOK THREE

ALEXA B. JAMES

Hunted Princess

Published in the United States by Alexa B. James and Speak Now.
Cover design by Fantasy Book Designs

ISBN: 978-1-945780-69-1

Trigger warning

This book features material that some may find offensive, including violent dubcon and extreme taboo. If you have hard limits, I recommend returning this title for a refund

ONE

Itzel
Princess, Ocelot Nation

MY DEATH WAS QUICK, IF NOT PAINLESS. THE PAIN came at once, like a blow, so intense that it obliterated my entire being. One moment, I was a human, scared and screaming as an enormous tiger leapt at me. The next, I was only pain. There was no scream. No sound could give voice to the pain of a dozen dagger teeth sinking into my throat at once. My voice was gone the next instant, my throat ripped from my neck in the smash of teeth, the sanity-erasing wall of pain.

And then it was over. The teeth. The pain. My life.

DARKNESS.

Darkness.

Darkness.

"No!" The voice was not mine. The sound startled me back to a reality I shouldn't exist within. It wasn't a sound at all, not one I could hear with my ears. It was more of a sensation. The knowledge that someone was protesting my departure. Or...

Arrival.

The world came back into focus around me, but it wasn't the world I knew, the one I should inhabit. At least not the one I thought I should inhabit. There was nothing around me but vague shapes, like shadows shrouded in fog.

I was myself, and yet... Different.

"Itzel."

A familiar voice spoke my name, one I had never forgotten, one I thought of every single day.

"Mom?" My voice quavered like the little girl I had been when I lost her. I'd had one moment with her before I'd had to go the last time. This time, I had a feeling my time in this place might last a bit longer. My throat threatened to close, but I wouldn't think of all I'd left behind. I'd only think of her.

Suddenly, my mother was in front of me, taking my hands in hers. "What are you doing here?" she asked, her eyes full of anguish. "You shouldn't be here. Not so soon... Surely not yet."

"Where am I?"

Her gaze turned sympathetic, and she pulled me into her arms. I didn't remember the smell of her until that moment. When I'd walked in the spirit world before, my sense of smell must not have accompanied me. Now, I was enveloped by the sweet, slightly spicy scent I'd forgotten that I'd ever known, like cinnamon and oranges.

"You've just come through the veil between worlds," she whispered into my thick, dark mass of hair. "You're in the spirit world now."

"It's not possible," I said, the ache of tears building behind my eyes. "I was just alive. I was going to get the next amulet. Everything was..."

I couldn't finish that sentence. Everything hadn't been good or normal. I'd just shoved my sister, the heir to my nation's throne, out of a helicopter. I had stolen the amulets halfway through her Amulet Tour. I had become the thing she'd accused me of—a traitor.

"What happened?" Mom asked, stroking my hair.

Tears filled my eyes, spilling over my eyelids and down my cheeks. I was sure they did because I knew I was crying, but I couldn't feel their wetness against my skin.

"I don't know," I said, my breath catching. I didn't want to know. I couldn't. One minute I'd been alive, and now I was... Here.

"It's okay," she said. "You can remember later, when you're ready."

"There's nothing to remember," I said. Hearing myself, I sounded like the petulant child who had pretended she didn't care that the other shifter kids wouldn't invite her to their exclusive shifter-only parties. Denial was a survival mechanism for me, which was ironic considering that I was still doing it even though I hadn't survived. Apparently, I didn't cope well with my own death.

"Do you want to go somewhere to talk?" Mom asked. "Is there anyone else you'd like to see or speak with?"

I remembered my last visit to the spirit world, how rushed it was. I hadn't had time for questions then. Now, I had time until eternity. For a moment, I thought of Tadeu. I'd tried to summon him last time, but he'd refused to come. The rejection still stung, and I shook my head, refusing to think about what that meant. Denial seemed to be the theme of my death, and I was sticking with it for now.

"No," I said. "But let's go talk. Can we eat here?"

She smiled. "Of course. Anything you want."

She took my hand and squeezed. I had been so focused on her that I hadn't noticed that our surroundings had stayed sort of... Vague. Now, as she pulled me along, everything filled in around us. Suddenly we were on a narrow, winding path that led to an open wooden gazebo next to a blossoming cherry tree. It was nothing I'd ever seen before, and I wondered if my mother had conjured it from her past, from a world she'd known before I existed.

Inside the gazebo, which was shaped a bit differently than the ones I'd seen before, we sat on a bench made of woven bamboo. Mom patted the spot between us, and I looked down to find two plates with small cakes on them, and two saucers holding full, steaming teacups.

"One of the benefits of the spirit world," she said with a small smile. "It's not all bad here, Itzel. I don't mind it. You should know that. I'm happy here."

"Is that why you didn't want to go back?" I asked, picking up the tea. It felt weightless in my hand. I could taste the tea, and I knew that it was hot, but it didn't burn my tongue as real tea might.

"Prince Kwame should have protected you," she said. "I thought he would do it better than I ever could. I don't know why that didn't happen."

"It's not his fault," I said. "He would have protected me. It happened too fast. Like an ambush."

Mom sipped her tea and looked pensive. "I don't suppose I could have saved you from that, either," she said. "At least we have some time together now. I hate to say this, but I hope it isn't too much time. I hope he can find a way to bring you back, just as you did him."

"Is that possible?" I asked, tears aching in my throat as I reached out to squeeze her hand. I loved my mother, and I

5

wanted to cry like a baby because she was here, but I didn't want to stay here forever. If there was any chance that I could go back, I'd do it in an instant. I knew that with every ounce of certainty I possessed. I didn't belong here. I wasn't ready.

But was anyone ever ready? That wasn't the sort of thing people got to decide.

"Itzel," Mom said, setting down her tea and taking my other hand in hers. "In case we don't have much time, I want to tell you something. I should have told you last time, but there are laws that govern me even now."

"Don't tell me the spirit world has something scarier than an ocelot guard," I said, trying to lighten the moment. I could feel the impending truth pressing in, a heavy truth that would soon be mine to bear. Fear made me want to turn away from what was coming.

"An ocelot guard is a kitten compared to Lilith," Mom said with a small smile.

"The queen of the spirit world?" I asked, remembering Kwame's elusive answer when I asked if someone ruled here.

Mom nodded and squeezed my hands. "If we have all the time in the world, I can answer every question you ever have," she said. "But if we don't, I want to tell you what I think is most important first. If you have a chance to go back, I want you to know who you really are."

I waited for my heart to hammer in my chest as I held my breath, but with a shock of horror, I realized that I couldn't feel my heart beating.

"Who am I?" I whispered, too disconcerted to collect myself. So many times, Balam had told me that I was more than human, that I had magic, but it had hardly seemed important with all the other things happening around me.

"That is something a mother cannot define for her daughter," Mom said. "Only you will discover who you truly are. But know that you are the child of great magic, Itzel."

"Because my parents are both shifters," I said carefully.

"A shifter possesses a great amount, it's true," she said. "To be able to shift from man to animal, and their other abilities depending on what type of shifter. But there is hidden magic everywhere, the kind you don't see with the eyes alone."

"You're saying I have... Magic of some sort?"

"Surely you must know that by now."

"It was mentioned a time or two," I admitted.

"Have you seen its effects for yourself yet?"

I shifted my position, angling my knees toward hers, wanting to hold onto her and stare into her kind eyes forever. "I gave someone the True Mate mark."

Mom's eyebrow arched, and she gave a small smile. "Really?"

I nodded, feeling unaccountably shy, as if I were showing off high marks from a tutor and waiting for her praise. "Apparently."

"Prince Kwame said as much," she conceded.

I nibbled at the corner of my lip. "It's possible I gave two men the mark."

Her eyes fixed on me with greater intensity. "Two?"

"Well, it marked them. It only hurt like hell for me." I pulled up my sleeve as I spoke.

My mother froze, a gasp escaping her lips before her fingers covered them.

Slowly, I raised my eyes to hers. "What the hell does this mean?"

Apparently, I *had* been marked. I'd been so drugged and out of it that I hadn't even looked at what had caused the searing pain up my arm. It had been covered by Camila's cardigan, and then a pair of pajamas that someone had put on me. Someone who knew that I had the True Mate marks, too. And not just two of them.

Climbing my arm like a procession left by a vicious cat were four glowing pawprints.

I swallowed hard, panic rising in me. "What the hell does this mean, Mom? You told me to surround myself with men, not just one man. But how can I have True Mates? I'm not even a shifter."

I was breathing hard by the time I stopped speaking and stared up at my mother with wide eyes, so grateful she was here to comfort me and give me answers when no one else could.

"Perhaps it takes four shifters to protect you," Mom said, wrapping her hands around mine and squeezing.

"Obviously it takes more than that," I grumbled.

Mom shifted on the bench and slid a gentle arm around me. "Tell me about these men you've marked."

"Well, I barely know Prince Kwame," I said. "Before the tour, the last time I saw him, you were still... In our world."

Mom nodded for me to go on.

"And I'm not sure about two of these." I ran my fingers over the marks, watching as the full-moon glow flickered under my fingertips. Both the marks and my fingers tingled for a second when they came in contact with each other. Lord Balam had told me outside Sir Kenosi's that he didn't have a mate, and I'd seen every inch of his glorious body a hundred times. I'd also seen Sir Kenosi, who had no mark and who said the panther amulet hadn't shown him a True Mate.

"The last one?" Mom asked, looking at me with unsettling intensity.

"I accidentally opened the panther amulet, and it marked a panther named Shadow," I said. "Though he said he'd already opened the amulet and knew we were mates. But I saw his body, and he didn't have the mark. It only appeared when I opened it."

Mom looked stricken. "You opened the panther amulet, and it marked someone?"

"Is that bad?"

"Were *you* marked when *he* opened the amulet before that?"

"No," I said, a creeping unease settling into me. "Why?"

Mom swallowed. "So, he opened the amulet and saw that you were his True Mate, but it didn't mark you," she said, speaking slowly as if to clarify to us both. "But when you opened it, he was marked."

My eyes narrowed as I stared back at my mother. "I thought only panthers knew about the curse on their amulet."

"There is one other person who knows about the curse."

"You," I said slowly, tension coiling inside me. I had believed Shadow's insistence that his people didn't kill my mother, and she'd confirmed as much. But had she come in contact with the panthers? "Mom, how do you know about the curse? Are you the queen who opened the amulet too soon?"

She shook her head. "I was a queen, but I was never an heir. I have no royal blood. Your father had an Amulet Tour, not me."

"And you're not a panther," I said. "So how do you know about the curse?"

"Itzel." Mom set her tea down on the saucer. "I know about the curse... Because I'm the one who cursed it."

I stared at my mother, trying to make sense of the words that had just come from her mouth, trying to back up and remember what Shadow and Lord Balam had said about the person who cursed the amulet.

"Wait," I said. "Let me get this straight. You're not a shifter? You're some kind of sorceress?"

"I was both of these things in your world," she said. "I can answer your questions about that if you stay. But if you go, there's something else you should know about this curse."

"What?" I asked. "Because it already seems pretty unfair that a random, unsuspecting human can get caught up in it so easily."

"There's only one person who wouldn't be marked as a True Mate when someone else opens the amulet," she said. "Only one person who the curse should affect at all. And it's not a random human."

"It's Camila," I whispered, horror rising inside me. Even after all she'd done, Camila was my sister. I couldn't undo eighteen years of wanting to protect her.

Mom's lips tightened. "No, Itzel. The curse only falls on the one who opens it. You can't hurt your sister with it. You can only hurt yourself."

"Then I don't understand," I said, jumping to my feet, wishing I could feel a heartbeat drumming the rhythm of my dread inside me. "The curse is supposed to fall on the heir if she opens it too soon, but Camila is the heir, so how can I be cursed?"

"She may be the heir now," Mom said slowly. "But the magic is never wrong. You will be the one to take the throne, Itzel. You will be the next ocelot queen."

TWO

Lord Balam
Curandero, Jaguar Nation

ITZEL WAS DEAD. IT WAS CLEAR IN MY MIND EVEN though my jaguar hadn't caught up yet, even as I clutched her to me and snarled at the others when they tried to pull her away. They crowded around me, each as panicked and hopeless as I was. None could question whether she might recover. This was not an infection, not a jagged panther bite torn during rough sex. This was an execution.

"Put something on the wound," Sir Kenosi ordered, desperation in his voice. "Maybe we can stop the bleeding."

There was no stopping the bleeding. She was human, and most of her neck had been torn away. Only her spine was intact, keeping her from a complete beheading.

Fate could not be this fucking cruel. My heart thudded in my chest, beating hard enough for both of us. It pounded out the rhythm of my jaguar's claim.

My mate. My mate. My mate.

I knew it, but she didn't. I hadn't gotten the chance to tell her, and now I never would. It shouldn't have happened this way. It was all wrong from the start. The way we'd started out just fucking because it was what she needed, and I wasn't the type to feel used. I was the type to fuck a beautiful princess if that's what she wanted. But it hadn't marked us. That was what I didn't understand. We'd been fucking for months, until it was more than just fucking, and no mark had appeared.

Until it did.

I had wanted to tell her, but someone had interrupted each time I drew close. It wasn't something to blurt out as if meaningless. A True Mate was a bond deeper than love, than life and death. I knew that now. I felt it now. But I hadn't told her. I had been waiting for the right moment, and now that moment would never come.

Had she known? And if she had, was she pleased?

It didn't matter now. That was the truth of it. It didn't matter if she'd been happy, or pissed, or scared out of her mind. Now she was none of those things. She was only dead.

"I'm going after him," Prince Kwame said in his deep, accented voice.

My brain began to wake from its shock. Sticky warmth trickled down my chest, plastering Itzel's wild mane to my bare skin.

"There's a chance," Sir Kenosi said, staring at her as if her death had ripped out a part of him, too. "It was a tiger."

"Was it?" Shadow rasped.

"I'll go with you," I said, feeling the tremor in my sanity at the thought that this was more than a random animal attack. At the thought that someone had done this intentionally, with knowledge and foresight. That it really was an execution.

"I'll stay," Sir Kenosi said, prying the body from my arms.

Instinct drew my lips back in a feral snarl. Sir Kenosi's stricken face turned savage, and he bared his teeth back at me, a sharp hiss flying off his tongue.

"Whoa, there," Prince Kwame said. "We're all on the same side."

"Right," I said, forcing my jaguar down. "Apologies, Sir Kenosi. My jaguar wasn't ready to let her go."

"Understood," he murmured, his eyes locked on the princess. He accepted her body as if he were taking something as fragile as a dove instead of a sturdy human body, one who had withstood our poundings night after night. In this moment, she could have been a butterfly, and I wouldn't have treated her with any more care.

"I'll keep watch," Shadow said. "I can cloak us with invisibility if anyone tries to get to her again."

I didn't say anything, but I knew his concern was unwarranted. No one was coming after Itzel. They'd already done the job.

"Hurry," Kwame said. "We can't let the killer escape. Either they will have answers, or we will have revenge."

Revenge. Such a hollow concept now.

Revenge didn't reverse time or even erase regret. Revenge didn't replace a throat that had been torn out or replace her with one of us. I would have stepped into that tiger's path, would have taken her place, in an instant. Revenge couldn't make that happen. It could only add one more to the death count.

But I understood the desire to act. We could do nothing here, and the helplessness was torture. We had two choices. Sit here and accept this new reality, or go after her killer.

I pulled my jaguar cloak around my shoulders and let it sink into me, wrap around me, hold me like a pair of arms. My jaguar accepted me like an old friend, a friend who offered comfort and a sense of oblivion. Though I retained much of my human mind, the pain and shock were numbed by my animal senses taking over. I welcomed the relief.

With a hiss of magic that distorted the air around him, Prince Kwame became a lion. I had never seen him shift, and it was different than my own transformation. I would consider it later. Now, we had a tiger to catch.

Together, Prince Kwame and I bounded into the forest. There was one answer that could make this better, one answer that could bring our mate back. That hope drove me forward through the unfamiliar, sweltering jungle. If the tiger had no answers, if it was simply an animal, its victim would become a tiger shifter, undead as all tiger shifters were. But if it was not an animal, if it was a tiger shifter, answers were no better than revenge. Knowing who or why didn't bring breath into Itzel's lungs, didn't put the fierceness, loyalty, and spark back in her eyes. Only her spirit could do that, and her spirit had already passed through the veil.

A scent found my nostrils, caressing my muzzle, and I turned and let out a huff to the great lion who bounded beside me. I had found the trail. Prince Kwame veered right to follow me, and we scrambled over logs and squirmed under vines, our bellies scraping dirt, our pelts scratched by thorns.

As the scent grew stronger, so did the sick sense of dread gripping my gut like a malady. It seemed more and more unlikely that an animal had randomly attacked Itzel out of everyone in our group. I realized as I closed in on the attacker that this could very well be a trap. If Shah Tiger knew we were coming, and he very well should, he might want to lure us in. But he already had the upper hand. He had the amulet. Why assassinate a princess instead of making her bargain for it? Itzel wasn't a commoner, despite her human blood. She was royalty. If this was ordered by the shah, it was an act of war.

Still, a trap wouldn't stop me. I'd walk into hell if it gave me a chance to get Itzel back. If it gave me a chance to do it over, to read the oracle and see what was coming. Why hadn't it shown me this? Her death was the death of my soul. The oracle should have told me, so that I could prevent this. I didn't care if it meant interfering in fate. I would have disrupted the entire cosmos to stop her death.

Prince Kwame bounded past me, skidding to a stop below a sprawling tree, its trunk as wide as we were long. Vines wound up the trunk, and in the canopy above, I could hear a shrill bird call.

I could also smell the trail I had been following. The bastard had gone up a tree, knowing only one of us could follow. Lions didn't climb trees.

But I did.

I gripped the trunk, my claws extended for purchase, and began to climb. Prince Kwame growled his frustration behind me, but I didn't slow. I should have foreseen this, should have brought Shadow with me. There was nothing to be done about it now, though.

Leaves showered down as I scrambled over a branch, catching my first glimpse of the enormous orange cat above me. I was a big man and a big cat, but tigers were bigger. I'd had dealings with the Tiger Empire before, but rarely a tiger in its animal form. I couldn't help but be impressed by their size, despite the advantage it gave them.

I snarled at the tiger, which had reached the highest limb that would support its weight. It twisted its head around, baring saber teeth as its lips pulled back in a warning snarl. Gripping the bark, I scrambled up a few more feet. The tree groaned under our combined weight, but I inched forward, reaching up to slash at the tiger's hind leg. My claws raked through its fur and flesh, and blood splattered down on me. The tiger screeched in fury and twisted around, dropping onto a branch below me.

I leapt after it, a growl tearing from my throat. The bastard wouldn't get away.

The branch sank under us, but I crept out along it, backing the tiger toward the end. Suddenly, it slashed out with its massive paw, clubbing me and slicing open deep furrows in the muscle of my shoulder. I lunged forward, sinking my teeth into its leg. The tiger growled in fury and clamped its teeth down on the back of my head. I wrenched away, ripping my skin and ear to tatters on its teeth.

The tiger leapt at me, but I darted out of the way, throwing myself at the trunk of the tree. His teeth sank into my haunch, and I turned and slashed at his neck, my claws sinking into the thick ruff around his face and neck. I dug in, burrowing the sharp points into his flesh, seeking an artery. The tiger jerked backwards, opening its mouth in a snarl that showed blood-streaked teeth. But I could see the fear in his eyes.

I sprang from the tree and slammed into the tiger. My teeth and claws sank through skin, ripped into muscle, spilled blood. The tiger jerked backward, and I went with it, slashing and snapping. I heard the crack of the tree's limb a second too late.

Before either of us could react, we were falling through the air. My body twisted to land, but I kept my teeth clamped into the tiger, refusing to release him. We hit the ground in a spray of leaves and twigs. The tiger instantly went limp, still as death in my grip. I unclamped my jaws and stepped back.

Prince Kwame, now in human form, bent and pressed a hand to the tiger's throat. He looked up at me and shook his head. Frustrated, I shook my head back. Fuck if I was going to return to human form and risk the tiger playing a trick, waiting to jump up and rip my throat out the way he had Itzel.

"He's gone," Prince Kwame said. "To the spirit world."

I shifted back to a man, adjusting my cloak over my shoulders. "You're sure? I killed him?"

The lion shook his head. "He's already dead. Feel how his blood is cold? Only his spirit went back. He's a bridge, like me."

"Fuck," I said, burying my hands in my hair and staring down at the massive, still form. "Fuck. Fuck."

"I will follow him," Prince Kwame said. "He's not the only one who can move between worlds."

"It doesn't matter," I growled. "I can cut his fucking throat out and burn his body so he can't come back here, but *she'll* still be gone."

"I don't care," Kwame said, his eyes burning with his lion. "I had a mate for one day, Lord Balam. Nothing can stop me from avenging her killer. And in that world... We can be together again."

"You just got your human life back," I said. "You'd give it up to stay there with her."

"I'd give up the life of every human on earth to be with her again," he said. "Believe me when I say it's worth it."

A growl threatened to tear from my throat. At least he'd gotten a mate for one day. I'd had her for months, and I'd squandered it all. I hadn't been her mate for even a day. Not even a moment when she knew, when we were together as True Mates. It had happened amid the chaos, so that the only one who had a chance to be with her since we'd been claimed as True Mates was this guy. This guy who didn't even know Itzel, who now acted as if he alone mourned her loss and treasured their bond.

I knew Itzel. I knew what she was worth, far more than I'd ever shown her. I knew every inch of her inside and out, the way her eyes burned with ferocity when someone threatened her sister, the taste of her sweet cunt, the force of her determination, the moans that escaped her throat when she was cumming on my cock, the wildness of her laugh. I *knew* her. I should have seen this coming. I should have known she would destroy me.

"Carry him back," he said quietly. "Tie him up in case he escapes me in the spirit world and returns here. Do not kill him. I want answers."

I dropped my hands to my sides and stared at my companion. "Answers won't bring her back, Prince Kwame."

"If there is even a one-percent chance that they will, I'll take that over the ninety-nine percent chance that you're right."

I nodded, understanding him even as my own hopes died. As hard as it was, I had learned long ago to accept things as they were. That didn't mean other people didn't need answers, didn't need closure. And he deserved that even if it was meaningless to me. To me, all that mattered was that this fucking bastard tiger wasn't a wild animal. It was a shifter, one who had committed premeditated murder. No matter what he had to say for himself, no matter if we followed him to the ends of the earth and the spirit world and the heavens above, it wouldn't change what truly mattered. This time, I didn't know if I'd ever be able to accept the reality. My mate was dead, and she wasn't coming back.

Three

Itzel
Princess, Ocelot Nation

"Okay, I don't know how to respond to that," I said to Mom, my tea and cake forgotten as I stared at nothing, trying to comprehend the impossible thing she'd just told me. "When you said you were going to tell me who I really am, I wasn't expecting to be told I was going to usurp the throne. I mean... What?"

"I wish I had all the answers," Mom said, staring off with me. "I don't know what the future holds. I only know the intricacies of my own curse. It has to be so."

"But... How? I'm not a shifter, Mom. I'm not an ocelot."

We sat in silence for a long while, staring at the foggy nothingness beyond the cherry blossoms hanging over us like an umbrella.

At last, she spoke. "If it hasn't been too long, and your body is still in a state to sustain life, it's possible you could live again. But you should hurry. If your body goes without life for too long, your organs will be too far gone, and you cannot inhabit your human form again."

"Is there any way to get back from here?" I asked.

She bit at her lip. "No," she said at last. "Lilith is the only one who might be able to help us, and we are not allowed to ask for an audience with her. When she's ready to see you, she'll come to you."

"Then what can we do?"

"We'll have to wait for Prince Kwame," she said, wringing her hands. "I pray he's resourceful enough to figure out a way to get you back in time."

I swallowed hard, frustration and helplessness gnawing at me.

Come on, Kwame. You're a bridge. Come and see me. Take me back.

I turned to Mom. "Wait, back up for just a minute. You didn't know about my mates until I told you?"

She shook her head, a look of resignation filling her eyes. "No, Itzel."

"Then that's not what you were going to tell me."

"No."

"Then what?"

She sighed and took my hands. "First, I want to tell you this, Itzel. I love you and your sister more than anything in this world or the next. Don't ever doubt that."

"Okay..."

"How much do you know about the ocelot amulet?"

"More than enough," I said. "It's basically a love potion."

I stopped there, not telling her what I knew beyond that. She already knew our father had murdered her. She didn't need to know that after that, he'd started using the amulet to make young women fall disgustingly in love with him against their will.

"And how much do you know about a True Mate bond?" Mom asked.

"I know our father wasn't your True Mate," I said, shifting uncomfortably. "And I'm assuming he used the ocelot amulet on you to make you fall in love with him."

She nodded. "It's hard to describe what it does as anything other than love. But it's not the same love as when you meet someone, get to know them, and truly love who they are as a person. What the amulet does is create the same chemical response in your body that you get from falling in love. It creates an instant bond, the high of falling in love. But it can't force you to truly love the person inside the one you've been bonded with."

"You didn't love our father?"

"I certainly believed I did," she said. "It's powerful magic, Itzel. Dangerous magic. But what I was... The High Priestess... That magic had similar properties. It manifests in each High Priestess differently, but one thing is a constant. Men didn't fall in love with me instantly, but they were powerfully drawn to me. That included your father. When he saw his chance to claim that for himself, he took it."

"He made you fall in love with him."

"I truly believed that he loved me," she said. "But magic is not an exact science. Just as it manifests differently in its host, so it affects people differently."

"Like making them lose their mind and murder you?" I asked bitterly.

"This isn't easy for me to tell my daughter," she said. "And it won't be easy for you to hear. Do you want me to continue?"

"Yes," I said without hesitation. If I somehow got back to the human world, if I was truly going to be the one in power, I would be in charge of sentencing my father. I needed to know his crimes.

"The magic I had is the magic of creation. In a large part, it is sexual in nature. It is both released and strengthened by the female orgasm."

"That's pretty personal information, Mom."

She smiled. "I know. I told you it's not a conversation that I wanted to have when you were younger. I always thought I'd have time to tell you when you grew older. And now I suppose you have."

"Okay," I said. "So, what then? You got more powerful than him, and he was pissed?"

"Oh, I was always more powerful than him. We were both shifters, but I was so much more. It didn't threaten him... At first. But then, yes, he grew threatened, not by me but by the interest men took in me. I spent so much of my day reassuring him, and my nights satisfying him to prove that I was interested in only him. It was exhausting, but he was inexhaustible. And the more he wanted, the stronger my magic became. Eventually, it was too much for the two of us to handle."

"So... What then? He killed you?"

"I had an affair."

"Oh," I said, drawing back. "That's not what I was expecting."

"It's a shameful thing to admit," she said. "The magic had taken over our lives. It was making us both sick in different ways. Your father was dangerously obsessed, so much so that he couldn't stay away from me. But the more we were together, the stronger it grew. I couldn't contain it, and the more I released into him, the worse he became. The only thing grounding me was your sister, and your father was jealous of even her."

"How old was she?"

"Just a year or so," Mom said, smiling as she stared out into the distance. "We'd left her with a nanny at home and flown to a conference of the ICFN in the Tiger Empire. That's where I met him."

I swallowed, my head spinning at the mention of the place where I'd been attacked.

"A tiger?" I whispered.

She shook her head. "No, he was a god."

"A god?"

"A snow leopard," she said. "They're the children of gods. He was... Oh, he was magnificent. I'd felt the effects of my own magic, but nothing like this. This... Itzel, it was the most devastating thing I'd ever experienced. Because he wasn't just a demigod. He was *my* god. The entire world shifted when we met. It wasn't just my magic that claimed him. It was my soul."

"Your True Mate?" I breathed. It was too terrible to imagine. Lord Balam had been married when his wife met her True Mate, and she'd left him. I'd never considered what would happen if a married woman met her True Mate and *couldn't* leave.

Mom nodded, her lips tight. "I wish I could say I was stronger than my animal instincts, but there was no conscious decision. We had to be together as much as the moon must rise each night, as the sun must take its place in the morning. I would never have hurt my husband that way if I could have thought it through, resisted it. But the mate bond is not rational. It defies logic. It's a law of nature in itself."

"But if Camila was just a baby, then he didn't kill you then," I said. "Did it take him ten years to find out?"

She shook her head. "No. I went to him while we were still abroad, told him that I had found my True Mate. There's an unspoken law among shifters to honor that above all else. But King Ocelot refused to let me out of our marriage."

"You couldn't get that decision overturned or something?" I asked. "Isn't there someone you could appeal to?"

"He's a king," she said, giving me a sympathetic smile. "I came from nothing. Perhaps I could have gone to the ICFN. Perhaps I could have stayed, remaining legally married to him while I made a life with my mate. But there was one person whose happiness meant more to me than my own."

"Camila," I said, my throat tight. "You went back for Camila."

Mom nodded. "I'd have done the same for you. I couldn't leave her without a goodbye, and I knew that if I stayed, your father would never let me see her again. I couldn't give up my daughter, not even for the one love I'd ever be allowed. Because once I met him, once I knew how that felt, I knew that I'd never felt that way about your father, and I never would. I couldn't. You can't love anyone the way you love a True Mate."

I felt simultaneously guilty and left out. I had two True

Mates—maybe four—and I didn't get to feel for them the way they apparently felt for me.

But it didn't matter, did it? Because I was dead. Their one and only chance at true love was already over.

"What happened?"

"I snuck away to be with my mate every chance I could get. We had those two weeks. That one conference. I knew I couldn't stay, but I couldn't stop myself from going to him. He managed my magic so well. Just having someone to help me contain it, someone else to take on some of the burden. The day we left was one of the worst days of my life. And when I got home, I found out that he'd been killed in a random attack as he was leaving the conference."

She paused and reached for her teacup.

"That's an awfully big coincidence," I said slowly. "Or... Not a coincidence at all."

It had my father written all over it. He'd probably sent one of his guards or hired a hitman. He did that kind of thing all the time. If there was one thing my father knew how to do, it was to dispose of his enemies.

"We'd already left," she said. "So there was nothing pointing to us as responsible. But I knew. And there wasn't a damn thing I could do about it. It changed me, though. I sank into despair, not caring about anything. I was your father's pawn. I let him have whatever he wanted. I didn't think I'd ever come out of it."

"Mom, I'm so sorry," I said, hugging her hard. I wished I could tell my mates how sorry I was that I'd done this to them, widowed their souls.

Mom hugged me back with equal strength. "And then a miracle happened," she whispered into my hair.

"He came back?" I asked, pulling away, wondering if this story had more purpose than to tell me what my father had done. Was this a lesson that would lead me back to my mates?

"No," Mom said with a small smile, cupping my cheek in her palm. "You came."

"The second child of a pair of shifters," I thought aloud. It made so much more sense. No shifters had a second child. It was almost unheard of in our country. No one wanted a common human child who couldn't attend their parties or inherit their titles or property. Not to mention that it made the parents look impulsive and irresponsible, like they couldn't control themselves.

Tears pooled in my mother's eyes. "I'm sorry I never told you, Itzel. You were a child, and King Ocelot was the only father you'd ever have or know. I thought I'd tell you when you came of age, but I never got the chance."

"That's what you meant about telling me who I am," I said. "I'm not Camila's sister. I'm not a princess at all, am I?"

"She's your half-sister," she said. "You don't have to have royal blood, Itzel. You're the child of an ocelot and an elusive snow leopard, a High Priestess and a demigod. You have incredible power inside you, my daughter."

"Is he here?" I asked, standing. "I want to meet him."

She nodded. "There was one silver lining to my death. It joined me back with my mate, and although I would have given anything to go back and raise my girls as I'd always planned, he made death bearable. I know that sounds ludicrous, but it's something that only a True Mate could offer."

"Let's walk," I said, too restless to sit with all the new information crammed into my brain. "Tell me the rest. I want to know everything. Even the ugly parts."

She rose, and we left the gazebo and began to walk along a winding stone path through the soft green grass. "When we got home, your father locked me up in the castle," she said. "I told him you were his, and I think he believed me. His pride wouldn't let him believe anything else. But he never trusted me again. He liked us to have the appearance of being happily married, but I was a prisoner in my home. I wasn't allowed to go anywhere without guards escorting me or waiting outside my door. He wanted to know my every move. And then he began to get suspicious of the guards. He'd have one killed because he imagined he was looking at me the wrong way.

"My magic took a while to build up to what it had been before," she said. "But eventually, it built up again. Your father didn't want to share that with anyone. At that time, the Panther Nation was being ripped apart by storms and floods. Some panther leaders came to visit the castle, asking if their people could seek asylum in our nation. When I dared to take their side against our king, he flew into a rage. He accused me of an affair with the panther chief even though we only saw the panthers every few years, and he killed their chief and seized all of their diplomats."

"Oh my god," I said, my mind racing. "Did he start a war?" Of course I knew my father hated the panthers, and I knew other Feline Nations hated us. Sure, we were seen as isolationists who wouldn't help other nations in need, but I hadn't realized we'd done something as extreme as murder their leaders. Until I met Shadow, I'd never heard anything but my father's side of the story. As the saying went, history was written by the victors.

"No," Mom said, shaking her head. "You would remember a war. Without their leaders, and with hundreds of their people dying every day, the Panther Nation couldn't retaliate. Their people probably didn't realize what had happened at first. When you're fighting for survival, and every moment is life or death, you pay little attention to political maneuverings. I'm sure some diplomats had remained, and they probably contacted your father. I don't know what he told them. It was too late for the visiting dignitaries, and too late for most of their people."

"You couldn't get them out?"

She shook her head. "He threw me into a cell under the castle that night, and I never saw them again. He told me a few days later that he'd had them all executed as invaders of our nation. As for me, he said the only way to keep my magic in check was to isolate me so that I would never see anyone but him again. I begged to see you girls, but he refused. He was maddened with jealousy and the magic. He brought in sorcerers to siphon off my magic, telling me that he'd protect you girls only if I cooperated."

"And he killed you anyway?" I asked as we reached the top of the slope and a small house with a pointed bamboo roof appeared.

"Maybe we should stop here," Mom said. "The rest is... Maybe unsuitable for my daughter to hear."

"I want to hear it," I insisted, grabbing her hand. "I want to know. I need to know, if I'm going to take his place one day. Tell me."

Mom hesitated before giving a reluctant nod. "He would force himself on me each day, at first just once and then with increasing frequency until he barely left my room. And then one day he got carried away, as shifters do on occasion, and he bit me. But he didn't stop at that, like a typical love bite."

I wrapped my arms around myself, wracked with shudders. "He's the one who did that to you? He told us panther rebels ate your body."

Mom shook her head. "I'm sorry. I know it's not something you want to know."

"You're wrong," I said, taking a deep breath to steady myself. "I'm glad I know exactly what kind of monster I'll be up against."

"And you will," Mom said, placing her hands on my shoulders and staring straight into my eyes. "You will go back, Itzel. One way or another, it'll happen."

"Thank you," I said, emotion choking off my throat. I took her hands in mine and squeezed, a smile inching onto my face. "I'm ready."

"Are you ready to meet Tsewang?" she asked, searching my face. "He's dying to meet you."

"Dying?" I asked, cocking an eyebrow. "Really, Mom?"

"An unfortunate word choice," she admitted.

I squared my shoulders and stood up straight. I was going to meet my father for the first time. I hadn't even gotten used to the fact that the man I'd always known as my father wasn't the man who had given me life. Somehow, I was ready anyway. Maybe it was the fact that I'd always felt a bond with my mother and a distance between me and King Ocelot. There had always been a very clear divide. Camila was our father's daughter, and I was my mother's. We even looked like them. Camila had Father's pale hair and fair complexion, while I had Mom's unruly hair and dark complexion. And while I had never questioned whether I was his daughter, I found myself less surprised than one might expect when I found out I wasn't.

"Okay," I said. "I don't know if I'm ready, but this might be my only chance. If I get an opportunity to go back and save my country from King Ocelot's reign, I'm going to take it. And if anyone knows how to get me back to the human world, it's probably a god."

FOUR

Sir Kenosi
Entrepreneur, Cheetah Nation

"WE SHOULD FIND SHAH TIGER," I SAID, PACING back and forth next to the body of the murdered princess. "He might have surgeons, healers, something. At least we can put the body somewhere cleaner than the dirt."

"No," Shadow rasped in that voice that didn't match his boyish face. "We don't know who attacked. It could be them."

"It's not," I growled, turning on my heel. "The shah can be a bit eccentric, but he's not a ruthless killer. He was generous with his aid when my people needed it. He would not murder someone in cold blood."

"You're not an ocelot royal," Shadow pointed out. "You're a cheetah peasant."

"Peasant?" I asked, turning on him with a scoff. "I could buy your entire clan and the swamp they live in."

"And you'd still bleed red like the rest of us," Shadow rasped, sitting on the ground next to the princess, his legs folded and his head bent forward so his hair covered his face. "You can be knighted and earn a thousand titles, buy your country house by house, but your blood will never be gilded like royalty."

"I thought you didn't care about that kind of thing," I said, narrowing my eyes at the panther. I was fairly certain he was, as he put it, a peasant, too. And he'd stayed that way while I'd become a Sir, while I'd bought up enough land for my entire clan, gained worldwide notoriety, and fucked my way through every tight pussy in Africa.

"I don't care," Shadow growled. "But other shifters do. The shah might give charity to a nation that poses no threat to his, but he's still a king."

"The miniscule Ocelot Nation doesn't pose a threat to him. The Tiger Empire is the most prosperous feline nation in the world."

"You don't know what their relations are."

I knew enough to know that Shadow was right. It could have been a political move that left our mate dead on the ground. The Tiger Nation had given aid to the persecuted cheetahs in our clan, had given us food, supplies, even books. I owed Shah Tiger my life as well as the empire I'd built from knowledge gleaned by reading those books. Their king could be a bit depraved if his sexual tastes were any indication, but he had a good heart behind that stiff cock. I hoped so, anyway. I'd modeled half my life after his example—take what you can and enjoy the fuck out of it every step of the way.

But what if I'd been wrong? I'd never questioned my choices. Fame, riches, adoration followed me everywhere I went. Paparazzi followed me around the city, flashbulbs going off when I walked by. The most coveted designers sent me their wares in the hopes that I would sport them in public. Women from all over the world spread their thighs, took pictures, and sent messages begging for the chance to be pounded into the bed by the famous Sir Kenosi. And I was more than happy to fulfill their every desire.

Princess Itzel had made me question that lifestyle, though. She had pointed out the emptiness inside the shimmering bubble of my existence. Underneath the glitz and glamour, no one actually cared about me. They loved my fame, my money, my image. Not the guy I was under it all.

The princess's death seemed to confirm that I had been right all along. It was better not to care. It was better to name a woman for the month when you'd fuck her along with twenty others. It was better to have pleasure without torment. Attachment to someone meant being hurt when they were gone.

Except...

Except she *wasn't* wrong. How could I deny that now, when I knew what it felt like to know a True Mate, if only for a moment? I hadn't believed it when the amulet had shown me only the human princess. But when she'd opened the amulet and given me a mark, I could no longer deny it—at least to myself. I hadn't told anyone, but I knew. Magic didn't make mistakes.

"We'll stay here and wait for answers," Shadow said after a short silence. "Balam will be back."

I needed to do something, to act. I was tired of prowling back and forth in the small clearing, charged with energy and helplessness to change what had happened. I cursed myself for not joining Kwame on his search for the killer. Doing nothing while our mate grew cold on the ground was a torture worse than death itself.

I stopped pacing and turned to Itzel, staring down at her glorious body, now drained of life. If my fate was worse than hers, wouldn't I trade places with her? If knowing a True Mate for only a moment, not even long enough to consummate the mate bond, was worse than death, wouldn't I choose death instead? It was the only way for us to be together. To go to the spirit world and join her.

I stared at the bag sitting next to the princess, discarded as if it didn't contain four of the most precious items in the world. I would have traded them all without a moment's thought to get her back, to know how it felt to fuck her as a mate, not just a man. To do more than glory over her helplessness as I held her captive and made her beg for my cock, and then filled every tight inch of her with it until she begged for mercy. I would take time to appreciate that her cunt tasted like honey, and I'd know why she was the best fuck I'd ever had.

As if in a trance, I took a step toward the bag, blood drumming in my ears. She wasn't a shifter, but she had marked us. I was her True Mate. My amulet... Could it heal a human?

Before I could do anything too crazy, my phone went off in my pocket. Shadow's head shot up, and his nostril's flared as if it were an insult to carry technology while holding vigil for the dead. I slid my phone out, turning my back and pacing to the edge of the forest before answering. A pale, flavorless blonde face stared up at me from the screen, as far as you could get from the succulent, wild woman who had claimed me and then promptly and spectacularly died in front of me.

"Hello," I said carefully, brushing the fog from my brain.

"Hello, Sir Kenosi," Princess Camila said. "I'm so glad to see that you're unharmed. Though I admit to being slightly surprised."

Blood rushed in my ears, and I rubbed at my chest, trying to relieve the tightness that squeezed it. I could barely speak, and I was not the kind of man who stumbled over his words. "Did you—Did you order that attack?"

"What attack?"

"Shit." Though I was no fan of Princess Camila, I didn't relish the thought of telling her that her sister was dead.

"I'm sure you were taken hostage by my sister and her poor, misled band of rogue shifters," Camila said. "That's the only explanation. Otherwise, you'd be in violation of our agreement. You do remember promising me the use of your helicopter for transportation, don't you?"

"Your Grace," I said. "Camila, if I may…"

"I don't believe our relationship warrants that kind of informality. Perhaps after you've returned with the promised vehicle, and we've spent the remaining stops on my Amulet Tour as a team and gotten better acquainted, it would be acceptable for you to call me by my given name."

"Your Grace, your sister was attacked by a tiger when we reached the Tiger Nation."

"What?" Camila's voice was blank, unbelieving. For a long minute, neither of us spoke.

"I'm sorry, Your Grace."

"Oh," she said. "Oh. Then you absolutely must come and get me. I'll need to speak to King Tiger about this right away. And it will take my father too long to arrange for a plane to fly here from the nearest city and then take me to the Tiger Nation."

I glanced across the clearing to where Shadow sat with Itzel. He'd lifted his head, his eyes fixed on me with their eerie, otherworldly green glow. Despite Camila's businesslike response, I knew that everyone dealt with their own shit in their own way. Still, I didn't much like her way.

I wrapped my hand around the phone and lowered it from my mouth to speak to him. "Do you think we should return for Princess Camila?" When Shadow glared at me, I shrugged. "She's her sister. Wouldn't Itzel have wanted her here?"

"Mistakenly," Shadow growled. "Camila has no heart. She's not above hiring a tiger to ambush someone. We have the amulets. She would think nothing of killing her own sister for them."

I shrugged like his words meant nothing, but my fingers returned to rub at my sternum, attempting to loosen the crushing tightness that had risen again. He'd confirmed the momentary suspicion that Camila's first words had raised in me. I lifted the phone back to my mouth. "I won't be coming back for you, Princess Camila. I promised the helicopter because I wanted to be closer to Princess Itzel, so I might get to know her better. Not you."

I relished the indignant huff on her end of the phone. There was little that could satisfy me more than knocking a spoiled princess down a notch. And while seeing Itzel on her knees choking on my cock had been irresistible, Camila held none of that appeal. She probably had shark teeth that would slice my dick like salami. But there were other ways to bring a princess to her knees

"You've created an enemy in the ocelots," she hissed at me through the phone.

"If I recall correctly, your kingdom has already created an enemy of... Everyone. You're giving me far too much credit for the tension between nations."

"You'll regret this day, you worthless upstart." Her voice grated like chewing a mouthful of ice.

"I assure you, I'm far from worthless," I said. "In fact, my net worth is more than your entire kingdom."

"I command you to bring back the helicopter," she gritted out. "A man of your station is required to obey my orders. I am a *princess,* Sir Kenosi."

I laughed at that. "You're not my princess. I use your title out of deference to the predecessors in your position, not because you've earned it, and certainly not because I believe you somehow superior. You have no power over me, *Princess* Camila."

"You stole the amulets," she fumed. "Those are mine, and you know it. I earned them. You won't get away with this. I've already spoken with my father. If he hasn't already contacted the shah, he will. And trust me, you don't want to make an enemy of me or my father, Sir Kenosi. All the money in the world can't get you back into our good graces."

"Your good graces?" I asked with an incredulous laugh. "That's the best threat you can come up with? Princess, I couldn't give two shits about your good graces. And if I recall, your sister was the one who earned the Cheetah Amulet."

"I was treated like a servant. I worked for that!"

"It wasn't given to you," I said. "It was given to your sister, and trust me when I say that she earned every ounce of it. She knew how to work for a mating amulet."

"Ugh, you're disgusting," Camila said. "You deserve each other."

"And it was Itzel who marked a mate when she opened the cursed amulet," I reminded her. "Something that, if I recall correctly, only the future queen can do."

I could hear sputtering on the other end of the line. Shadow studied me as if waiting, watching intently as the realization dawned in my mind. We stared at each other across the clearing. I'd just put it together, but it was clear that he was one step ahead of me.

Camila's voice trembled when she finally spoke. "She can't be queen. She's not a shifter."

"If a tiger killed her, she would be."

"She'd be a tiger," Camila said. "A tiger can't rule the Ocelot Kingdom."

When I didn't answer, she went on. "I'm coming for those amulets. Gabor will get them from you. You have no idea how ruthless an ocelot guard is, Kenosi. You don't know what he's capable of. My father will send more guards, too. You won't get away with this. Those are my amulets, and I'm going to get them back."

I didn't know if she was trying to convince me or herself, but I didn't have time to talk her through it. I needed to see what else Shadow knew about the curse, about my mate. *Our* mate. She'd marked him, too. He hadn't been afraid to tell her, even when I was still in denial. I didn't know how it was possible that someone could have more than one True Mate, especially a human. But magic didn't lie.

I ended the call without another word to Camila. Shadow watched as I strode across the clearing to him. "What does this mean?" I demanded.

Before he could answer, Lord Balam appeared, the body of a tiger who must have weighed four times as much as him draped in his arms. I sprang to his side as he dropped the enormous beast, its legs trussed with vines and its fur streaked with blood. "You killed him?"

"He's not dead," Lord Balam said, his deep, rich voice thick with disgust. "He's a shifter. He escaped into the spirit world."

"Fuck." I cursed our rotten luck. If only he had been a real tiger, one who could have given Itzel a second life. I stared at her body, swallowing at the thought of what I'd considered earlier.

"Where's Kwame?" Shadow asked, never moving from his vigil by her side.

"In the spirit world," Lord Balam said glaring down at the murderous tiger at our feet. "But here's our answer."

"The curse," I said, turning to Shadow. "It says Itzel will be the next queen."

He nodded.

"Well," I said. "Things just got interesting."

Lord Balam scowled. "How is that possible? If she was killed by a shifter, she won't come back as a tiger."

I swallowed, my pulse painful in the side of my throat. "There is one thing we haven't tried."

Both men turned to me. "When I used the Panther Amulet, I saw Princess Itzel," I said. "I didn't believe it, but... Maybe it's true."

Lord Balam nodded, no surprise on his face. "I thought that might be the case."

"How does that bring back our mate?" Shadow asked, his face going still as he swept aside a strand of hair that had blown over Itzel's cheek.

"It doesn't," I said. "It's my amulet that might bring her back."

FIVE

Itzel
Princess, Ocelot Nation

I APPROACHED THE MAN STANDING BEFORE THE wide, open windows of his house. His hands were clasped behind his back, and in front of him stretched an endless orchard.

"This is your father, Gao Tsewang," Mom said gently, guiding me forward. "Tsewang, this is our daughter, Itzel."

The man turned from the window slowly. He was short and black-haired, with a round face and Asian features. "Itzel," he said, a smile breaking onto his face. "I have waited eighteen long years to meet you."

"You knew about me?" I asked, swallowing hard.

"Of course," he said, clasping his hands in front of him and giving me a small bow. "I know all about you."

I glanced at my mother. "I thought you said you didn't get to watch over us from this world."

"I'm not a god," she said, a slight twinkle in her eye that hadn't been there before. I could see it now, how her whole being was both relaxed and lit up in his presence. I felt a strange, irrational pang of sympathy for my father—no, not my father. King Ocelot. And just as quickly as it had come, it was replaced with fury at all he'd done. Yes, it would be heart-breaking for the person you loved to find their True Mate. But there were people like Lord Balam who loved their wife enough to let her go, so she could marry the person she was meant to be with. And there were people who didn't.

"I'm the daughter of a god," I muttered, my head spinning with this knowledge. I'd always felt so...ordinary.

"And of the High Priestess," Tsewang said, a note of pride in his voice as he smiled at my mother. "That's even more rare. There is only one of those in the world at once."

"Who is it now?" I asked.

Tsewang frowned up at the ceiling as if in thought. "There's a little baby girl with the power inside her right now," he said. "When she grows into that power, she will have to be careful not to meet the same fate as your mother."

"Did you know what my mother was when you met her?"

"Yes," Mom said. "And so did your father. I felt it only fair to inform prospective lovers of the potential consequences."

"Like pissing off King Ocelot," I said, glancing at Tsewang.

To my surprise, he laughed. "Yes. I'm overjoyed that I was able to make your acquaintance at last. I'm sorry that I was not able to do so in the human world. I would have liked to be your father, Itzel. I have a feeling you would have challenged me even more than my son."

"Your son?" I asked, my throat tightening. Awe and loss filled me at once. I had a brother as well as a sister. There was so much I had missed by not knowing who I was, so much I had missed because of Tsewang's death. So much that King Ocelot had taken from me. My real father, my mother, the chance to know my brother.

"Ah," Tsewang said, his head jerking up. "We've got company."

"Lilith?" my mother asked, her eyes widening.

Tsewang's eyes sparkled and he lifted a finger. "What do a ghost, a lion, and a prince have in common?"

"Kwame," I said, an ache twisting in my chest that took my breath. I hadn't expected to be so affected by the thought of one of my mates. But he was someone I knew, someone familiar, even if I hadn't known him long.

"What a wonderful match you have made, Princess. I couldn't have chosen a better mate for you if I'd tried."

"You know Kwame?"

"Well, of course," Tsewang said. "He's royalty and a shifter—as much as we call ourselves that here, when only the spirit is present."

Mom had said something like that, that she had been the High Priestess and a shifter in our world, but now she was neither.

Kwame appeared in the room before I could ask more. "My queen," he said, rushing to pull me into his arms. "I have never been happier to be a ghost."

"But I gave you your life back," I pointed out. "Why are you here?"

"I can still travel between worlds. I imagined I would have more time in the human world before I came back here, but if you are here, I have no reason to stay there."

"Your family," I said, my throat thick with the words. "I didn't save you so you could come back here."

"There's nowhere else I'd rather be," he said, taking my face between his hands and kissing me softly. His lips were warm and full, and I had to fight the urge to sink into him instead of standing on my own two feet. I had to be strong, though.

"What aren't you telling me?" I asked, pulling away.

"Why must there be more?" he asked. "You are my mate. I would do anything to be with you. Remember, I even tricked you into coming here with me the first time so we could be together. I would risk you hating me because I know that I can only be happy when I'm with you. If that means never returning to the human world, so be it. I'm satisfied with you by my side."

"Kwame," I whispered, getting all choked up again. "That's crazy."

"I'm crazy," he said. "Crazy for you, my queen." He kissed me, and again I felt that spiraling, hypnotic attraction.

"I'm not used to men being so..." I shook my head and laughed. "I don't even know the word for it."

"You're not used to being treated like a queen?" Kwame asked. "Then shame on your other mates. You should never be treated as anything else. I will spoil you into eternity, Princess Itzel."

"Wow," I said. Because what else could I say? It wasn't like a man had never sweet talked me before, but this was a bit overwhelming. He wasn't just trying to get laid. He really meant these things. I was used to men like Tadeu and Lord Balam, with their dirty mouths and rough exteriors. Men who might have emotions buried somewhere under there, about as deep as the earth's core. Even Sir Kenosi was more familiar, with his sick games and tests. I could negotiate with a man like that. Only Shadow was still a mystery to me, but I understood mystery better than... Adoration.

"You came here prepared to give up your human life and stay forever?" I asked, halfway in awe and a bit appalled that he'd die so quickly for me.

"Of course," he said. "There's nowhere else for me now that we've met. You're my True Mate, Itzel."

"But... You wanted out of here so badly. You wanted your human life back."

"I know what I am doing," he said. "No matter how painful it is to give up a chance at a human life, it's infinitely more painful to give up a mate."

I couldn't believe it. He'd tricked me, fought so hard for his human life, and now he was ready to give it up in an instant to be with me.

"I have to tell you something," I said. "When I marked you, it meant I was going to be queen. Somehow, I have to get back to our world."

Kwame gave me a sorrowful look. "I'm sorry, Princess. But the tiger that killed you was a shifter. You won't come back as a tiger."

Mom was instantly at my side, laying a hand on my arm. "I don't know if Itzel is ready to look that closely at her death yet, Prince Kwame."

"Of course," he said. "I'm sorry I mentioned it. I simply didn't want you to place your hopes in that."

My eyes narrowed as I looked at him. "You're a bridge between worlds. You came to the human world and brought me here, and that allowed me to choose someone to bring back. Could you bring a living person here to get me out?"

"If only it were that simple," he said. "But alas, I was allowed that privilege only one time. Since lion shifters are the ghosts of our people's royalty, our amulet has a power that revolves around the spirits of our dead. It allows its user to bring a True Mate to their world for one day only. Most use it to say goodbye and reassure their mate that they are safe here."

"But we didn't say goodbye," I said. "I brought you back to life."

"It was *your* magic that allowed that to happen," Mom said quietly. "I told you when you visited that only someone strong enough can bring a soul back to life. You're stronger than you know, Itzel. That's why it was so dangerous for you to come here while still living. You have the magic of life running through your veins."

Her life, I thought. If it weren't for her magic, she'd still be alive.

"I could bring Lord Balam here," I said. "He's strong. He could take me back."

"It is not about physical strength," Tsewang said. "It is about the strength of your magic."

"Otherwise, there would be countless ghost people walking in your world," Mom said.

My eyes widened as I stared at her. "Could I use it to bring myself back?"

"Perhaps your power and Kwame's together," she said. "Although... Your magic may have returned to the human world when you passed into this one. It would be helpful if one of your other mates is undead as well. With the strength of two shifters moving back into the human world, it might be possible to blast through the veil between worlds."

"That's very dangerous," Tsewang said, laying a hand on my mother's waist. "Are you sure we should try this?"

"What choice do we have?" she said. "Itzel has been here too long already."

"Why's it dangerous?" I asked.

"If you fail, you could be lost in the veil," Mom admitted, her voice soft. "It's a place between this world and that."

"Limbo," I said.

"Yes, like that," Mom said. "Do you know anyone else who might travel between worlds, someone whose magic you can feed off for the transition?"

"No," I said desperately. I could feel it somehow, some undefinable current of energy draining from me. Was that my magic?

Mom took my hand and squeezed. "If you can bear to relive your last moments, you might be able to go back with the tiger shifter."

My body quailed at the thought of facing my killer so soon. "I don't know if I'm ready," I said with a weak laugh. I took a breath to steady myself. "But I need to get back, and if my death has answers, I'm going to have to face it now. There's no time to get ready."

"When you look at something so intense, it puts you back in that moment," Tsewang said. "You'll need to latch onto that tiger when he goes back to the human world. Kwame will hold onto you as well, helping propel you through. You must focus all your power, and don't let go."

"I will return and bring you the Lion Amulet," Kwame said. "You aren't bringing a mate here, but it has strong magic associated with traversing the veil."

"It may not work," Mom warned gently. "Magic doesn't follow us here for long. It drains away, back through the veil to the human world."

"If there's a chance it can help me find a way back, I'll take it," I said.

"Then do it now, while you still have magic left."

"Seeing won't help you," Kwame said. "Maybe it is better if you don't look. It can be upsetting to know who wishes you dead. And I don't think that person will help you go back."

It struck me then that Kwame really was dead. He had come back, but he was a ghost. He had died, and I didn't yet know how, but he did. He had seen his own death, and judging from his words, his own killer. Now I had to find the strength to do the same.

"I have to try," I said.

"When you get back, you must find my son, Gao Jetsun," Tsewang said. "It's of utmost importance."

"Will he know who has the snow leopard amulet?"

"He has it," Tsewang said. "Find him."

I nodded, knowing there was more that I should know, but also knowing the time for questions and answers was over.

"I will be with you," Kwame said, stepping behind me and wrapping his arms around me, holding on as if I might evaporate into thin air.

"Close your eyes," Mom said. "Meditate on that time, and you will be there again."

My knees were trembling, but my determination was unwavering. I had to do this. I had to get back to our world, to rid it of my father. I didn't know where Camila fit into all this, how she would react to finding out what our father had done, but I couldn't dwell on that now. I didn't want to think about the prophecy that said I would be queen because that meant she'd been right all along. I was the one who would take her throne just as she'd feared. My sister may not have been strong, but she was smart. She'd known the truth about me before even I did. I was a usurper.

"Focus on your last moments," Mom murmured, rousing me from my crushing guilt and pulling me into the present. "Go back to that moment fully."

I let my mind circle back to the helicopter. The trees and grass and dirt blowing as it descended to the ground. The green of the jungle so lush it almost hurt my eyes to look at it. A giant tiger leaping at me. My lovers trying to block its way but failing. It had attacked me. Not us. Me.

"It was... Intentional," I whispered.

"Who would send a tiger after you?" Mom asked, her voice slight even as she took my hand in her firm grip.

"A tiger shifter," Kwame murmured. "It must be someone from the Tiger Nation."

"No." My eyes opened, and I stared ahead, unfocused. I could still feel the complete and utter shock, the sense of betrayal that had stunned me as my consciousness blinked out. As I'd tumbled into this world, into the blackness, the veil that had swallowed me between worlds.

I knew who it was.

A man who had been killed by a tiger, therefore turned into a tiger.

I knew only one man who had been killed by a tiger, a man whose eyes had burned hatred at me in the last moment of his life. A man who had refused to see me the last time I was here. The man I'd never forgotten, who I never would forget. He had promised to make a life with me, to give me the life I wanted. Instead, he'd given me death.

SIX

Sir Kenosi
Entrepreneur, Cheetah Nation

THE OTHER TWO MEN STARED AT ME. I WAITED FOR them to tell me I was a sick fuck, and that they'd rip my dick off if I put it near our mate now. But no one said a word. I'd never used the amulet before, since it only worked for True Mates, and I'd never imagined that I'd be lucky enough to have one. I certainly hadn't imagined putting my cheetah inside her when she was already gone, trying to bring her back to life.

"You know it might be too late," Lord Balam said, eyeing me and then Itzel.

"I know."

Shadow shielded his eyes and peered up at me. "You're going to do it?"

"It might not work," Lord Balam warned.

"But it might," I said. "My cheetah is strong. He might heal her."

"He might," Shadow said slowly. "But according to the curse, if the heir opens the amulet before the tour is complete, she can never mate until they've passed into the spirit world."

"She's already there," I said. "The only question is, what happens to me?"

Shadow's young face was somber. "If you do it, you may or may not save her. Either way, you'll die."

We stood surrounding her, watching her body for a moment. There was none of the fire and spark in her anymore. It wasn't Itzel. But if it could be... If there was even a chance, I had to do it, and I had to do it now. Each moment that her body lay dead, that her organs were deprived of oxygen, made it less likely that I could heal her.

I retrieved the Cheetah Amulet, then paused with it cradled between my hands. "Are we really doing this?"

Shadow gave the slightest nod. Neither man pointed out that they weren't doing anything except observing. I was the one doing it. It was my amulet. I was the one trading my life for hers.

I recognized the cruel irony. If I brought her back to this world, we'd trade places, and I still wouldn't get to be with my mate. If I didn't? Well, I'd fucked just about every kind of woman in the world, but I'd never fucked a dead one.

If my cheetah was strong enough to bring her back, to heal her body from death, that would be the last time I fucked her. I wouldn't get to fuck her as a True Mate, now that we'd been bonded. I'd never get to taste that dripping, delicious cunt again. I was bringing her back for the others, but for myself? I would not only live a life without my mate, but I wouldn't live life at all. I was giving up everything. My empire, my fame, my businesses. My *life.*

The others could have used it for the same purpose. But neither of them was volunteering to die for the princess. Maybe it was my penance for what I'd done. I'd never even started to make it up to her for what I'd put her through. I kept telling myself she'd liked it. At least part of her had liked being at my mercy, completely under my control. I couldn't deny the feeling of power had been addictive, too. To make a princess beg for my cum inside her, to hear her screaming my name with helpless abandon.

Yeah, I'd liked it.

And maybe that was why I was the one who had to die to bring her back. Because I had liked bringing her to her knees, breaking her will. Because I had relished her helpless whimpers without revering her for the goddess she was. I had scorned her even after the panther amulet had revealed the truth. When I found out, I hadn't groveled and begged her forgiveness. I had pretended it wasn't true. My mate could not be the woman I'd bent over a table, holding her face in filth while I stuffed her tight cunt with my cock. My mate couldn't be the woman I'd degraded and shamed.

And yet, she was.

I wasn't a man who would say the words a woman wanted to hear, the words a True Mate deserved. I probably couldn't even say I was sorry. But I could do this. And maybe, even if she never saw me again, she'd forgive me. Maybe this would be enough. She would see what she meant to me, even if I could never say it.

Taking a deep breath, I knelt beside the dead princess. If I didn't look at her face, at her torn throat, at the blood, it would be okay. I'd fucked her before. Steadying myself, I took hold of the hem of her shirt and pulled it up, revealing her glorious breasts. They jiggled slightly as they were freed from the fabric and exposed to the afternoon sun. Her dark nipples stood out against her tan skin, and I swallowed at the sight of them poking up at me, begging me to stroke them with my tongue.

Shadow let out a low growl, his eyes fixed on her body as I crouched over her and gripped the waistband of her pants. With a trembling breath, I drew them down over her hips, baring her luscious mound. My mouth watered at the sight of her naked body, at the scent of her sex.

I glanced up at the others, expecting them to curse me and shame me, but they were staring transfixed at the buffet of naked glory in front of us. I held up the amulet, turning the delicate gold filament holding the oversized ruby. It gave easily, and I lowered my head and inhaled deeply. A rich, sweet scent invaded my nostrils and filled my sinuses. I fell back, gasping to draw a breath of the dense jungle air into my lungs. When I did, I felt the vapors fill and expand my lungs, and I was instantly lightheaded. A strange feeling of detachment settled over me, and I capped the amulet and slid it into my pocket.

"What happens now?" Shadow asked.

"Now I fuck the dead princess," I said.

I slipped out of my clothes, dropping them to the ground beside me. My body shone in the warm rays of evening sun, dark beside the princess's golden tan. I'd fucked dozens, maybe hundreds of women with an audience, but this time, unease flickered inside me. I would die whether or not Itzel lived. Was it really worth taking the chance?

One look at the princess gave me an answer. It was worth any risk.

I bent over her, seeing my body as if from above as I leaned down and pressed my mouth to her smooth mound. Shadow drew a sharp breath, but I didn't look up. The scent of the princess's addictive cunt invaded my nostrils as effectively as the potion, and I was gripped with a blinding urge to drink from her juices, to lap up every drop of her sweet nectar. I moaned and opened my mouth, sliding my long cheetah tongue through her lips from her clit to her ass.

She still tasted like our princess, the sweetest nectar that made every thought disappear from my mind except the incessant drive for more, more, more.

I parted her legs, buried my face between them, and lapped at her tender flesh, sucking her clit between my lips. I sucked harder, expecting her to yelp in pain until I remembered that she couldn't. I drove my tongue into her opening, wetting her folds until they were as slick as if her own juices ran through her crevice and dripped over her ass, wetting the dry ground beneath her.

My tongue stretched further, becoming rougher and longer as I let my cheetah surface. I tasted her, tunneling into her, then withdrew. Cradling her big round ass in my palms, I stretched her pussy lips wide with my thumbs and began to fuck her with my tongue. It thrust into her until she was warm and wet as a living body. My cock throbbed with each pass of my long, cat tongue into her depths.

"Give her your cheetah," Lord Balam commanded, his voice cutting through my hypnosis.

I dropped back from her, breathing hard and wiping my mouth with the back of my hand.

"Fuck her," Shadow rasped, his eyes burning with pure, raw lust. "Or I will."

As if I expected her to wake up, I lowered myself over her carefully. Reaching down, I gripped my cock and slicked it through her wet folds. Pressing the head to her opening, I sucked in a breath. Her pussy was cold against my fevered skin.

"Fuck her," Shadow rasped again, his breath coming short as he knelt beside us, watching my cock strain against her tight opening.

With a groan, I shoved forward, burying my cock inside her. I shuddered with horror at the cold clench of her walls around me, but also at the knowledge that it still felt good. God, it felt good. Her pussy was slick and tight, straining around my thick cock. I thrust into her again, helpless to keep the pleasure from rippling through my body. I didn't want it to feel good, but it did. Oh, fuck, I was sick, but her cold pussy felt so horrifically taboo that it made my cock swell even harder as I drove into her, unable to help myself.

That had been it all along. I wanted her to feel as helpless as I felt in her presence. One taste of her honeyed cunt, and I'd lost my mind, lost all control. I'd wanted to make her feel just as powerless. Now I had the power.

"Harder," Lord Balam rumbled, his breath hot against my ear as he leaned in, watching my cock driving to the hilt inside her. I thrust harder, pounding into her with a wet, slick sound. He drew her knee wider, giving me easier access. I could feel my cheetah straining inside me, ferocious and maddened with a desire to claim our mate. I gripped her hip and slammed into her motionless body harder and harder, pleasure driving me like a cruel master.

"Give her your cheetah," Shadow growled.

I pushed my cheetah to leave me, but he only urged me to fuck our mate more viciously. I dug my hands into the dirt, ramming into her with such force that she scooted across the ground with each savage thrust. I had all the power now. The power to put more than my cock into her. To put my cheetah into her, to take over her entire body with mine, to own her to the furthest stretch of every hair on her head. She was mine. Ours. We possessed her.

My balls filled, ready to spill our seed into her. I heard a rumbling and looked up to see the tiger staring at us, a low growl building in his throat. Shame shot through me like a geyser. This was a ritual meant to be witnessed only by Itzel's mates, not her murderer and enemy. Instead of making me slink away in humiliation, the knowledge that someone else was witnessing this violation squeezed a shot of cum from my cock. I let out a giant roar and pumped into the dead princess, grinding her ass into the dirt as spurts of hot cum flooded from my turgid cock into her limp, cold cunt.

I felt a strange separating sensation as my cheetah raced into her with the tide of my seed. It wasn't just as if I were looking down on myself from outside my body. It was as if half the life had been snatched from my body. Maybe it had. For one moment, my mind grew as sharp and clear as a diamond. I saw everything. My life had been empty, and now it was over. There was no redeeming myself, no second chance to live better. I had given her my cheetah, and she had no cat to give back. My body felt small and vulnerable, as if it could be overpowered at any moment by anyone.

I heard a rasping voice speak, coming from beside me but simultaneously as meaningless as a sneeze on the other side of the world. "The tiger's gone."

I lifted my head and blinked, uncomprehending, at the pile of vines where the tiger had been. Lord Balam gave a bark of rage and shot to his feet.

I rose from the princess and knelt on the ground beside her. I wondered if my cheetah would come back to me when she'd healed, if I'd get to have him in the spirit world at all. As I knelt there, I knew I wouldn't get answers here. If my cheetah could heal her, it would take time, and I didn't have time. I wouldn't get to see Itzel come back. I'd have no last moment with her to tell her it was worth it, to ask her forgiveness. My life had been big, glorious, glamorous. My death was quiet and unremarkable.

SEVEN

Itzel
Princess, Ocelot Nation

PAIN AND CONFUSION WARRED IN MY MIND. EACH time I would think that I needed to remember—something, I didn't know what—the pain would wash away all conscious thought. It seemed to have no end, only a razor continuously sawing through my throat and the knowledge of some invasion I was helpless against.

At last, I felt something besides pain. I opened my eyes.

The first thing I saw was a curtain of long, black hair hanging over a man's face. I sucked in a breath, and his head shot up, his gemstone green eyes fixed on me with such intensity it nearly knocked the breath right back out of me. I opened my mouth, wanting to say his name, but my throat screamed in protest at the very thought.

"Itzel," he said, staring at me like... Well, like I'd just come back from the dead.

I nodded, and Shadow slid from the stool where he'd sat, leaning over me. His fingertips whispered over my cheek, and I closed my eyes and drew another breath, this one trembling through me.

"You're alive," he said. I wanted to ask how, how it was possible that my body could support my life, but then a strange thought invaded my mind. Was I in someone else's body? I felt like myself, but not like myself. There was something different, some uneasiness at the edges of my mind, as if someone unseen were breathing over my shoulder.

My lids fluttered open, and I stared up into Shadow's unfathomable gaze. His eyes burned into mine, a tumult of emotion swirling there. For a long minute, neither of us moved.

"Thank you," he whispered, the raspiness of his voice smoothing out. He leaned in and gently swept his lips across my forehead.

"What for?" I whispered, even that sending a bolt of pain through me.

"For coming back," Shadow said, crouching so his face was level with mine, his chin resting on the edge of the bed.

I smiled, a warmth filling my chest until I thought it would overflow.

"I'll get you medicine," Shadow whispered, gently stroking a hair off my cheek. "Then you'll rest and heal."

I wanted to tell him I loved him, to thank him, but I couldn't. Not yet. I was too tired.

I slept again. When I woke again, I had the presence of mind to look around. I was in a bed with thick pillows and a soft mattress. Rich, jewel colored velvet curtains covered the windows, and an intricately designed rug shot through with gold threads covered the floor.

"Here, drink," rumbled a deep, rich voice. I turned to see Lord Balam lying propped on the pillows next to me, a book in one hand and his head resting on his other palm. He reached behind him and produced a glass of water, which I quickly drank.

I lay back on the bed after downing the chilled liquid. Lord Balam studied me expectantly.

"Hi," I said.

"Hi." He smiled and leaned down, pressing his full lips firmly against mine.

When he pulled away, he sat up. "I should get the others. They'll want to know you're up and about."

"What'd I miss?"

"Not much," he said. "Your death hit us all pretty hard."

"Is Kwame back?" I asked, an irrational dart of fear shooting through me. What if he'd tried to drag me back here, and I'd somehow trapped him back in the spirit world?

Lord Balam nodded, pressing a kiss against my lips again before speaking. "He's here. We're at the palace in the Tiger Empire. We thought maybe they'd orchestrated the attack, but after seeing your attacker, we realized it had nothing to do with Shah Tiger."

"Tadeu," I said, my chest tightening. I pressed a fist to my heart and closed my eyes.

"When I saw him emerge from the tiger, I realized who he was, though I only saw the last minutes of his human life. I realized then that the attack had been... personal."

I nodded, my throat aching from more than the wound he'd caused.

"How did I heal?" I asked. "How can my body have recovered from that?"

"Sir Kenosi," he murmured, covering my hand with his. "He gave you his cheetah."

"How?" I whispered, realizing that was the presence I felt, the restless feeling that something foreign hovered around me. It wasn't around me, though. It was inside me.

"He used his amulet," Lord Balam said soberly, his eyes full of concern as he watched my reaction.

"He... Fucked my body?"

Balam nodded.

A shiver went through me, and I gripped Lord Balam's hand. "Is he okay?"

Some part of me knew the answer to that question, though. Because I still had his cheetah. He wouldn't have simply left it with me. I didn't know if that was even possible.

"There's something you should know about the curse on the panther amulet," he said.

But I already knew. There was so much about the curse that they should know, and the first thing was that no one could fuck me.

"But... He's not my mate," I said. "He said he didn't have one. That he didn't see anyone when he opened the Panther Amulet."

"He lied."

"But... Why?"

He shrugged one hulking, tattooed shoulder. "That's something only he knew."

"Did he know about the curse?" I asked, staring at the jaguar with stricken eyes.

He nodded again. "He knew."

"He knew I was his mate? And that he'd die if he gave me his cheetah?" Even though part of me had known it all along, another part of me couldn't believe it. Sir Kenosi was nothing if not hedonistic and selfish in his pursuit of pleasure. He was certainly not the kind of man who gave part of himself to a girl he'd fucked, even if she was his mate. He hadn't even accepted me as his mate. He'd denied it.

Lord Balam nodded again. "There's something else."

"What?" I asked, my mind skipping from one of them to the next. Shadow was okay. Lord Balam was okay. Prince Kwame was okay.

Sir Kenosi was dead.

Lord Balam wet his lips with his tongue, almost as if he were having trouble speaking. Which was not something he did.

"Is it Camila?" I asked, flooded with guilt at what I'd done to her, and the guilt at knowing her accusations about me were right. I would be queen. I didn't know how, but I prayed it didn't mean that she wouldn't make it home from her tour. Death was the only thing that could keep her from the throne. Had I hurt her when I pushed her from the helicopter?

But no. We hadn't been in the air yet. If something had happened, though, if she died because I'd left her stranded in the Lion Kingdom...

"No," Lord Balam said, shaking his head. "But I hear she's arriving today."

I sat up, amazed at the solid feeling of my own body. In the spirit world, I had been myself, and I'd seemed to have substance. But the weight of my human body here was different somehow. It felt comforting and secure, like wearing a heavy blanket on a cold night.

"Camila's here?" I blurted. "She's going to kill me."

"Is there any chance... That she already tried?"

I started to protest, to say of course not, she would never do such a thing. We were sisters. We loved each other. We looked out for each other.

But I'd pushed her from a helicopter. I'd stolen her Amulet Tour.

And she'd... Well, she hadn't done anything but accuse me of a few things that turned out to be true. That was the thing, though. She hadn't done anything. She'd been more than happy to let me do the hard things on her Amulet Tour, only appearing to collect each clan's amulet.

She had tried to stop me from going to Africa on that leg of the tour, though. She'd been prepared to do it alone. I couldn't blame her for what had happened to me at Sir Kenosi's. She hadn't bitten me, hadn't given me an infection. She hadn't forced him to hold me hostage. If I hadn't inserted myself into her business, she would have been there on her own, without me.

And maybe she'd have gotten it just the same if I had stayed home when she'd told me to.

"I don't know," I admitted after a long silence. Saying those words, admitting that truth, hurt worse than her worst betrayal. Because now I was the betrayer.

The truth was, I didn't know Camila as well as I'd always thought. I'd seen a side of her on the tour that I'd never seen before, a side that I wouldn't have believed existed before I'd seen it with my own eyes. Camila could be conniving. She could be as cold and heartless as our father.

Maybe I could, too, but that wouldn't have surprised most people. I had always been prone to losing my temper, to passionate outbursts. People knew what they were getting with me. I'd always thought the same about Camila, but now... Now I knew she was more than I'd given her credit for. She'd make an excellent queen. I'd just never realized that she would be an opponent, not an ally.

"We better get ready," I said, throwing off the blankets. I was naked under them, and I remembered again what had been done to me before I woke. Part of me was horrified by the violation, but I couldn't exactly be angry at a man who had sacrificed his life so that I could live.

"I still don't understand," I said as I searched for clothes. "Why would Sir Kenosi die for me? He didn't even like me."

"He doesn't have to like you. You're his mate." Lord Balam paused, watching me wrap a patterned skirt around my hips. "Our mate."

My hands stilled, and I looked up from what I was doing. Lord Balam sat on the bed, his hands folded in his lap, his steady gaze fixed on me.

"Your mate?" I asked, my voice catching. Lord Balam was the man who had been with me from the start—or what felt like the start. He'd freed a part of me that I'd never explored before. He'd shown me the heights of pleasure, and some pain along with it. He'd been exactly what I asked for every step of the way while never compromising the truth of who he was. But he wasn't my mate. He'd told me as much.

He nodded, pushing back his jaguar cloak to show me a tattoo among all his others, this one glowing like moonlight.

"You lied to me?" I asked, hurt digging its claws into me like the tattoo.

"I didn't," he said. "I wasn't your mate then. At least, I didn't know I was. Not until you opened the amulet. It marked me, too, Itzel."

"I thought that was supposed to happen when you had sex with someone?"

"It is," he said. "Maybe it's the curse. It held the mark off any of us until you opened it. Then it marked all of us."

"It marked me, too," I admitted, sinking onto the edge of the bed. I turned and showed Lord Balam my upper arm, the four cat paws climbing my skin to my shoulder. One of them had turned the inky black of a midnight sky.

I raised my eyes to Lord Balam, running my finger across the print. "Kenosi?" I whispered.

He nodded.

Pain and regret twisted in my belly. I hadn't known Kenosi well, but I knew why he was the way he was. I knew that despite what he'd done to me, he'd been the one willing to give his life for me. And now his mark was on me, black as the loss it represented.

I knew I was lucky—unbelievably lucky. I didn't have to live with one black mark and nothing else for the rest of my life. I had life. And I had three other marks, where other shifters had only one. But even knowing that, I couldn't help but ache for the loss of my cheetah mate. I'd barely scratched the surface of the famous Sir Kenosi, and now I'd never know him further than that.

Or maybe I would. I wasn't going to say never. Not after what had happened to me. If I could bring Kwame back, I'd find some way to bring Kenosi back. It felt wrong to go on with life as if he'd never existed, to be happy with my other mates at his expense. Because he wouldn't be happy. He wouldn't get a lifetime to bond and get to know his mate, to make love to her, make children with her. How could I do all that knowing that a man had sacrificed his life to give me those things?

I would find a way to bring him back, to give him all those things just as he'd given me the chance to do. I wouldn't give up until he was beside my other mates, just as he should be.

"Come here," Lord Balam said, taking my arm and pulling me down on the bed with him. "Let me look at you before you cover up. I can't quite believe you're healed."

"I can't either," I said, skimming my knuckles over my bare belly.

Lord Balam's eyes followed the movement, and his lids became hooded. Warmth flooded my limbs as my body remembered how to live again, how to love. I slid my hand lower, undoing the tie in the wrap I'd secured around my waist.

Lord Balam drew a breath, and a deep, satisfied rumble started somewhere deep inside him. Keeping my eyes locked on his, I slid my hand lower, cupping my bare mound.

He growled and slid a warm, rough hand across my belly and up to my breast, palming one and squeezing gently. Leaning down, he captured my nipple between his thick, hot lips. I gasped as his tongue rasped across the bud, and my other nipple became instantly hard. He pinched it between his thumb and forefinger, squeezing hard enough to make me yelp. My clit throbbed, and my knees opened instinctively, aching for him. My own fingers felt small and cold compared to his thick, skilled ones.

Lord Balam tugged a mouthful of my breast into his mouth, twisting my other nipple until I whimpered and squirmed against my hand. I spread my pussy lips and felt the cool of the air hit my hot wetness. After what I'd been through, nothing could make me feel more alive than being claimed by this rough, primal man. I needed him, needed his torturous girth to rip me open, his powerful body to pound me until I exploded, reminding me that I was alive, solid, and real.

I rolled over onto him, straddling his hips even as he adjusted his position to keep my nipple in his mouth. He teased it with his teeth, sending another throb straight to my core. I rolled my hips on his, relishing the hard ridge of his cock swollen inside his pants.

"Lord Balam," I gasped. "I need you to throw me down and really fuck me."

He groaned and wrapped his arm around me, flipping us over in one motion and grinding me down into the mattress. "God, I want to," he growled. "I want to fuck you so hard I tear you in two. I want to hear you crying for mercy while your cum squirts all over my cock because you like it when I really plough that pussy and leave you wrecked."

"I don't like it," I breathed. "I love it. Now fuck me. I'm so wet."

He reached between us and sank a finger deep inside me. "No, Princess," he said. "You're not wet. You're dripping."

I spread my thighs and arched up, clutching his shoulders so hard my nails dug into his skin.

"I'd kill to fuck you like that," he said into my ear. "But you know the curse. I can never fuck you again."

Eight

Tadeu
Shifter, Tiger Nation

"I KILLED THE WOMAN WHO KILLED ME," I SAID TO the interviewer, some cheetah chick working for one of the reality shows about felines. When they found out back home that I'd killed Itzel, it would blow up in my face. Everyone in the Ocelot Nation loved her. I wanted a chance to share my side of the story before they called for my head. Not that I'd be in danger here. What could the Ocelot Nation do to me now?

Nothing, that's what.

"Are you sorry?" asked Ebele, a thin cheetah lady with medium brown skin and lemon-yellow curls cut close around her head. I'd agreed to an exclusive interview for her show, something that famous cheetah Sir Kenosi owned, in exchange for a chunk of money that I could use to buy my own house here. One day, maybe I'd have a few horses and a stable of my own, just like I'd dreamed about back home—with Itzel.

"No," I said. "No, I'm not sorry. She deserved it."

"She deserved to die," Ebele said. "Because she killed you?"

"She didn't just *kill* me," I said. "I didn't get to die like a regular guy, pass on to the spirit world, and make peace with it. I woke up in this body the next day, this body that started growing like I was fucking twelve instead of twenty-five."

"You don't want to be big?" Ebele asked, her small eyes widening.

"That's not the point," I said. "Tigers are undead. We're the fucking vampires of the feline world."

"But the Tiger Empire is the biggest of all the Feline Nations," Ebele said. "The most powerful and prosperous of all."

"I'm sure they are," I said. "But I never asked to be a shifter. I'd rather have died. I hate shifters."

"A shifter who hates shifters," she said with a grin for her cameraman. "This is a first."

"Because I'm not a shifter," I said. "I don't have that mentality. I don't have that entitlement. I was born human, and I should have died human. Itzel knew that. That's why she chose such a fucked up way for me to die."

"She chose the tiger?" Ebele asked.

"Yeah, but first she had me convinced she was going to give herself to me. That little cock-tease strung me along for years, promising me more than a taste of her pussy. And I followed along like the pussy-whipped idiot I was," I said, shaking my head in disgust. "Am I allowed to say cock on your show?"

"Just be yourself," Ebele said. "We'll edit."

"Thanks," I said, shifting my huge, foreign body in my seat. "Anyway, I don't know what I did to make her hate me so much. The fucked up part is, I don't think she did hate me. She just didn't give a single fuck what happened to me. It was all a game to her, to see what I'd do. And I guess she got tired of her little game and fed me to a fucking tiger. If that wasn't bad enough, I became the thing I hated most. And she knew it. She knew how I felt about shifters."

"What happened once you woke up?"

"The Ocelot Nation didn't want me," I said. "They offered me to Shah Tiger. Itzel was done with me, so she had me shipped to this place, clear across the world to a nation I don't know, a culture I don't know. I didn't understand this society. And unlike her, I wasn't tutored in the customs and languages of the world. But there's one thing I do know. One thing I understand. Revenge."

"Are you afraid she'll come back as a tiger, since you were in tiger form when you killed her?"

"No," I said, shaking my big head. "It has to be a real tiger, not a shifter, to make you come back. That's how I know she meant for this to happen to me. Why else would she choose a tiger of all things to kill me? She could have scraped up a pack of wild dogs on the streets of the Ocelot Kingdom. They don't want you to know they have that kind of thing there, but they do. In the poor human neighborhoods? Shit, you can find anything."

"What about here?" she asked. "Were you poor here, too?"

I shrugged. "Yeah. It's hard to get a job when you can't speak the language. The shah speaks many languages, so he gave me a job, but I'm worse off here than back home. There, I was skilled. Here, I'm a fucking janitor. And it's not like I have my boys to go out with. I'm a transplant. I'm not even the same race as the other tigers. I don't know why the shah didn't just tell King Ocelot to keep me. I'm sure Itzel could have found some new torture for me there."

Shah Tiger owned my life now. He was twice as perverted as King Ocelot but not near as bloodthirsty. I'd take it, if I had to stay in this world.

"The shah, is he good to you?" Ebele asked.

I knew a trap when I heard it. This damn interview was going to get me killed. Oh, well. The shah had given me permission to do it.

"I haven't been beaten here," I said. "I haven't been forced to fight to the death with no chance of winning. In fact, I've never heard about the shah ordering a single execution in all the months I've been here. I've never even gotten wind of a death under mysterious circumstances—King Ocelot's

86

favorite. That way, he could also execute some guards or a few others he pretended to suspect."

"It sounds like the Ocelot Nation is a dangerous place," Ebele said. "They won't accept foreigners to film or interview anyone there, so this is a rare glimpse into their kingdom. Can you tell us some more about that?"

"I wasn't part of palace life," I said. "I was in the stables, just outside it. Sometimes we heard gossip, or we heard about the big things, like when the queen died. The guards who were supposed to be on duty the night she was kidnapped, they were all strung up and shot by the new guards taking their place. No one will ever forget that day. I think that's when we all realized exactly how disposable we were to the royal family. How obedient we had to be, and what could happen to us if we weren't."

"Were the guards celebrating their promotion?" Ebele asked. "The ones shooting the bodies as they hung. Were they proving how loyal they were?"

I shrugged. "They're shifters. I didn't know them. But if they were smart, they were following the king's orders and praying like fuck they didn't end up there next. The guards usually work the streets for a while. A palace guard position is a huge promotion. But it's probably the most dangerous job in the world. In the stables, we called them 'dead men walking.' We took bets on how long they'd last before the king had them executed."

"Why would they want that position?"

"Money," I said. "Money to send back to their families, if they have someone to take care of at home. Prestige. The hope they might be moved off guard duty and into the court itself, be given land and a title. The chance to one day sway the king's decisions... If they live that long."

"Was that your goal?"

"Fuck no," I said, shifting in my seat. "Even the stable boys know not to get too close to the royals. Anyone in spitting distance is in blaming distance. The minute one of them annoys a royal, he ends up where I did. Hell, he might end up there for no reason other than he was the first person the king saw when he needed someone to blame for a murder *he* committed."

"That does sound like a dangerous job," Ebele said. "But let's talk about your job. You said even a stable boy knows not to get too close to the royals. And yet, that's exactly what you did."

I cracked a grin at her. "I never said I was smart."

"What made you break your rules and befriend the princess?"

I laughed, but there was no humor in me. "I was twelve. I didn't have rules of life back then. If I had, I wouldn't have lost my life. But she came out there crying one day, must have been about five years old, wanted to hide in the loft. You try saying no to a crying kid—even a princess. At first, she was more like the annoying kid sister who liked to tag along. But she grew up good."

"As her friend, did you enjoy certain... Privileges?"

"You mean, did I fuck her? No."

"Anything else, though?" Ebele pressed. "Maybe some leniency, a little more freedom?"

"I guess so," I admitted at last. "In a country where you're so unimportant that you can be killed and no one blinks twice, but so dangerous that even speaking the king's name in vain earns you a death sentence, you take whatever protection you can get. Even if it turns out to be a trap."

"You think Princess Itzel planned to have you killed all along?"

"Not all along," I said. "But at some point. I don't know when. I only know that she set me up that night. She lured me into thinking she was going to give herself to me, that we'd really be together. And then she sent ocelot guards after me."

"You still don't know why?"

I shook my head, my fists clenching on the table between us. "No," I said. "The guards grabbed me out of my apartment, but they wouldn't tell me what I'd done. Later, one of them brought me dinner and told me that Itzel had ordered my arrest. She'd told her father that I'd offended her with my presumptuousness because I'd thought I was good enough to fuck her. She couldn't believe I thought I had the right to her virginity. She wanted to give it to someone important."

"Did that sound like something she'd say?"

"I didn't believe it at first," I said. "But he knew how I'd die, what she'd ordered for me. I don't think I believed it still, not until I was led out and killed for sport in front of an entire arena. And the princess, she just sat there in her fancy dress with her royal family, in the best seats in the house, and watched me die."

"That convinced you," Ebele said. "Because you saw that she was like her father after all."

"That, and one more thing." The memory made me see red, anger pulsing in the corner of my vision like an exposed heart.

"What thing?" Ebele asked, leaning forward, her inky eyes alight with eagerness. She wanted the good stuff. The stuff that turned to poison in my veins, burned like cinders in my throat.

"That night, after I'd been killed," I started, grinding out the words. "I asked to see her. The guard left and came back with her sister—Camila. She said Itzel didn't want to see me. That she was done with me, and she'd ordered me shipped out so she never had to lay eyes on me again. When I told that bitch I didn't believe her, Camila said Itzel wanted me out of the way. She'd already set her sights higher, and she wanted me gone so the rumors about our relationship wouldn't tarnish her reputation or make her new lover doubt her *purity*." I laughed, the sound slicing at my throat like razorblades.

"Because rumor had it, you'd already been with the princess."

"I hadn't fucked her, but there was nothing pure about Itzel. She'd been sucking my dick for years, just stringing me along until she was ready to move on to more important men, ones with titles, who could give her the status she'd been so desperate for all her life. I'd never finished the job and fucked her properly, but she was anything but innocent. And not just in terms of sex. She was always scheming, wanting closer to the throne. Wanting influence."

"That's why you don't feel any remorse for killing her?"

"I'll pay for what I did. The shah will make sure of it. I accept that. But feeling remorse? Why should I? She felt none for killing me."

NINE

Itzel
Princess, Ocelot Nation

"OH MY GOD," I GROANED, COVERING MY FACE WITH both hands. "The fucking curse."

And then I started laughing. Because what else could I do? I'd come back from the dead, but I could never mate with my mates. I was still cursed. My pussy literally brought death to the world. Well, maybe not the world, but all the men I loved.

Not to mention that we'd once called them the "fucking amulets," which was just about as fitting as calling this the "fucking curse."

I got up from the bed and started dressing, ignoring the swollen ache of arousal between my thighs. "I don't know how long I'm going to last before I think one last fuck is worth dying for," Lord Balam said, watching me re-wrap the silk dress around my body.

"Can we do other stuff?" I asked. "Maybe we can still fool around. Can you consult the oracle or something?"

"You want me to ask the oracle if I can still fuck you with my fingers and my tongue?"

God, yes. I'd have let him ask my own mother that question if it meant he'd satisfy the hunger to be filled.

He ran his tongue slowly along his upper lip, his eyes hooded as he stared at my bare tits. My clit throbbed, and my gaze was captivated by the obscenity of his pink cat tongue stroking the flesh of his mouth.

"I'm sure it's not worth asking," I said with a shrug, as if he had no effect on me.

A soft tap sounded on the door, and Shadow stuck his head in. When he saw that I was awake, he stepped into the room with Kwame on his heels.

Kwame came to me and took both my hands in his. "My queen," he said. "The king is requesting your presence at dinner."

I'd barely gotten back on my feet, but I knew there was no time to lounge around and recover. I'd already been in bed for too long.

"I owe him my gratitude," I said. "We'd better make an appearance."

"Yes," Kwame said. "He's been most hospitable while you recovered."

"We should go and see the king before Camila gets here," Shadow said.

I stilled, pain squeezing inside me at the reminder of the rift between me and my sister. A strange sensation rippled through me following the pain, defensive and alert. Something that didn't like that I was hurting.

I realized with a jolt that it was Kenosi's cheetah. He may have been gone, but he'd left a piece of himself with me—inside me.

The knowledge unsettled me, but not as much as the meaning of Shadow's words.

"You think I'm going to try to steal the tiger amulet from Camila?"

"You already have four of them," Lord Balam said, nodding to the bag containing the amulets. "You only need two more."

"And the ocelot amulet," I pointed out. "You think Camila's going to hand that over to me willingly?"

"If we can get the tiger amulet before she arrives, we can start for snow leopard territory," Prince Kwame said. "We'll be a step ahead."

"We'll need it," Lord Balam said. "The snow leopard amulet is owned by a hermit monk who makes Shadow look like an international celebrity. Finding him will be the real challenge."

My heart skipped. "A hermit?"

My brother. I knew nothing about him. All Tsewang had told me was that he had the amulet, and I had to find him. But right now I had something else to think about—my sister.

I stared at my men, anger building inside me. Camila might think I was a usurper, but I wasn't. I wouldn't be. If that's how I had to get to the throne, she could have it. I had no right to that throne. I didn't even have ocelot royal blood. I was the upstart, the common human born from her non-royal mother's affair with a man from another clan altogether.

I had no claim.

If fate was going to put me there, it could do that, but I wasn't going to murder my sister to make a curse come true, especially since that curse was on me, and it wasn't doing me any favors. I turned to my men, planting my hands on my hips. "You're all serious? You think this is decided, and I'm going to steal the throne from my own sister? She's still the rightful heir."

"The curse says otherwise," Shadow reminded me, his gaze unflinching.

"The curse said someday I'll be queen," I said. "It doesn't say when. If somehow that happens, which seems impossible since I'm not an ocelot, it won't happen like this. I'm not going to stab her in the back to get there."

Shadow's brows lowered. "Have you forgotten what she did to you?"

"I pushed her out of a helicopter."

"For a reason."

"Look, I'm not going to argue with you about this," I said. "I don't expect you to understand, but I love my sister. Even if she's weak, and even if that hurts me. I left Camila in the Lion Nation because I didn't want her to come here and get herself killed. I haven't changed my mind. I'm going to get the amulet, but I'm getting it for her."

"Are you fucking kidding?" Shadow growled.

The muscle in Lord Balam's jaw tensed, but he didn't speak.

"It is most noble to protect one's family," Prince Kwame said. "I also wouldn't want the throne if I had to murder my sister to get it. A reign that begins with bloodshed ends with bloodshed."

"Thank you," I said, taking his hand and squeezing. He beamed like he'd won a prize, and Shadow growled in disgust.

I turned to Lord Balam. "Do I have your support?"

"Always," he said simply.

The sincerity in his gaze reminded me of his unwavering presence throughout the whole tour, and a flood of warmth filled me. I took a breath and turned to Shadow.

"You said you'd do anything to make your mate happy," I reminded him. "I won't ask you to support me in this or to like my sister. But this is something I have to do. Please let me do it."

He stared at me a long moment, his green eyes electric. My pulse pounded as I waited, sure he'd say no. He was going to walk away. I'd asked too much.

"Why do you insist on being a martyr for your sister?" Shadow hissed. "You know she wouldn't do the same for you."

"I'm not being a martyr," I snapped. "But if I don't get the amulets, my father will stay on the throne forever, and I'm not about to let that happen."

"You should be on that throne. You've done what was needed to get the amulets. She hasn't."

"Because she can't," I blurted out, finally admitting a truth I hadn't even accepted for myself yet.

I stood staring at my men, the truth of my words sinking in. I wasn't just getting the amulets to protect her. I was getting them because I didn't believe she was capable of getting them.

"And you're sure you want her on the throne?" Lord Balam asked at last.

"I want my father off it," I said. "And truthfully, she's probably better equipped to lead the ocelots than I am. I'm not one of them. They've known Camila all her life. They trust her. If they want her, I'm prepared to give them what they want. If she fucks up? Then we can talk about the prophecy."

Finally, Shadow nodded. "The prophecy will come to pass one way or another. You're prolonging the inevitable."

"You're probably right," I admitted. "But I won't be the hand that makes it come true."

"I think we're all in agreement about one thing," Lord Balam said. "Let's get the amulet before Camila gets here and does something stupid."

Shadow picked up the small velvet bag Camila had used to store the amulet and slipped it into his pocket.

"You know I have to give those back," I said, fixing him with a stern look.

"I know."

"We shouldn't keep the shah waiting," Kwame said, swinging open the door.

I took a deep breath to steady myself, feeling the odd and somewhat invasive restlessness of the cheetah still inside me. I wasn't sure how long he was hitching a ride with me, or if I wanted him there, but for now, I had him. From the way he reacted to my emotions, he wanted to protect me. Sir Kenosi was gone, but his cheetah felt like another member of my team, someone who was on my side just as Prince Kwame, Lord Balam, and Shadow were.

As we strode toward the dining hall, my nerves settled, and I felt strong again, stronger than I had before. I was surrounded by three strong, incredible men. As my mates, I knew they would do anything for me. And even though I could feel a gaping emptiness where Kenosi should have been, the presence of his cheetah comforted me.

I mentally replayed the basics of what I knew of the Tiger Empire as we approached the court. The largest of the Feline Nations, it had a complicated government that I should know better than I did. Unlike a lot of other Feline Nations, tiger shifters didn't separate themselves from humans or other supernaturals. The Tiger Empire was a part of the larger country of India, like a state within the country. Humans and other supernaturals of all types all lived together within the empire, but Shah Tiger only governed the tiger shifters, while human laws governed humans. The shah's rule extended to all tiger shifters in the world, even the ones who didn't live within the borders of his empire.

My thoughts were interrupted by our arrival at the end of the corridor. There, we were ushered through a tall set of double doors into the dining hall. The large hall was circular, with windows high in the ceiling. Wall sconces provided ambient lighting to the diners, who were seated around the outside of a long, U-shaped arrangement of tables. We'd entered at the opening to the tables, directly opposite the shah's seat. A long rug of gold-colored wool led down the center of the room between the tables, leading to his seat at the apex of the arrangement. Everything in the room—the table setup, the rug, the entrance—led the eye directly to the shah.

"The princess has arrived," he said in a creaky old voice that was tinged with humor and thick with an accent. "Let us have a look at you."

Though he was a small, stooped old man, his eyes were alert and watchful with an edge of cunning. Everyone in the room had turned to stare at me as I stopped at the entrance to the walkway between the tables. I had a feeling I shouldn't take the attention off him for long. I swallowed my nerves and started forward, Lord Balam on one side of me and Prince Kwame on the other while Shadow loped behind.

This was the first time I'd appeared before a king who was as intimidating as my father, and I couldn't help but wonder what else they had in common. Besides that unfounded paranoia, there was the very real problem that he might not want to hand over the amulet to a mere human.

"Your Majesty," I started, bowing when I reached the end of the row of tables that led to his. "Thank you."

The diners, an assortment of people with defining features of various supernaturals as well as some that appeared human, paused in their meal to watch our exchange.

"It's not often we get visitors from the Ocelot Nation," Shah Tiger said, stroking his chin. I could hear his fingers rasp against the silver stubble on his pointy chin.

"That's true," I said. "But my sister and I would like to remedy that."

"I'm sure you would," he said, a gleam of mirth in his eyes.

"After all, we're the most powerful nation in the ICFN, and you're the smallest."

"What the Ocelot Nation lacks in geographical size, it makes up for in resources and innovation," I answered.

"Is that right?" he asked. "I'll have to take your word for it. I haven't set foot in it for almost a decade."

I winced. This guy was nothing like the head of the Lion Court, or even Sir Kenosi. I knew how to play Sir Kenosi's games.

I knew how to play this game, too, though. It had been a while since I'd been required to do so, but I'd grown up deflecting that kind of veiled accusation. I called on my inner Camila, the poised princess that I'd tried to emulate for half my life before realizing I'd never be a match for her in this department.

Still, I could usually maneuver my way through the minefields of a political dinner.

"We'd like to invite you to visit as soon as Her Grace Princess Camila takes the throne. In fact, we hope to gain the tiger amulet as a show of trust and improved future relations between our nations."

"Really?" he asked, raising a thin eyebrow. "You might want to inform her that you're working together. She seems to think you've stolen the world's most precious artifacts from her."

Fuck. Of course he'd talked to her, or at least my father, before she started for the Tiger Empire.

"I didn't steal them," I said. "A mistake was made, and they ended up in my possession. I have them right now, ready to give back to her when she arrives."

I gestured at Shadow, who grimaced before giving the shah the slightest of nods.

"That's too bad," the old man said with a twinkling smile. "I was hoping to watch the drama unfold when she arrived. I do so like a good show."

"My apologies, Your Majesty," I said. "But I'm simply completing the challenges needed to gain the amulets so my sister will not be overtaxed by some of the more demanding tasks."

"Ah," he said. "But if she's to be queen, she must be willing to make these sacrifices, don't you think? She should be willing to make hard choices and do hard things."

"Oh, she is," I said, an ache building in my chest as I forced out the next lie. "My sister and I are very close. It's devastating for her to see me go through any hardship."

Shah Tiger studied me for a long moment before nodding. "Very well. If you can't give me a show with your sister, then perhaps we'll find a different way for you to entertain me and my guests during our dinner."

I swallowed, my eyes darting around the tables on either side of me. "You want me to dance for you?"

"This is one of the sacred mating amulets," he said. "It takes more than a dance to seduce it from my hands. But I have spoken with your sister, and she said something similar about the future relations between our nations. I expect a lavish welcome when I arrive there."

"So, you'll come?" I asked. "Thank you so much, Shah Tiger. No expense will be spared to welcome Your Highness. We are so grateful for your interest in our humble nation."

"Now, as far as getting the amulet, I believe tonight I'd like a live show. I may look old and worn out, but I assure you, the right entertainment before bed can get me started and keep me going through my entire harem." He gave me a grin, his wrinkled lid dropping in a lewd wink.

I gulped, pretty sure I knew what he was asking. I glanced at my three lovers. "You want us to have sex for you?"

"Unless you can think of something better."

"We'll do it," Lord Balam said, his thick fingers wrapping around mine. I knew what he was thinking. It could have been a lot worse.

"Oh, not you," Shah Tiger said with a sly smile. "Let's make things interesting."

Fuck. It was about to get worse.

"Trust me, watching me with Lord Balam would be more that entertaining," I said. "But if you require all of us..."

"That's no sacrifice on your part," the shah said. "I like to see more drama unfold than just seeing a woman and her mate. I want to see the drama of a moral dilemma unfold before and during the act."

"Moral dilemma?" I asked, a knot forming in my stomach. Was he going to make me choose something horrible, like which of my lovers I wanted to fuck my sister while I watched?

"Besides," he said with a mirthful smile. "You haven't really been fucked until you've been fucked by a tiger. We are the biggest of all the species, in more ways than one."

Shit. I glanced around the table, wondering which of his court he was going to give me to. Two maharajas sat on each side of him, his sons from his various concubines. Was he going to make me choose between them? Or what was the drama?

The shah turned to the row of guards that stood behind him. "Bring the prisoner."

TEN

Gabor
Royal Guard, Ocelot Nation

"THAT THIEVING WHORE," THE PRINCESS CAMILA fumed, flinging open the door to the tiny cockpit. "After everything she's done, she gets to ride in comfort while I, the crown princess of the most refined nation in the world, am stuck with this piece of shit."

I wasn't sure that she required a response, but I nodded nonetheless. Her emotional state worried me, but I knew better than to suggest she talk to someone more qualified to calm her than a palace guard with a traitorous heart. I stared out the front of the old cargo plane that had arrived on King Ocelot's order to the nearest city. He'd asked for the best for his heir, and this was what they'd sent. I had tried to dissuade the princess, not sure that the plane was safe or even able to stay aloft, but she had ordered me to fly it to the Tiger Empire. So, that's what I'd done.

She stared at me through narrowed eyes, breathing hard. "Say it."

"Yes, Your Grace."

"Call her a thieving whore."

I was ten thousand feet above the ground with a woman whose mental state seemed less stable than ideal for the situation. So, I forced the words out, sure that my own mental state must be compromised if I was feeling more guilt about calling a human woman a name than about all I'd done to betray our crown. "She is a thieving whore."

"Hmph." Princess Camila crossed her arms, looking less than convinced. She stooped and squeezed into the empty copilot seat beside me. For a minute, neither of us spoke. I began to think she was calming down at last, something she'd been unable to do since we'd been stranded in the Lion Kingdom.

The plane lurched under us, despite the clear sky. I checked Her Grace, but she didn't seem to have noticed. She stared ahead, a calculating expression on her face. That was good. I didn't want her worried about the plane on top of everything else on her mind.

I had checked the fuel myself, but my knowledge of the mechanical aspects of the plane needed improvement. Most of my experience with aviation was confined to flying, along with a rudimentary knowledge of the mechanics of the much more modern planes King Ocelot had at his disposal.

When I'd joined the Guard at age sixteen, developing flight skills had been the thing I most looked forward to. Its allure had been just part of what led me to the high-level position of guard, but I had excelled at it. It wasn't as if I could pass up the opportunity to work inside the palace gates, anyway. One did not refuse an offer from the royal family. I would be paid handsomely, taught an impressive number of skills at the hands of the masters, from aviation school to sniper training, hand-to-hand combat, knife play, and horse-manship.

But no skill was more important or more necessary than keeping quiet, forgetting what one's eyes had seen and one's hands had done. Above all, a guard must have unwavering loyalty and unquestioning obedience. That had not been listed as a privilege granted, nor a skill required, in the letter of summons from the king, but I'd learned it soon enough. We all had.

"You know she's a traitor," Princess Camila said suddenly, turning to me.

"Yes, Your Grace."

"Even if she's a princess, she's not a *real* princess. She's not an ocelot. She can still be tried. For a crime this big? My father will have her imprisoned for life. And not just in a convent. Not that they'd take her after she screws her way across the entire globe."

Princess Camila might have lost her confidant, so she'd confided in me, but I'd never had one. A guard wasn't allowed the luxuries of family or love. I had only my own servitude, my honor, and the throne. The throne above all else.

"Yes, Your Grace," I said.

She crossed her arms again and threw her shoulders back against the seat. "You know," she said slowly. "I'll be the one who sentences her. Sure, he'll toss her in jail when she gets home. But before she's tried, I'll be coronated. I'll have her dragged out of her cell and shot on the street like the common whore she is." A self-satisfied smile played across her lips. She stared off as if imagining the scene exactly how she wanted it to play out.

After a minute, she fixed me with a glare. "She deserves it," she snapped, as if I'd protested her planned treatment of her sister. "She stole the most sacred objects in the world from me. And she pushed me, the heir to the throne, out of a helicopter, Gabor. She tried to kill me!"

I clenched my teeth together and didn't speak.

Her eyes narrowed. "I'm going to have you do it."

"What would you have me do, Your Grace?"

"I'm going to have you execute her," she said. "To prove your loyalty."

"I've sworn my life to the throne," I said. "It belongs to the crown until I die."

"Does it, though?" she asked, watching me as if waiting to pounce. "You haven't shown yourself loyal to me on this tour. Not the way you should be. Does the body, heart, and mind of both your human and your ocelot still belong entirely to the Ocelot Throne?"

I inhaled slowly, silently, through my nose. "Yes, Your Grace."

We both knew I lied. I had learned to have no heart, to take the thing I'd been born with, as flimsy and delicate as paper, and fold it into smaller and smaller squares until it was something as hard and impenetrable as steel. I felt only loyalty, pride, and honor for my country. Nothing else was allowed.

And yet, somehow, the other princess, the simple human princess, had plucked it up and unfolded that paper heart as if it were the most meaningless thing she'd ever done. She tied it to her kite string and flew it high, where everyone could see it, as if she were as proud of that steel-grey heart that had lost all feeling as she would be of a bright yellow one with as much light and passion as the sun.

Princess Camila had seen that kite, and she knew what it was. She knew what it meant.

A royal guard should have no strings to pull but the one tied to the throne.

I'd made that mistake, the mistake of thinking this was a job that would feed my family. It wasn't a job. It was a contract, a selling of the soul. And it hadn't provided for my little sister, the human who would unfairly be denied the opportunities the rest of my family, the ocelot shifters, were so eagerly handed. Her screams still haunted my sleepless nights, even though I hadn't been there to hear them. I hadn't been among the guards who had dragged her out of bed, accused her of treason, and beaten her to death.

But I might as well have been.

I had sent her money. Letters showing concern and love for her. I'd asked for days off to visit her, to attend a ceremony in which she was receiving an award for community service. I had dared to care about someone more than the king, and that wasn't simply treason, it was dangerous. A guard who loved someone more than the king could be blackmailed and bribed. But he couldn't be fired. Not after so much expense had been spared to train him in the skills a guard needed to be able to protect the king, to give his life for the king, to take lives for the king.

Princess Camila shifted in her seat to watch me. "Prove it," she said. "Prove your loyalty."

The plane lurched, but she didn't seem to notice. I wondered how much Princess Itzel would hate me if I didn't make it to the Tiger Empire with her sister. If the plane went down, killing us both, I would lose nothing. I'd already lost everything that had ever mattered.

I hadn't gone to my sister's funeral, and I'd never visited my parents again. One death had taught me enough. Guards didn't have families.

But Itzel did. Camila did. I wouldn't add her blood to the countless layers already on my hands.

"Your Grace, I would be happy to renew my vows to the throne," I said, as if it were a marriage.

It was a marriage. But in this marriage, someone whose heart strayed from the throne was executed as a traitor. Princess

Camila was allowing me leniency, and I owed her nothing but gratitude for that.

"Not to the throne," she said quietly. "To me."

I turned from my seat to stare at her, the lurch inside me instead of the plane this time. What she was asking was impossible, not just treason for me but for herself. The throne, the country, came before the individual who ruled it. For a moment, I wondered if she was testing me. Her eyes said she wasn't, but she wouldn't commit treason in front of one of the king's own guards. My heart began to hammer in my chest. I could have her removed from the throne, even imprisoned, for such a request.

But no. Of course I couldn't. There was no one left but us. No witnesses. No one, especially not her father, would believe me if I came forward. I could swear on the throne itself, and all I'd get in return was a firing squad for accusing the heir of betraying her own crown.

If I swore an oath of loyalty to her, though, I would lose the only part of myself I had left, the only thing the king hadn't erased completely. My honor.

And later, she could execute me for betraying the throne, even though I was obeying her orders. She could claim she'd been out of her mind with grief, and in her time of need, I should have upheld the oaths I'd taken to protect the throne from every threat, internal as well as external.

"Your Grace," I said quietly. "You know I am bound to the nation's throne."

"The throne will be mine," she said. "You're bound to my throne. You need to be loyal to me until that happens. While we're on this tour, you're not my father's guard. You're mine. I need to know that you won't betray me like you have before."

"I have made mistakes," I admitted. "You may punish me for them as you see fit. But I will swear loyalty only to the Ocelot Throne and Crown. I will never betray my country. Now, I need to land this plane without distractions, so please allow me to convey Your Highness safely into the Tiger Nation. I don't think it will stay up a minute longer."

Camila's eyes widened as she finally registered that the plane was not supposed to be experiencing turbulence.

"Swear loyalty to me," she demanded. "You have to do it now, or I won't leave."

"Your Grace," I said. "My life counts for nothing, but yours would be a great loss not only to your family but to your nation and the world. There is no time to argue. You need to be seated and secured in your seat."

"You will swear before we get off this plane," she hissed. "You'll swear or—or—."

Her eyes widened as an alarm began to sound. Without another word, she ducked out of the cockpit and back to one of the two seats behind it. I wondered if she knew that there was nothing she could add to the end of her threat. She could take nothing from a man who had already lost everything.

There was a reckless, terrifying freedom in having no heart. She had nothing to hold over me but my own life, and I'd long ago decided I would willingly give my life to keep my honor.

As the plane sped toward the jungle, I thought once more about the price of the lives on this aircraft. One was worth so little that even his own parents wouldn't mourn his passing. The other was worth so much to so many.

For one careening moment, I held not only Her Grace's life in my hands, but the lives of everyone who would live in our nation under her rule. For one moment, I had more than honor. I had power. I felt what the king must feel every moment, the sickening high of knowing that at the snap of my fingers, I could control the world. I wasn't just a man or a shifter or even a king. I could choose who lived and died. I was a god.

As I leveled the plane and aimed it for the clearest spot I could find, another thought flashed through my mind. I had the choice. I held our lives in the balance. The only question was, which decision let me keep my honor?

ELEVEN

Itzel
Princess, Ocelot Nation

MY HEARTBEAT SLAMMED INTO HIGH GEAR. INSIDE me, I could feel Kenosi's cheetah straining as if trying to rip through my chest and attack the shah who was apparently going to make me fuck some kind of convict.

Two of the guards exited the room while Shah Tiger turned back to me. "I owe you an apology, too," he said. "I believe you were greeted in a most inhospitable manner upon entering our country."

My head swam, and I could barely keep my feet. "Yes, Your Highness," I agreed, taking courage from the strength of my own voice. "But no apologies are necessary. As you can see, I'm fine now."

"Still, I would like the chance to make it up to you," he said, motioning to the door behind us. "Please allow the man who attacked you to do that. He's prepared to show you the warm welcome he failed to give you when you landed here."

"No," I whispered, stumbling back against Shadow. His strong hands caught my waist, and together we turned slowly to face my attacker.

A man stood in the doorway, a guard holding each elbow while his hands were bound together by a pair of steel cuffs. He was bigger than I remembered. No, that wasn't exactly right. He *was* bigger than he had been. Tadeu had been strong from hard work and naturally on the tall side. Now he was at least seven feet tall, straining with muscle from head to toe. His eyes, though. His eyes were fixed with the same murderous hatred I'd seen in them the day he'd died.

My knees buckled. Shadow's hands kept me upright, his grip tightening on my waist, his voice rasping in my ear. "No fucking way."

"Tadeu," I said, my voice coming out strangled as tears sprang to my eyes. "You're really alive." I was scared, yes, but more than that. So much more.

This man had been my childhood. For every party I hadn't been invited to attend, for every tear I'd shed, Tadeu had been there. He'd been the one I ran to when my entire family, even my mother, went to ocelot-only events. And there were plenty for the royal family.

My mother had apologized for having to leave me. She'd brought me back gifts when the obligations took her away for more than a night. When they went visiting the other families on their tours of the country, she'd bring me back fancy pastries, little stones she'd found in a streambed, even the gifts the family had bestowed upon the queen.

But Tadeu had never left me. He had been there to wipe my tears when the royal procession disappeared through the palace gates. He had taught me to curse so that I could express my feelings about the snobbery, to despise their status so it didn't hurt me. He'd made up games to distract me when they were gone, never failing to invite me along when he snuck out, even though most of the things he wanted to sneak out for were scandalously inappropriate for a princess. He'd never treated me like a princess. He'd treated me like a person, one he wanted to protect and care for as an equal, not someone he had to bow and scrape before.

What had happened?

Death, that's what.

Tears blurred my eyes as I stared at him, at the inhuman coldness in his gaze, the inhuman size he had grown to as a shifter. This was no longer the boy who'd given me my first kiss and my first orgasm. He wasn't the boy who had taught me how to spit watermelon seeds, hide from angry tutors when I skipped a lesson, and saddle a horse. The world had lost that boy. In his place was only a ferocious animal, a cold killer.

My killer.

At the shah's signal behind me, the guards began to march him forward. His jaw clenched, his nostrils flaring as he approached, but he didn't fight. He wore only a pair of loose trousers, so I could see every inch of his gigantic form, so I could tremble at the thought of enduring his wrath in a much more intimate way than a beheading.

A flicker of movement beside me caught my eye, and I glanced over to see a sleek black panther beside me, baring its teeth. Its coat glistened under the lights, its eyes gleaming green at the approach of danger. The panther was powerful and majestic like all felines, but he had a stillness about him that made him unique. He was the watchful one, my shadow guardian.

"Take the panther," the king said, sounding bored.

"No," I cried.

A net dropped over Shadow from out of nowhere. I wanted to scream, but before I could even draw breath, six men leapt across the tables and landed around him. Shadow hissed and bit at one of them, but another stuck a dart into his haunch, and the next second, the panther collapsed at our feet. The men started to drag him away, and when I tried to leap after him, Prince Kwame grabbed my hand.

"He's okay," he murmured. "They won't hurt him."

I took a shaking breath. Fuck. I'd almost lost it. I couldn't do that. I was the princess. I was being tested. They were watching my every move for worthiness. This was all a game, one that Sir Kenosi had prepared me for. He'd told me it was all a game, and now I was grateful as I pulled on that knowledge. The other kingdoms weren't so open and honest about it, but it was the same at each.

I squeezed Prince Kwame's hand to thank him, glad for the anchor as the guards holding Tadeu resumed their procession. When my first love drew closer, I could see the thin scars across his broad, tan shoulders—the ends of the lash marks that marred his entire back. Scars he'd gained at the hands of brutal ocelot guards for daring to love the king's daughter, insignificant as she was.

But that wasn't true, was it? If I was being honest with myself, I had to admit this part, too. I was responsible for every one of those scars. I might as well have held the whip in my own hands. In fact, he'd have been better off if I had. I wouldn't have struck him as hard as the ruthless guards.

When they whipped him, they'd done it for me. He hadn't been whipped because he dared to love me. He'd been whipped because I dared to love him. I had dared to love a stable boy. I had snuck out to see him. I had defied the king. But he couldn't order me to be whipped in the square without causing public outcry. As much as the ocelots of the nation knew and respected Camila, the human majority knew and embraced me. So he'd taken out his rage over my rebelliousness on Tadeu, knowing that if he hurt the man I loved, it would hurt me.

It had. But I hadn't stopped him. Sure, I'd cried and pleaded with my father to spare him, like any other teenage girl would. I hadn't been extraordinary. I hadn't summoned some unknown magic to protect Tadeu when the whip fell. I hadn't made him unnoticeable, almost invisible, the way Shadow could when he wanted. I hadn't murdered King Ocelot in his sleep.

Which made each of those scars mine to bear.

"Don't come closer," Kwame said in a low, strong voice.

The guards halted a few feet in front of me, their gazes moving between us and their ruler behind us, waiting for his instruction.

Sir Kenosi's cheetah was struggling furiously inside me, writhing for revenge. Our murderer stood in front of me. I might have been responsible for the beatings Tadeu had gotten, but he was responsible for my death, and now that I was alive, Sir Kenosi's. And the cheetah was pissed as fuck about that.

Apparently he was not alone.

Lord Balam turned to the shah with a murderous expression. The tattoos on his face seemed to have flowed into the lines of his fury, making this usually imposing man terrifying. His skin had gone red under the brown complexion and black tattoos, and his fists were clenched so tightly he was shaking.

"You can't mean for the princess to allow her own murderer any closer to her than he is now."

I'd never seen Lord Balam angry. Through this whole trip he'd been my rock, standing by me with calm that bordered on nonchalance. When Shadow had grabbed me and fucked me on the plane, he'd done nothing. When I'd told him what had happened when Sir Kenosi locked me up for days, he'd comforted me, but he hadn't hunted him down and kicked his ass, either. Lord Balam was the kind of guy who accepted things and moved on instead of fighting them.

Or so I'd thought.

The tiger shah scratched his head, grinning. "Who are you?"

I expected Lord Balam to back off at the reminder that although he was esteemed in his own court, he was still well below a king. Not only that, but he was a visiting noble, not in his own kingdom. Hell, he wasn't even from the Ocelot Kingdom, who would have more say in what happened to their princess than a random jaguar.

"I'm her True Mate," Lord Balam growled, the rage in his expression only darkening.

"And you think that puts you in a position where you can tell the Great Shah what he *can't* do?"

Before Lord Balam could speak, I grabbed his arm. When he didn't even move, his bulging muscles taut under my grip, I stepped in front of him. I took his face in my hands and lowered my voice, though the cats in the room could probably hear me anyway.

"It's okay," I whispered. "I promise."

"It's not okay," Prince Kwame murmured.

Lord Balam didn't relax, but his gaze moved to mine.

"I can do this," I said firmly, reassuring us both. "It's part of the game. He made his move, and now I make mine. Understand?"

Lord Balam swallowed, his gaze full of anguish that pierced straight to my heart. I leaned in and kissed him, hard and quick, on the mouth.

"It has to be done," I said. "It's what the king wants for the tiger amulet, and I'm going to do it."

"Your most esteemed and majestic Shah," Prince Kwame started, bowing deeply to the king. "If we may present a plea for your mercy—"

"I'll do it," I cut in, spinning away from Lord Balam.

"What?" Kwame asked, looking bewildered at my lack of hysterics.

"Your princess is eager to experience the true power of the most majestic of all beasts," Shah Tiger said. "The mighty tiger!" He swept his arm out, his oversized silk sleeve fluttering like a flag signaling the beginning of a race.

Go.

It was my move. A stark clarity entered my mind, and I began to unwind the dress I'd secured around my body. I didn't know if it was the cheetah inside me giving me strength or my own new understanding of the political world of felines, but any hesitation was gone.

"Seat the princess's escorts close to the exit so you can remove them if they distract from the wonderful show I've arranged for my guests," the shah said.

As guards escorted away my last two protectors, I wanted to offer them some comfort, but I had to focus on the task at hand before I lost my nerve. There was no easy way for them to watch this. I just had to get it over with so I could be with them again. I had to finish undressing, to pretend that I'd never known Tadeu, never promised him this night, this privilege. He was a stranger now.

But even as he stood watching me undress in front of the entire Tiger Court with zero fucks evident in his eyes, that became impossible. He may have been bigger and angrier, but he was still the man who laughed with me on his last night on earth, who I'd promised my virginity. That was long gone, but I'd always meant to give myself to him. Not like this, but nothing ever worked out as planned. So, I would have sex with him for the tiger king, put on a show for his guests. It was still Tadeu. If I'd been willing to do it with Lord Balam, someone I'd only known a few months, it should be nothing with Tadeu, who I'd known since I was old enough to sneak out of the palace and run to the stables to hide from the sting of rejection.

I'd been old enough for my mother to explain things to me, but not old enough for logic to ease the ache. Only Tadeu's jokes, the forbidden rides on the ponies and races up haystacks with other servant children, could make me forget and laugh again.

I turned to him, the last layers of silk sliding from my body and pooling around my feet. I heard a murmur of approval as the royal court surveyed my ample curves, but my eyes were fixed on Tadeu. "You're alive," I whispered. "It's really you."

"Don't act surprised," he said, his voice hard and accusatory.

"I just never imagined it like this," I admitted. I closed my lips, not willing to admit more. To tell him that if I'd let myself even hope that he was alive, it would have killed me. I'd have pictured myself running to him, throwing my arms around him, and sobbing until the tears were gone. That then he'd lay me down and make love to me, telling me he loved me even after death.

My virginal fantasies were obviously not coming true.

There was no love in Tadeu's eyes, not even understanding. No sympathy showed in this giant who had swallowed my childhood love. This was a transaction and nothing more. I took a deep breath, pushing down the swell of emotions that threatened to wash away my sanity, to make me throw my arms around him anyway, beg for forgiveness.

His gaze traveled slowly down my body, the weight of it making me come alive. As his eyes swept over my breasts, my nipples hardened, and a chill of fear and desire wracked my body. I knew this man's touch, knew his mouth and his hands, the pleasure they could give. He wasn't my True Mate, so I didn't endanger him. I'd promised him this, and even though my virginity was long gone, I owed him my body.

I stepped forward, a tremor going through me when his lids lowered halfway. He watched me close the distance between us. I slid my fingers into the waistband of his pants. I could already make out the ridge of his familiar cock through the fabric of his pants. Maybe it wouldn't be so bad. So it was in front of an audience this time. Still, I'd been fooling around with this man for years. I knew every inch of his scarred, work-hardened body. We were only taking it one step further, and though I didn't love that the entire Tiger Court was watching our first time to fully possess each other, maybe it would be kind of... Hot.

Tadeu lifted a hand, sliding it behind my neck. He gripped my hair, gathering it at the nape of my neck, and spun me around, pinning me to him. My head barely reached his nipples. Fuck, he was big. I bit back a cry of pain as his fist tightened in my hair, dragging my head back.

"Bend over," he growled in my ear.

"Wait," I said, grabbing his forearm. "I'm not ready."

"You think I was ready to die?"

I heard a small commotion to my left, but he was holding my hair too tightly for me to turn my head. My scalp stung and tears wet my lashes. Only when I heard the king order them to take him away did I realize my men must have moved to protect me.

"Okay," I whispered. "You're right. I deserve this."

"You fucking deserved to die," he growled. "I ripped your throat out. What voodoo is keeping you alive?"

Before I could answer, he wrenched my head forward so I was forced to bend over. The court cheered, hungry for the show. Ripping his pants down, Tadeu grabbed my hip and drove into me. A shock of pain tore straight through me, and my body clenched against the invasion. The head of his cock was so big it felt like a fist forcing its way into me.

I cried out, dropping to my knees to escape him, but he dropped with me. Yanking my hair, he forced my head back, making my back arch. Tadeu thrust forward, ripping into my unyielding flesh. Tears of pain leapt to my eyes, blurring my vision, and my mouth dropped open in a silent scream. He pumped into me again, his huge cock filling me and reaching my depths. His huge body and powerful muscles contracted, forcing his cock in deeper, past the point of pain, until his hips met my ass.

I clenched my teeth, swallowing my screams as tears poured from my eyes, dripping down my face. I couldn't open my eyes, couldn't see the room full of people watching my punishment.

"Oh fuck," Tadeu groaned. "I like virgins, but even a whore tightens up if you fuck her right."

He gripped my hip with one hand, yanking back on it as he began to thrust into me again and again. Pain washed over me with each punishing blow of his hips against mine, and I forgot the spectators, forgot everything. Blackness swam in my vision, and pain seared up my arms, up my legs, into my core. A roaring in my ears swallowed me, and for a minute, nothing existed.

I'm dying, I thought. *He's killing me again. First he ripped my throat out, and now he's ripping my insides out.*

I was vaguely aware of a change in the way his cock felt inside me, in the places it strained against the confines of my walls. A collective gasp went up around us, murmuring voices invading my torture. His cock swelled even further inside me, and I felt wetness as he pumped into me even deeper. I didn't know what was happening until I felt the brush of soft fur against my thighs as he drove his cock to the hilt inside me. The hand in my hair loosened, and a paw so big it covered the entire top of my back crushed me to the yellow carpet, grinding me into the stone beneath.

Razor claws pierced my skin, and then his huge jaws clamped around the back of my head and neck. My blood mingled with his saliva, trickling along my jawline and dripping off my chin. His cock swelled impossibly inside me, ripping me apart at the seams, and a scream tore from my throat as his massive tiger cock pumped relentlessly into my frail human body.

I screamed again, and again, and again, until he drove his hips against mine and held. Shots of scalding cum erupted into me like a volcano, burning through my veins and along my limbs. For a second, everything blurred, swaying sickeningly around me. My vision dimmed. Inside my head, an instinct whipped relentlessly at my nerves.

Fight. Fight. Fight.

I opened my eyes, aware that I could now see both rows of tables, one on each side of me. Some people began to clap and whistle, others looking stricken. They all looked... Strange, somehow, as if distorted in a funhouse mirror. I turned my head, which felt woozy and clouded.

I could see my sister sitting there, her face a perfect blank, and I knew that was wrong somehow, and it should matter, but I didn't know why. Beside her sat Gabor, his face like a stone statue. He was bleeding. I could smell it. I was bleeding, too. The scent of our blood together smelled right, as if it had been made to mingle, to complement the other's...

Wait...

How could I tell he was bleeding? I looked down at my hands in disbelief.

Not hands. Golden paws with small black spots.

TWELVE

Holy motherfucking shit. Sir Kenosi's cheetah had just...possessed me.

Bite.

Tear.

Slash.

Instinct urged me to act, but I knew I couldn't. I had to finish this, but I couldn't remember why. The pain exploding in volleys through me made me snarl and spit, my lips drawing back from my teeth and a hiss rolling off my long tongue.

My claws extended, digging into the yellow carpet underfoot. Tadeu's claws extended, too, his paws covering mine and pinning them to the floor while his hips flexed, and his cock continued spurting cum into my tight cheetah opening. I screamed again, this time a screeching cat sound that echoed through the high ceilings, wordless except for the urging in my mind.

Teeth.

Claws.

Speed.

Tadeu's tiger teeth clamped onto the back of my neck, and I arched up and then down, bucking to get him off me. His hind legs crouched low as he maneuvered to keep his cock inside me until he'd filled me with every last drop of his seed. He clamped my skull between his powerful jaws, grinding his throbbing cock deeper still.

Tear.

Wound.

Kill.

The instinct to fight screamed through my every limb, and finally, my human hold snapped. My claws shredded the carpet as I shot forward, adrenaline, fury and pain striking me like lightning. I surged from under Tadeu, springing free and whipping around to face him. My body crouched low, my fangs bared as I hissed ferociously.

Everyone at the tables began to applaud now, even the ones who had been silent before.

I focused all my attention on Tadeu, but I could still feel the Tiger Court around us. Tadeu stalked forward on giant paws.

I gave one more warning hiss, but he didn't slow. I leapt at him.

My paw swiped his face like a slap, my razor claws slicing open his skin. He snarled and lunged at me, but I was quicker. Holy shit, I was fast. I leapt to one side, sliced into his shoulder with my claws, and darted away before he could turn his huge body. The next time I darted in, he was ready, though. He batted me out of the air so hard my body went flying over the tables, twisting and turning before slamming into one of the columns at the edge of the hall.

Pain obliterated all else for a second. When I opened my eyes, I saw a tiger hurtling for me. I rolled away just as he leapt. His body slammed into the stone so hard the hall shook, and a roar ripped from his throat. I dove in, clamping my teeth under his neck. I barely broke the skin, getting a giant mouthful of the thick ruff of fur around his neck instead of his jugular. Tadeu grabbed me between his front paws, pinning me to the floor. My hind claws raking along his underside, but it was no use. I was quarter his size.

He lifted his head and roared triumphantly, then opened his mouth wide, and his jaws dove for my throat.

Before he could rip out my throat for the second time, something zipped through the air and planted in the side of his neck. Tadeu's massive head lifted, and he stared across the room at the offending royal. Swaying on his feet, he took one step before collapsing with a giant thud.

I scrambled away from him and onto my feet.

"I knew it," Camila shrieked. I spun to face her, but she wasn't talking to me. She was accosting Gabor, who sat beside her with a tiny pipe clenched in one fist.

A blow gun. He'd been the one to tranquilize Tadeu.

That's when I saw that his other hand held Camila's.

Confusion tumbled through my mind. Was he with her? Did he love her? And if he did, why had he saved me?

I loped toward them, stopping several paces back when the scent of his blood found me again. That's when I saw that he and Camila weren't holding hands in the way lovers did. She held his hand, but she had let a single ocelot claw extend. It pierced through his palm and out the back of his hand like a hook that held him to her. A slow trickle of blood had stained the table under their linked hands like it had happened a while ago, but neither showed the slightest sign of pain or pity.

Camila reached into her bag and tossed a few worthless coins across the table at me. They tinkled against the stone floor before silencing when they met the yellow carpet. "That was quite a show," she said. "Although I hardly think it's fair for you to get the amulet for something you've been desperately chasing since you were five years old."

"All that wanting led to a marvelous show, didn't it?" Shah Tiger said. "Now, let's mingle."

On his cue, everyone set down their utensils and pushed back from their plates. The shah stood, and then everyone else stood. I went to the dress I'd left crumpled on the floor and stopped. What now? I'd never shifted, and I wasn't sure how to shift back.

I could already feel more of my human mind than I'd had during the fight with Tadeu.

I'm safe, I told the cheetah. *Let me go.*

A moment later, I felt him sliding back from my mind, resting at the edges how he had before. My body began to sink toward the floor, and for a second blackness swallowed me. When it receded, I found myself crouching naked on the floor, my hands helping me balance. I grabbed the dress and pulled it around myself, feeling more vulnerable and exposed than I liked. My hands were shaking, and my legs wobbled as I stood and tied the dress. Instead of feeling powerful for doing this impossible thing, I felt dirty and ashamed. I could feel blood and Tadeu's sticky, hot cum trickling down my legs as I turned to search for the king.

I found him chatting to Camila, who looked as she always did—blonde hair twisted into an elegant updo without a hair out of place, tasteful powder blue wrap dress that matched her eyes and acknowledged the Tiger Court style without looking like she was copying it or trying too hard. She smiled serenely and sipped her water, her attention rapt on the shah.

Suddenly, all I wanted to do was turn and run away from this horrible place. Mom was wrong. The curse was wrong. I couldn't do this, so there was no way that I was supposed to. I just couldn't. It was impossible. I'd never make half the queen that Camila would, with all her polish and poise. I was a mess.

But it wasn't over. I couldn't leave until I had the amulet. I took a step forward on wobbling legs and then another, leaking cum and blood with every step. Camila gave a small, musical laugh and laid a hand on the shah's arm. I'd just been fucked on the floor in front of his entire court. I didn't want to mingle. I wanted to take a long, long shower the way I had after being with Shadow the first time. I didn't want to be queen. I wanted to hide with my men and never have to face any of these people again, let alone chat and laugh with them like nothing had happened.

At last, I reached the king and my sister, who each stood with a guard flanking them. I couldn't look at Gabor. Not after what he'd seen. It was one thing for him to know I'd fucked Shadow and Balam. It was worse for him to have seen security footage of me servicing Sir Kenosi. Seeing the live show was a whole other thing. I would never be able to look at him again. So, instead, I looked at the shah.

I had tried to prepare myself for what I would say on my way over, but I couldn't come up with anything. I was ready for the king to refuse me the amulet because Gabor had interfered. I was ready for more games like Sir Kenosi had played, but I didn't know how I'd convince him of anything. I had nothing left to give him.

"Ah, here she is," he said, interrupting something Camila had been saying. "The star of the show!"

A few people around us turned and applauded. Camila gave me a death glare, but she shouldn't have bothered. I already wished Sir Kenosi had left me dead.

"Go and fetch her escort," the shah said to his guard, flicking his fingers toward the door. "A princess should never be without her escort."

A guard disappeared out the door, and the shah turned to me and Camila. "Reunited at last," he said with a gleeful twinkle in his eye. "You must be so relieved to have joined forces again."

"We're not allies," Camila snapped. "She tricked you."

"Ah," the shah said, nodding. "Well played, Princess Itzel. This is the old way of the amulets. I do love the games."

"She's not the heir, though," Camila said. "As you saw, she's a cheetah, not an ocelot."

"Yes, that's true," Shah Tiger mused, his gaze turning to me. "How did that happen?"

"I don't know," I admitted. "I didn't know I could be a shifter. I'm the second child of shifters, so maybe I have some latent shifting ability even though I don't have my own inner feline."

"Fascinating," he said, studying me more closely. "Why a cheetah, though?"

"I was gifted my mate's cheetah when he died," I said, hoping he didn't know what that meant. In truth, I should have been an ocelot or a snow leopard, but since I hadn't grown up with this kind of spirit animal sharing my body, I didn't have either. It was an uneasy feeling to know he was in there, waiting to come out again. I vowed again to find some way to bring Kenosi back, to return his cheetah to him.

"Extraordinary," the shah said, his eyes shining with... Admiration. He didn't think I was a filthy whore worth only a handful of change. He was fucking impressed.

And Camila knew it. Her skin went pale, and panic flashed in her eyes.

"She obviously can't be the ocelot queen," she said quickly. "Since she'd not an ocelot."

"True, true," the withered old man said, leaning on his cane with one hand and reaching into his pocket with the other. He produced a purple velvet pouch with a silk cord and held it up, swinging it back and forth between us like a pendulum. "So, who gets the precious tiger amulet?"

Somehow, I had to convince this guy that I was more deserving of the throne than Camila. If even I didn't believe it, why would he?

"I do," Camila said, licking her lips nervously and reaching for it. "I'm the next queen."

The shah snatched it out of her grasp with surprising speed and grinned widely. "Then do we get a second show tonight? You haven't yet experienced the pleasure of a tiger lover."

"No," I said firmly. "The deal was one show for one amulet."

"Then I guess it's yours," the shah said, dropping it into my outstretched palm. "I'm a man of my word."

For a second, I was too stunned to move. It had been so easy. He had promised it, and he'd given it like the simplest thing in the world. A transaction. Which made me the whore Camila accused me of being. I'd fucked his prisoner, and he'd paid me with an amulet.

Just then, three men came running into the room, and my knees buckled with relief. Kwame scooped me up, catching me before I could fall. His ropy arms encircled me like a crown, as if I were already a queen. Shadow pressed in close at his side, offering me his silent strength. And Lord Balam took my hand, linking his thick, calloused fingers through mine without hooks or claws. It was the strong, gentle touch of a strong, rough lover. I barely held back the rush of tears that threatened as my shell-shocked heart filled with love for these men. My mates.

"I'm a cheetah," I said, laughing through the blur of tears.

"For now," Shadow murmured beside me.

I slipped the tiger amulet into his hand, squeezing his fingers before releasing it. Suddenly, my legs were shaking again. I had earned five of the seven amulets. There was only one more, and Camila would be queen. She had the seventh amulet already.

"Put it with the others," I said.

Suddenly, someone shoved through the crowd around us, the fae and vampires, humans and shifters, men and women. But this towering tiger made my heart kick into top speed.

Tadeu stood before me, naked and enormous, his fists clenched and his eyes blazing with hatred. "What did you do to me?" he demanded.

Camila shied away, slipping behind Gabor's shoulder, and my mates surged forward, blocking me from his reach, but no one else seemed at all frightened by this beast.

"What the fuck did you do?" Tadeu barked again.

"Nothing," I said. "Someone shot you with a tranquilizer. I had nothing to do with it."

"Not that," he growled, his eyes narrowing with a poisonous glare. "This."

He flexed his arm and pointed to his bicep, where a cat print glowed from his skin like the moon.

Thirteen

Gao Jetsun
Demigod, Snow Leopard Nation

"Your toe is twitching."

I opened one eye. "What?"

"You have been tapping your toe all morning," said the elderly monk, a smile creasing his wrinkles even deeper. "Perhaps you are restless."

Restless.

I'd never been restless in my life. That was something for other men. Men like my father were restless. I was not that sort of man. I didn't chase adventure. Everything I needed was right here on this mountain. Looking out over the valleys below and the peaks beyond, mountains formed by the colliding of tectonic plates millions of years ago, always brought a sense of peace. Even the addition of chasms torn during recent quakes, and trees bent and twisted by windstorms, were a part of the landscape I'd always known. I searched for the calm that always accompanied the timelessness of this view.

A deep, unwavering appreciation for the stark beauty of nature was a requirement up here, and that remained. But lately, a part of me had wanted—

That was it. I was not supposed to want. Part of the discipline of being a monk was teaching oneself not to want. Though our practice was somewhat different from our human counterparts, we all practiced peaceful nonattachment. I lived by that law. It was no wonder, after I'd seen the way it tore my mother apart. Her clinging, desperate attachment to my father had terrified something inside me even as a child. Later, I'd been disgusted by it. Now, I felt nothing when I thought of it.

I hadn't thought of my parents in a long time. But lately, I'd thought of my father several times, though I still hadn't been able to delve deep enough into my subconscious to find the reason. Maybe it truly was some sort of malady, the restlessness that my elder had suggested.

I stood and bowed to the man who sat behind me on the precipice jutting out on top of the cliff where we'd had our morning meditation. "I apologize for distracting you," I said.

He cracked one eye open, peering up at me without changing his position. "Perhaps a trip down the mountain is in order," he said. "Maybe you're due for a change."

Change? I didn't need change. Nothing in the monastery changed. That was the beauty of this life. It was perfect as it was. It needed no changing.

"Perhaps," I said to my elder before bowing and leaving his side.

"Change is the one thing that never changes," he called after me. "We are always changing, whether we admit it or not."

He was right, of course. I was no longer the eighteen-year-old boy who had committed to studying and becoming a monk. I wasn't the man who, after ten years of practice and study, had been accepted in the Order of the Snow Leopards, the only all-shifter monastery in the world, and dedicated my life to the practice of physical, spiritual, and mental discipline. I'd grown older and gained knowledge, dealt with my childhood, and helped build the lab where our brightest minds worked to earn money to keep the monastery going. But my heart had not changed.

I was where I was meant to be, doing what I was meant to be doing. I was a man of science, magic, and religion. There was reason and order in all these things, though people often missed it. I lived by reason, practiced reason, studied reason. I liked the order of the monasteries, the unchanging, timelessness of them that matched the landscape. Everything here made sense. It had a purpose. It had reason. I had chosen the right path, and I had never strayed. I would never stray.

The old monk was right. Much had changed, both outside and inside me since I'd come to the mountain. Change was inevitable and constant. But he was also wrong. I wasn't restless. I simply needed to focus. The heart of a man like me would never change.

FOURTEEN

Itzel
Princess, Ocelot Nation

FOR A MOMENT OF STUNNED SILENCE, NO ONE
spoke.

"No," I muttered, stumbling back against Kwame's comforting hold. "Just no. I quit. Not fucking doing it."

I was so done with this shifter mating shit. I wasn't even a shifter. Not a real one. I'd borrowed an animal, but I wasn't one of them. And there was no fucking way I was taking this brute for a mate. Not even if he had been my first love, my childhood sweetheart, or the last man on earth.

"It can't be him," I whispered, shaking my head and backing away.

"This certainly is a show," Shah Tiger crowed. "Just imagine, if I hadn't asked for this exact pairing, you'd never have met your True Mate. I am guided by divine forces, indeed."

"It's not mine," I blurted. "I already found all my mates."

Four marks. Four mates.

Except... I'd never seen Sir Kenosi's. My head spun, and I clutched Lord Balam's fingers like they anchored me to this world. "It must have been Kenosi," I whispered.

"He had to be your True Mate to give you his cheetah," Kwame murmured. "And he died, which only a True Mate would, according to the curse."

"Well, wouldn't you know," Tadeu growled. "Fucking black widow."

"What?" Kwame asked.

"I'm not the first man she's claimed to love but murdered instead."

"I didn't murder Kenosi," I said. "In fact, if anyone's responsible for his death, it's *you*."

"Then who's his True Mate?" Shadow asked. I'd seen all their marks, and Sir Kenosi had died for me. They were my mates. This savage tiger wasn't my mate.

"Itzel," Lord Balam said quietly.

"She is," the shah insisted. "He was marked when he mated with her. That's how these marks are given. If you have the mark, you should know that."

Shadow hissed, and I was suddenly afraid my panther mate was going to go feral shifter on the crusty old king and kick his ass. Which would probably get us all executed, or at the very least thrown in prison for the rest of our lives while my sister traipsed off into the mountains to find the snow leopard amulet and get herself and Gabor killed.

I grabbed Shadow's hand again, stopping him from doing anything murderous.

"Shadow is my mate," I said. "Apparently, I don't mark them the way regular shifters do. I marked all mine at once, when I opened an amulet. If Tadeu wasn't marked then, he wasn't my mate."

"Then explain this," Tadeu demanded, thrusting his shoulder toward me.

Lord Balam took my arm and slid the silk of my dress up my arm, revealing my marks. I swayed on my feet, blackness threatening to swallow me again. "No," I whispered, closing my eyes so I didn't have to see it. Five paw prints marching up my arm, one black as a starless night, the others silvery as moonlight.

"That solves one of my problems," Shah Tiger said. "What to do with this errant tiger. Now he's your problem."

"No, no, no," I said. "I'm not taking him."

"Don't worry, you'll grow to love each other in time," the shah said. "It's impossible to do otherwise with a True Mate. And you'll thank me when you're on your next quest. The

Snow Leopard Kingdom is the most impenetrable of all. You'll need all the help you can get."

"Fuck that," Tadeu said, wheeling on me. "I'm not helping you."

"Good," I said. "I don't want your help. I've got enough protection already."

"Your first lover's quarrel," Shah Tiger said with a grin. "I am privileged to witness it."

"He's no lover of mine," I said.

"Gao Jetsun is the most reclusive man you'll encounter on your journey," the shah said. "The last feline heir took thirteen years to gain their amulet. If you want it, you'll take every advantage you're given."

Camila stepped out from behind Gabor, who hadn't once moved or looked at me. He was so still, I could almost forget he stood just a few paces off, his wounded hand hanging casually at his side, as if he couldn't feel it. I had ignored him, too, but now that I had given in and looked at him, I ached for him to look at me, even if nothing more than that could ever happen. Just to see something in his eyes, to know he felt something, even disgust, was better than that blank mask. But he stared straight ahead, his eyes as empty as glass.

"I'll take him," Camila said.

"What?" I yelped. "Did you see what just happened?"

She rolled her eyes. "Don't act like you didn't want it."

Blood roared in my ears as I gaped at my sister. "Did it look like I was enjoying myself?"

"It looked like you got what you asked for," she said. "And not nearly as much as you deserve. Now, give me my amulet."

"Your amulet?" I asked. "The one I just paid for with my body and my dignity?"

Camila snorted. "Dignity? You lost that long before you ever saw an amulet. You were always common, and you always will be. You're only keeping the amulets from me because you're jealous."

I waited for the pain of her words to knife into me, but to my surprise, the pain was brief before being replaced by anger. She'd hurt me too many times, her blows landing on my heart until it grew calloused, immune to the blade of her betrayal.

I faced her squarely, my voice steady as I hit back for the first time. "You can't hurt me anymore, Camila. You can't break me, because I've already been broken."

"And nobody wants a broken princess," she said. "The only people you can get to support you are a bunch of men who want to get in your pants. The sad part is, you don't even realize that they're just using you. They don't care about you. They just want a whore to pass around. And you..." She gave me a disgusted, pitying look and shook her head. "You actually think they're your mates. As if a human could have a True Mate."

"I don't care if they're my True Mates or not," I said. "That means nothing to me. What matters is that they love and support me, which is more than I can say for you."

"You're right," Camila said. "I'm not completely brainless. Of course I don't support a usurper who is trying to unseat me, who stole the amulets—which is pretty much like stealing the crown off my head—and tried to kill me by pushing me from a moving helicopter. Now, give me my amulets."

"You're right about one thing," I said. "I have no claim to the throne. I'll get you to the throne because you're the rightful heir, and despite your accusations, I'm not trying to steal your crown. But make no mistake. I do this out of duty to my country, and because it's the right thing to do, not because I think you deserve it."

"Oh, a common whore thinks she's better suited to run a country than an actual princess who studied and worked for it since the day she was born. Sorry to spoil your fantasy, but there's more to being queen than sitting on a throne with your legs spread and letting every man in your country come up to take his turn."

Anger flashed inside me, and I resisted the urge to slap my sister's pretty, toxic mouth. Instead, I drew myself up and squared my shoulders. "I remain loyal to you as our nation's queen," I said. "Not my sister. From now on, I will treat you as such, Your Grace."

"Good," Camila said, holding out a hand. "My amulets?"

I turned to retrieve them from Shadow, but he wasn't on my left, where he'd been minutes before. I spun around, searching for him but finding only Prince Kwame and Lord Balam. I looked from one of them to the other. "Where's Shadow?"

Prince Kwame shook his head, looking as bewildered as me. "I don't know. He was just here."

I turned back to Camila. "It seems my mate has disappeared with them."

"You expect me to believe that?" Camila hissed, her eyes flashing.

"Panthers," Lord Balam said with a shrug and a smirk at my sister.

"They're supposed to have powers of invisibility," Kwame offered.

"Filthy panther," Camila hissed.

"I'll find him," I said. "You saw me get dressed. You know I don't have them on me. I'll go look for him now."

"You're even stupider than I thought," Camila said, pursing her lips. "I guess I really don't need to worry about you trying to steal my country. If you'd entrust a panther with something valuable, you're never going to make it to the throne."

"Thanks."

"You'd better find him and bring him back right now," she said, her chin rising. "He stole my amulets. If the shah finds out, he'll have him executed."

Shah Tiger had wandered off, mingling with some of the other royals while we talked. Apparently, our squabbles were only interesting for so long.

"The shah won't execute anyone," Tadeu rumbled. "He's not the murderous type."

I glanced at him before returning my gaze to my sister. "I told you, I'll find Shadow."

"You better hope you do," she said. "Because if you don't, Gabor and I will hunt him down. I'll make sure he employs every torture before killing him. Ocelot guards know plenty of ways to make a man suffer."

I glanced at Gabor, my soul begging for some sign from him, but he gave me nothing. I didn't know why I couldn't let it go. He had chosen a side, and that's where he would stay. I wasn't going to convince him otherwise. No matter how much I yearned for his approval, his forgiveness, he would never grant them.

"We'll go find him now," I said, swallowing the knot in my throat and turning away from the guard whose love I ached for more than I could explain.

"Oh, no, you don't," Camila said with an incredulous laugh. "You might be stupid, but I'm not. I'll go with you. Come on, Gabor, Tadeu."

"Fine," I said, feeling so bone-deep exhausted that I couldn't find the strength to argue. Lord Balam insisted we go pay our respects to the shah, so we bid him goodnight and thanked him for his hospitality. Only when we were in the hall on the way back to our room did the night catch up with me. My body was battered and bruised, and walking was more painful by the moment. To make matters worse, the man who had done this to me was following me around, along with the last man on earth I wanted to see me in this condition, and my sister, who kept making snide comments.

When Kwame saw me limping, he scooped me up in his arms and carried me the rest of the way to my room. So grateful I nearly sobbed with relief, I buried my face in his chest and wrapped my arms around his neck.

"Where is he?" Camila demanded when we reached the bedroom. She dragged Gabor into the bathroom to check with her, then back into the main room, where they checked in every corner and under the beds before accepting that he wasn't there.

"I don't know where he went," I said. "You're welcome to stand watch outside if you're worried about it. Otherwise, we'll just have to wait until he shows up again. Now, if you don't mind, I'd like to get some sleep and recover. It's been a long day."

I took more pleasure than I should in closing the door in her face.

"You know they'll be out there all night, listening in on us," Lord Balam said, giving me a significant look. But I honestly didn't know where Shadow had gone, so I couldn't have said anything if I wanted to.

"Surely she won't do such a duty herself," Prince Kwame said. "She'll have her guard do it."

Once, she would have. Now I wasn't sure. I knew she didn't trust Gabor, but she hadn't dismissed him from her tour. She could have done worse. Maybe she was waiting until she returned home before she thanked him for his service by imprisoning him and having him executed. Or maybe...

My pulse quavered at the thought. Maybe she knew how I felt about him. Somehow, she had figured it out even though it was so complicated that even I couldn't figure it out. She had accused him of choosing me over her, and she wasn't wrong. He had. Despite that, she'd let him live, continued to order him to stay by her side. If she knew that I loved him, she could use him. Was that her plan? Or was I being paranoid and self-centered to even suspect it had to do with me?

"You're tired," Kwame said, scooping me up again. "Let me bathe you."

Another quaver went through me, this one laced with fear. I swallowed and pulled his head down, pressing my forehead to his scarred one. "Just a bath?" I whispered.

"Of course," he said, looking truly wounded. He squeezed me to him and carried me into the bathroom, running the tub full of water and soap until the bubbles billowed high and steam filled the luxurious bath. Kwame untied my dress and lowered me into the water. I gasped when it hit my torn and bruised places, trying to put away the memories of tonight the way I had with Shadow. Our first night had been wild and violent, and yet, it had never felt personal.

With Tadeu, it felt personal.

I squeezed my eyes closed, but a tear forced its way out onto my lashes. Kwame leaned over the side of the tub and pressed a kiss to my salty lashes. "I'm sorry," he murmured, his thumb stroking my forehead as he sat back, watching me.

"You didn't do anything to be sorry for," I said, resting my head back and drawing a deep, shaky breath to get myself under control.

"I should have been stronger," he said. "I should have stayed in that room, so I'd know what you went through. If you were strong enough to do it, I should have been strong enough to witness."

"It's okay," I said, cupping his cheek with my wet fingers. "I'm glad you didn't see it. I'm glad no one saw it."

No one in my party. None of my lovers. Only Gabor had seen it, and he was Camila's.

Kwame's skin was cool as always, the ghostly cool of the undead. For a minute he was silent, stroking my hair with gentle fingers.

"My people believe that pain and suffering are as much a part of life as happiness and laughter," he said. "I should have been stronger, strong enough to see yours. I hope one day I can be as strong as you."

I snorted. "I'm not feeling very strong right now."

"You don't have to be strong every moment of every day," he said. "You're allowed to break like the rest of us. Your suffering is real, Itzel. Your experience is valid. I should have stayed to bear witness if I could do nothing else."

I remembered Gabor sitting at the table like a statue at Camila's side, not looking away, not moving. Bearing witness. It wasn't the first time I'd heard that, but it was the first time I'd thought of Gabor as doing that, or even Lord Balam when he hadn't protected me from the other men who had now become my mates. Maybe he'd been doing that all along.

Gabor, though... I wasn't sure. Something had happened to him, something worse than whatever he'd gone through to become a guard, whatever he'd done since becoming one. He was different. He hadn't looked as if I disgusted him, like he couldn't bear to look at me, though. He'd simply refused to even acknowledge my existence. Somehow, that hurt worse than disgust. How could he bear witness, validate my experience, at the same time as he invalidated my very existence?

I'd always known he was loyal to my father, or at least to crown and country, but deep inside, I'd felt that he was on my side. Now, I didn't know anymore. I felt selfish and greedy for wanting more than I had, and guilty at the same time, as if I'd told my mates they weren't enough. But I couldn't help the hurt that came from Gabor's snub or the ache of longing for him to be with me and my lovers.

As I lay in bed later, Lord Balam snoring softly on one side of me and Prince Kwame lying still as the dead on the other, I couldn't fall asleep. I could feel the guard outside my door, could feel the pull of him like gravity, drawing me to him. I wanted to get up and go out and talk to him just as I had all those nights in Florida when we'd stayed up late, Gabor smoking cigarettes and pretending he didn't notice my flirting while I tried to draw him out of his reserved exterior and pry personal information from him. And later, I'd shamelessly scream with pleasure, hoping Gabor heard, wanting to drive him mad as Lord Balam fucked me senseless.

Fuck, I'd been so selfish, so naïve and young.

It seemed a lifetime ago, and I supposed that it truly was. I had died and started a new life since then. A life as a shifter. Maybe it was time to move on from fantasies about my father's guard and accept that we would never have more than we'd had on those fleeting nights on the balcony of a fleabag motel.

Fifteen

For the next few weeks, we stayed at the palace, which was a replica of the famous historical Taj Mahal, this one modernized and built after the original had been destroyed by the devastating earthquakes that had ripped apart the world decades before. Shah Tiger was usually occupied, so I didn't have to face him again, and he was more than happy to let our procession rest, recover, and regroup. We needed it. We'd been through a lot.

By day, we planned our next move, discussing how we would lure out the reclusive Gao Jetsun. Lord Balam spent a lot of time alone with his oracle. Prince Kwame doted on me, and we had long conversations about his family, whom he loved and missed, and mine, whom I was not too fond of right now. I'd never had a lover who was so open, so calm and steadfastly loving. I appreciated it, but I missed Shadow, who hadn't shown up again.

By night, I lay awake resisting the pull of Gabor outside my door, resisting the urge to sneak out and talk to him. I knew he wasn't alone, though. He'd never talk to me in front of Camila or even Tadeu, and I didn't want him to. I wanted him alone, when I could tease the truth from him drop by drop. And more than that, I wanted to forget him, to stop wanting and be happy with what I had. So each night, I forced myself to lie still until I fell asleep.

One day, a tiger news crew came by to interview Camila about her Amulet Tour. Another day, a cheetah interview show asked for an exclusive on my 'miraculous rise from the dead,' but I turned them away, and they went to find Camila instead. I wasn't sure she'd give them an interview, as it seemed like something she'd find distasteful.

Surprisingly, she seemed to enjoy the attention. A few days later, we watched the interview from our room, and I was surprised at how relaxed and charming Camila seemed in front of the camera. She'd make a good queen. I kept reminding myself of that.

One day, after we'd been there a few weeks, Lord Balam came in and sat beside me on the bed. "I'm sorry, but we're going to have to go on," he said. "I know you wanted to wait for Shadow, but I think we should start looking for the snow leopard amulet if you want to get it before Camila. And I think she's leaving soon."

"Did your oracle tell you she's leaving?"

He grinned. "Sure. Or maybe I overheard her talking with her guards."

Despite having protested when Camila had said she'd take him off the king's hands, Tadeu had joined her little party. I hated that I felt anything at all about that, but I did. Honestly, he terrified me, but the shifter part of me that must have felt the True Mate bond even when my human side couldn't, knew that it was a direct affront for him to follow her over me.

"Then we'll have to go without Shadow," I said, though a huge part of me balked at the thought. I knew that was irrational. He'd already left me. But I had never once wavered in my trust for him. I knew he loved me beyond anything else, that in his own way, he was trying to protect me. Camila could call me stupid all she wanted, but I knew he would never betray me. He was hiding somewhere, keeping the amulets from Camila. I wished I could tell him that it didn't matter when she got them. She already had the Ocelot Amulet, which none of us could even touch without dying. I would give her the others, let her take the throne as planned, trusting that eventually, the pieces would fall into place as they were meant to be.

"Sir Kenosi's helicopter can take us up into the mountains," Lord Balam said. "From there, we're on our own."

"What do we know about this guy?" I asked. "Gao Jetsun."

"Besides that he's a reclusive hermit?" Balam asked with a grin.

"Besides that," I agreed. And he was my brother. For some reason, I'd still not told my mates that part, though I'd told them everything else about my time in the spirit world. My mother's affair, being part snow leopard, and having a brother... It was something I needed to process before blurting out to anyone. I still wasn't sure how I felt about it.

"He's a monk," Lord Balam said. "The Snow Leopard Nation is very small in terms of population, and they don't live together like other cat clans. They're isolated from the world and each other."

"Sounds like the panthers," I said. "Maybe we can do what we did to Shadow." I felt guilty even suggesting it after what had happened with Shadow. He'd also been a celibate recluse, and I'd seduced him out of his lifestyle, his home, his whole life.

"A couple problems with that," Lord Balam said. "First, the jaguar amulet has been closed. It would take another virgin to open it."

A flicker of heat shimmered inside me at the memory of opening it the first time, the way it sprang open inside me, filling me with an incurable need to be fucked into submission.

"What's the other problem?" I asked, squeezing my knees together.

"Even if we found a virgin to open it, we can't give the potion to someone until we find him."

"Maybe the other amulets can help," I said. "What does the Tiger amulet do?"

"Kwame's finding out right now."

A few minutes later, Kwame returned from a lunch with the large family of tiger princes and princesses.

"It will be most helpful to lure out the next keeper of the amulet," he told us. "But it's risky for Itzel, and it might not work at all."

"What does it do?" I asked, my heart beginning to hammer.

"It puts you into a heat."

I gulped. "I can do that?"

"You're a shifter now," Kwame said, taking a seat on my other side and linking his fingers through mine. "You should be able to."

"Okay," I said. "Let's try it. How does it work?"

"It'll make every shifter male in the area go nuts when they smell you," Lord Balam said. "And that includes us. It's kind of like what happens when you open the jaguar amulet, except it's carried by pheromones. And it'll make you want to fuck anything that moves for about a week. You won't care who it is. We won't care if it kills us, and neither will you."

He let that settle into my mind for a minute.

Finally, I shook my head. "No. I can't endanger you. If you fuck me, you'll die."

He nodded. "And so would Shadow."

Kwame squeezed my hand. "I've already been to the spirit world with you. I'm not bound by the curse."

I hadn't even thought of yet. I hadn't exactly been in a feisty mood since the rough treatment I'd received from Tadeu, and my mates had all been wonderfully patient in helping me recover. Despite knowing that we could still be intimate, Kwame had never so much as suggested it. My heart filled with warmth and gratitude for my most openly loving and nurturing mate.

"Then you're the only one who can go with me," I said, gripping his fingers. Despite having found a group of steadfastly loyal men, I seemed to be losing them as fast as I could gain them.

"It will be my honor to guard you," he said.

"If we could get Kenosi back, he could go, too," Lord Balam said. "But if he came back, you'd lose his cheetah, and you wouldn't be able to go into heat."

"Damn it," I said. Despite our rocky relationship, I needed Sir Kenosi. He'd given his life for me, though, and I needed to remember that. I had forgiven any resentments I still had toward him—how could I not? The man had fucking died for me. Now, I would have given anything to have him back. He'd been a soldier for me, one willing to lay down his life to give me another chance. Now, I had to do something with it. I had to make him proud.

"Only a lion or a tiger could escort you," Kwame said, watching my reaction warily.

"Oh, fuck no," I said. "Tadeu is on Camila's team now."

"He is your mate," Kwame said. "When you are ready, he will have to accept that and come to your side."

"Besides," growled a voice behind me. "Aren't you on Camila's team?"

I nearly jumped out of my skin, my heart racing as I spun to see Shadow standing near the window.

"What the fuck, Shadow," I growled. "You trying to give me a heart attack? Where have you been?"

He shrugged one shoulder almost imperceptibly. "Around."

"Right," I muttered, rolling my eyes. "Well, how much of the plan did you hear?"

"Enough to tell you it's a bullshit plan," he growled. "You think what Tadeu did was bad? If you go up on a mountain with only one guard and go into heat, the entire Snow Leopard Nation is going to come running to rape you."

"Well, hopefully they won't all come at once," I said. "If we get within scenting distance of one, me and Kwame will fight him off. There's two of us, and Kwame is bigger than a snow leopard. They live alone, so it's not like an entire clan will find us at once."

"Remember how easily I took you?" Shadow asked, his green eyes going dark and his face sober with memory. "You had more than one guard then."

"What other options are there?" I asked. "Search for thirteen years while my father goes on murdering our people?"

Lord Balam cleared his throat. "You need to prepare for the possibility that Gao Jetsun will be locked up in a monastery somewhere, since he's a monk, and he may not be out and about to catch your scent. I'm sorry, Itz, but this isn't a guaranteed win."

"Anyone have a better suggestion?"

"If he's out, he'll come to you," Kwame said. "He won't be able to help himself."

He was my brother, so I knew he wouldn't do what Tadeu had to me. I just had to find him. It was probably a good time to tell the guys he was my brother, but for some reason, that felt too strange. I hadn't even come to terms with the fact that my father—the man I'd always known as my father, who had raised me—wasn't blood related to me. Sure, he'd done a shitty job of being a dad, and he was a murderous psychopath, but he hadn't kicked me to the curb when Mom died. Didn't that count for something?

Or was it just because he didn't know?

And having a brother somewhere, a brother I'd never met but who had been alive my entire life, felt even stranger. I wanted a moment to know him before I announced him to the world. It seemed somehow intimate and private, and there was a bit of shame attached to it, too, whether I wanted to admit it or not. My mother had conceived me through an affair.

This man I'd never met was more closely related to me than anyone in this world except Camila, but he might want even less to do with me than she did. After all, I was a bastard child, the result of an affair between his father and a woman who had lured him to be unfaithful to Jetsun's mother. Not only that, but that affair had cost his father his life, leaving Jetsun to be the man of the house and take care of his mother in whatever way she needed when her husband died.

"If you're sure this is what you want to do, I'll consult the oracle, find out as close as I can to where Gao Jetsun is," Lord Balam said after a long silence.

"I will find a map of all the known monasteries in snow leopard territory," Kwame said. "Most snow leopards belong to human monasteries, though there is one shifter-only one. The territory is large, but there aren't many snow leopards within its boundaries."

"We should follow at a safe distance," Shadow said. "We can move in if things go bad and head off Camila's crew if they get too close."

He was protecting me from Tadeu, and I was thankful for that, but I didn't like the thought of him and Lord Balam coming to rescue me from some snow leopards, only to be sucked in by the pheromones and end up dead.

"Far behind," I said. "I don't want any more of my mates dying for me."

"I'll go find some things you might need while you're backpacking around the mountains," Shadow said.

"Hey," I said. "Before you go, I'm going to need those amulets you stole."

"I didn't steal them," he said, producing a bag from his pocket and handing it to me. "I protected them from the thieving hands of your sister."

"Thanks for keeping them safe," I said, looping an arm around his neck and pulling him down for a quick kiss. "And thanks for coming back."

For a moment, he pressed his soft lips to mine, his hair falling around our faces like a curtain to give us privacy. His hands tightened on my hips, and I could feel the ache in him, could feel how much he'd missed me and the conviction it had taken to keep him away. At last, he stepped back.

"I was never gone," he said, disappearing out the window before I could press him for more answers. While he collected supplies, Lord Balam went to consult the oracle and Kwame went to research monasteries, leaving me alone in the room with my thoughts. One guard wasn't enough, but it was all I had, unless I took Tadeu, and I didn't think he'd come even if I asked. And I wasn't about to ask.

Sixteen

It was time to move on. I went to the door, the bag of amulets clutched in one hand. The emotional side of me balked at the thought of giving them to Camila after all I'd endured to get them. The rational half knew that it was the right thing to do no matter how unfair it felt. I had worked for them, yes, but I'd gotten each and every one of them under the pretense of giving it to her. So that's what I had to do.

When I opened the door, Tadeu stood in the hall, his arms crossed over his chest. He straightened when he saw me, a frown darkening his brow. "What do you want?" he snapped.

My heart lurched into my throat, wrestling to take me over, to turn us into the cheetah and run away faster than a tiger could follow. I had to reason with myself to get it under control. If Tadeu wanted me, he could have knocked down the door and come at me any time I was alone in the room. And this wasn't the first time I'd been there alone. I'd insisted my men not hover, not feel like they had to treat me as something broken. I knew that if I let them, I'd feel more broken than I was.

"I was actually looking for Camila," I said, crossing my arms to steady myself.

"And now you know she's not here," Tadeu said, glowering at me.

I hesitated, a masochistic urge inside me refusing to walk away without hearing the truth. "Why do you hate me so much?" I blurted before I could talk myself out of it.

Tadeu snorted. "You mean besides the fact that you're exactly like your father?"

"What?" I asked, recoiling.

"You could have just told me to fuck off," he said. "But you had to have a little fun with it, make it into a big spectacle. You couldn't be happy with just stringing me along for ten fucking years and then dumping me like a bitch. You had to throw me out for the rabid dogs to tear apart when you were done with me."

"What are you talking about?" I asked, gaping at my former friend and first love, who was now spewing venom and acting like he didn't know me at all.

"Did I say rabid dogs? I meant ocelot royal guards. Sometimes it's hard to tell the difference."

"I didn't throw you to the guards," I said. "I know you blame me, and I admit that it's my fault for not protecting you better, for drawing attention to you. Yes, I was selfish and blind and young, but I never wanted to hurt you, Tadeu."

He shook his head, looking disgusted. "But you never cared if you did, either," he said. "So long as I hung on your every word, flattering your precious ego every step of the way. The really pathetic thing is, I don't think you even know you're doing it. And even more pathetic, I didn't know you were doing it, either. All those years, I actually *believed* your lies. At least I know what kind of snake I'm getting in Camila."

I gripped the door handle, thankful I had something to hold onto. "I may be a lot of things, and I may have made a lot of mistakes, but I am not a liar."

Tadeu's eyes narrowed. "So, tell me this, Itzel. Did you love me?"

"Yes," I said without a second's hesitation. My heart still ached with how much I'd loved him, with the loss of not only him but the promise that love had held.

"Then how come, not five hours after I was murdered by your father, you had your legs wrapped around another man's head?" he said slowly, his eyes blazing with fury.

"What?" I whispered, stepping backward. My mother had told me she couldn't see what was going on in the human world. How could Tadeu possibly know that?

"You said you weren't a liar," Tadeu said, stalking a step closer. "So tell me it's not true, Itzel. Tell me you weren't screaming another man's name while he pounded that tight virgin pussy you'd promised to me a hundred times."

"I thought you were dead," I whispered, staring at him as if seeing a ghost. The ghost of the boy I'd loved. Could ghosts visit you while you were with the man you'd used to erase him from your heart so you couldn't feel it breaking?

"Well, you sure had yourself a good time at the funeral," Tadeu said. "You couldn't even wait until my body was cold. And here I really believed you were a virgin all those years. Must have been pretty fucking funny, how gullible I was. I actually thought you were saving yourself for me."

He looked me up and down like he might spit on me, like I was some diseased whore begging him for work. I shrank back further, my heart pounding and my breath coming short. How could I defend myself? His accusations were true.

Tadeu prowled forward another step, his eyes filled with so much rage, so much betrayal, that I could feel it sickening my own heart. He was right. It hadn't been a sacrifice I made for the amulet. I hadn't lain under Lord Balam, feeling nothing while he fucked me. I'd liked it. So how could I have loved Tadeu, if I could do such a thing on the very night he died?

"Tell me, Itzel," Tadeu snarled, leaning in so his face was a foot from mine. "How long had you been spreading your legs for your daddy's royal visitors? Since your mom died, I bet. Your dad never minded pounding a little preteen pussy. Why wouldn't you be thrown in the mix?"

"It wasn't like that," I choked out.

"Is that why you were always all over my dick when you were way too young to fuck? If I'd known you were already doing it, I wouldn't have been such a good guy. Did you like it the first time, Itzel? Or did you scream for them the way you screamed for me the other day?"

"Leave me alone," I whispered, my throat too tight to rage at him the way I wanted.

"Maybe it wasn't the king's idea at all," he said, his voice taking on a cruel, taunting edge. "Maybe it was yours. You always wanted to be a shifter. I just never knew you wanted to fuck them. You used to laugh at the kitty chasers, but you were just like them, weren't you, Itzel? I saw how much you loved it with my own eyes."

"How?" I croaked, tears aching in my throat.

Tadeu straightened, pushing off the door frame to step back into the middle of the hall. "That night when I woke up? The night I fucking *died*, Itzel. When I woke up, your sister said she had something to show me."

"No," I whispered, shaking my head slowly. I knew what was coming, but I couldn't bear it. Now I knew why she'd wanted him close to her, away from me. So I'd never know the truth.

Tadeu snorted with derision. "I was such a lovesick puppy, you know what I thought? I thought about you, Itzel. I was back alive, so maybe I had another chance. And even though the guards told me you ordered my execution, and they had no reason to lie, I didn't really believe it. Not until Camila took me into the room where you were riding that jaguar like a real cowgirl. I'm glad those fucking riding lessons I gave you came in handy."

"I'm—sorry," I choked out.

And then I couldn't say anything, because a sob rose in my throat like a primal scream from the center of the earth itself, one that would tear apart my entire world like Tadeu's words just had. I closed the door, sliding down the inside of it and curling in on myself like a broken thing. Big, earth-rending sobs wracked my body as I lay there, my heart imploding. Strong arms wrapped around me, heaving me up and carrying me to the bed. Shadow lay me down with him, wrapping himself around me, his forehead pressed to mine as he watched me shatter like glass in his hands.

Seventeen

Gabor
Royal Guard, Ocelot Nation

It had been two weeks since I had considered killing the heir to the throne. Two weeks since I'd landed a plane with flames consuming it by the second. Two weeks since I'd pulled the future queen from the wreckage and taken her to the shah's palace, where she made me witness to the most sickening scene of brutality I'd encountered in a decade of serving King Ocelot, where degradation and violence were so much a part of everyday life that I could walk by a hanging man without blinking—without even noticing.

I had sat in the cockpit of a plane with Princess Itzel after her first murder, and I'd wanted to say something, but I hadn't. There were no comforting words that would make me anything but a hypocrite. I'd wanted to tell her that the first one was the hardest, which was true. But I hadn't wanted to remind her that after my first killing, there had been many, many more. I'd wanted to tell her that it never got easier, but I couldn't lie to her. It had gotten easier. Frighteningly easy.

I hadn't realized exactly how callous, how *sociopathic*, I'd become until something came screaming like a meteor through the void I'd cultivated around my heart. No, not something. Someone.

Someone whose scream had hit with the impact of a bomb detonating inside my soul. Now a second nightmare had joined the one about my sister, a scene to plague my dreams and haunt my sleepless nights.

I threw the blankets off and climbed out of the bed that offered every comfort but no peace. The familiar, restless urge to reach for my slow and bitter poison drew me out of my room. And because I had been imploding incrementally since the day I considered whether to kill the queen, I didn't stop at one self-destructive urge. After lighting a cigarette, I let my feet wander down the maze of halls, past the concubines' quarters, past the rooms where the shah's guards slept and down the hall where the other princess slept.

Her Grace Camila stood guard, a job far below what should befall a crown princess. She leaned against the wall as if exhausted, her shoulders sagging and dark circles like bruises under her eyes.

"Your Grace," I said, giving her a slight bow. "Are you unwell?"

"Of course I'm not unwell," she snapped. "I'm just tired of waiting out here for that filthy panther to show up."

I kept my expression neutral as I took a drag of my cigarette, daring her to chastise me. "Yes, Your Grace."

Her face was haggard, but her eyes were shrewd as she gave me a long, calculating look, the one that made my skin cold and my balls try to crawl up inside my body.

"Break down the door."

I crushed out my cigarette. "Your Grace?"

"He's in there," she hissed, jabbing an accusatory finger at me. "I know he's in there. She's hiding him from me because she doesn't want me to know she has the amulets. She thinks I'm stupid. But I know he's there."

"What will you do to him, Your Grace?"

"Break down the door," she ordered, pointing to her sister's sleeping quarters.

"This is the shah's home," I pointed out. "Not ours."

"You think I'm stupid, too, don't you?" Princess Camila hissed, her eyes flashing with gold—a threat ocelots used to intimidate each other the way wolves might bare their teeth.

For a second, I did the thing I'd begun doing since we landed. I considered whether what I was doing upheld the vows I'd taken to the ocelot throne. Was obeying Her Majesty in opposition to that?

Princess Camila stomped her foot. "Break down the door," she commanded again. I wasn't the only one changing on this trip. I wasn't the only one slipping from the rigid ocelot ways. I was genuinely worried for Princess Camila, for the decisions she was making, the impression she was making on the other Feline Nations.

But it wasn't my place to worry about those things. My place was to serve, to protect, to mindlessly obey. The rest was the job of Her Grace. The problem was that it seemed Her Grace had forgotten that.

Still, it wasn't my place to remind her. I had tried to do so gently a few times, and she'd threatened to send me home and order my execution, or to leave me in the Lion Kingdom, or to take it out on her sister. Princess Camila was shrewd and observant as well as smart. She knew how to threaten me, how to gain my compliance when she could no longer rely on me for dutiful obedience.

Now, she turned and called down the hall. Moments later, Tadeu appeared as if he'd been waiting. Was he guarding her now that she didn't trust me?

Before he reached us, I gathered all my strength, the fury that had awakened as I sat at that table with Princess Camila's claw piercing through my palm like a gentle reminder of the true violence of which she was capable. She might as well have tied a noose around my neck and used it as a leash to lead me around. Her subtle threats were worse than brutality. I could take a beating. The thing she was doing to my head, that was harder to endure.

Stepping forward, I crouched for leverage and slammed my shoulder into the door. It flew inwards with a crash. Inside the room, Princess Itzel screamed and leapt from the bed as if she'd been waiting for an attack all this time. She probably had. She wasn't stupid, either.

Around her, three men had been sleeping, all of them in the big bed together, like a family. My chest tightened, and I stood frozen as Her Majesty stormed past me into the room.

"I knew it," she shrieked, pointing a finger at Shadow as he slid out of bed as if made of liquid. He was naked and already halfway shifted by the time I stepped through the doorway, blocking Princess Itzel from Tadeu's path.

"What the fuck are you doing?" Itzel demanded. She stared at her sister with wild eyes, her hair a sexy, tangled mane. Thank the stars she was wearing something, though the over-sized T-shirt she'd chosen barely covered the apex of her thighs. Below its hem, the expanse of her plump, golden thighs beckoned.

"Give me the amulets," Princess Camila ordered, holding out a hand to Shadow. "Or my guards dispose of you right now."

Princess Itzel's eyes flew wide, and I saw the anguish there at the thought of losing her lover. I shouldn't care. I should be able to kill any man in the world without blinking. I'd done it so many times before. But the idea of putting that anguish in the princess's eyes, of making it permanent, made my blood turn to ice crystals that tore at my veins.

I should have seen this coming from the very first night I worked in the palace, when the preteen princess got into the king's liquor and drank herself numb from the pain of her mother's death. When I found her passed out on the kitchen floor and carried her to bed, because I would want someone to do the same for my sister now that she no longer had someone to look after her. I could look after this girl. I could follow her when my night shift ended on too many nights. I could make sure she made it home every time.

And when my sister died a few years later, I was meant to care for nothing but the king. That was the purpose of her death, and I'd thought it wasn't for nothing. But it was. Because I hadn't lost all attachments. I'd simply transferred them.

Shadow dropped his front paws to the ground, fully shifted in a second's time.

"Kill him," Princess Camila ordered, aiming a finger at the threat.

"No," Princess Itzel yelled, jumping in front of a panther, as if her human body could shield him. Tadeu jostled me aside, shoving past and lunging at Shadow while still in human form. Camila turned to me, eyes flashing murderously as she screamed at me to shift. I barely heard her. My eyes were riveted on the scene behind her back. Tadeu was wrestling with the panther while Prince Kwame had thrown on a set of clothes and snatched up a backpack.

Lord Balam grabbed Itzel, kissed her hard on the mouth, and shoved a velvet pouch into her hands. I knew what it was. I'd seen it in Princess Camila's bag. It was the thing she was after, the thing she would kill for. One of the things.

I could have leapt past Princess Camila, ripped it out of their hands. Joined the brawl. Shifted first, ripped out a throat. I could have pulled out the dart gun I'd procured from the driver who'd brought us from the plane to the castle, knocked out the thieving princess, and been the hero.

Lord Balam pulled his jaguar skin around his shoulders, and I knew it was time to fight.

"Come," Prince Kwame said gently, taking the princess's elbow. Our eyes met, and I knew with complete certainty that I was on the wrong side of this fight. I had sworn to fight and die for the throne, though, so that's what I would do.

Princess Itzel had her calling. She had her True Mates to fight by her side, to love and protect her with their lives. I had no place in her rebel crew. My place was to die at her sister's side.

So, I dropped and shifted into fighting form. When I looked up, Prince Kwame and Princess Itzel were gone.

The familiar determination hardened the steel of my heart back to the way it should be, cooling it from the molten form it took when Princess Itzel looked at me to the impenetrable resolve of a proper ocelot guard. I leapt at Lord Balam, sinking my teeth into his shoulder. He struck at me, and I jumped back. Tadeu's enormous tiger form had emerged, and he threw Shadow across the room and leapt at Lord Balam. I dove after Shadow, who came up hissing and snarling.

I fought for the future queen and for the honor I would never forsake. Even knowing we were the enemy, we were the evildoers, didn't erase the oath I'd taken. I hadn't vowed to do what my conscience told me was right. I had vowed to serve another's vision of what was right. I was bound to that oath until the moment of my death. That was my life sentence. Princess Itzel wasn't my forever. This was my forever.

She was my never.

EIGHTEEN

Itzel
Princess, Ocelot Nation

"WE SHOULD GO BACK," I HISSED TO KWAME AS WE ran through the tiled courtyard after climbing out the window. "She thinks Shadow has the amulets. She ordered them to kill him. What if he's dead?"

"He's not dead," Kwame said, his cool hand tightening around mine. "Come, we must hurry."

"How do you know?" I asked, digging my heels in and yanking at his hand.

Kwame turned to face me, resting his hands on my shoulders and squeezing. "Itzel, this is the plan. He would give his life for you just like any one of us would. There is no greater honor than to die for your mate. Come. We must stick to the plan."

"The plan wasn't for someone to die," I said, but I let him pull me on, through the entrance to the palace and back out toward the helicopter pad.

Sir Kenosi's pilot came running from the other direction, gave a quick salute, and hopped in. He'd been told to be ready when we decided to go, and a rush of relief and gratitude swelled inside me when the chopper started up. The pilot had come through for us even when his employer had left this world, but I had no doubt it was because of his loyalty to Sir Kenosi that he was so willing and ready to help.

"The plan was for us to get to the mountains, and for them to stop your sister," Kwame said, lifting me into the helicopter. "Of course there are small hiccups, but we stay the course. Right?"

He searched my face, letting it sink in that this was my decision. I could go back now, give the amulets to Camila, and be done. I could let her pay for the snow leopard amulet however Gao Jetsun wanted to make her. But something had changed in me the night Tadeu had told me the truth. Camila had known all along that he was alive. She had taken him to see me while I tried to fuck away my grief over losing him with a complete stranger. She had set it all up so he would hate me, so he would never come back and so that I never knew he could.

She was the one who had separated us. I was pretty fucking sure she was the one who had ordered his execution, not Father. Sure, my relationship with Tadeu pissed off the king, but nothing had happened to make him suddenly want to execute him. Camila couldn't have known how it would all play out, but she must have seen him as a threat. He was a distraction, someone I loved that didn't benefit her. She knew I wanted to marry him, elevate him in status. She knew I wanted to give my virginity to him. And she'd known that I would be much more malleable if I didn't have my heart in two places.

Fury rolled through me, and I squeezed Kwame's hands before turning to close the helicopter door. "Let's go."

AFTER ALL THE CLOSE CALLS AND BIG SCENES WE'D had trying to leave the last few territories, I kept looking out the window, expecting to see Camila, Gabor, and Tadeu charging for the helicopter, determined to stop us. Only when we were high above the Tiger Palace did I finally relax back into the soft, leather seat. Kwame slid an arm around my shoulders and squeezed me to him.

"You're safe," he said, kissing my forehead. "We're going to go find Gao Jetsun, get the last amulet, and then we will make you a queen."

"A queen of what?" I asked, drawing back to look at him.

"When we marry, you will be the Lion Queen, of course."

"I'm going to find a way to bring Sir Kenosi back," I said. "Then I won't be a shifter."

"I don't care," Kwame said. "You will be my queen either way."

"Would your people allow that?"

Kwame smiled, revealing the slight gap between his white teeth. "Of course," he said. "My people are mostly human. Only when people from the royal families die do they become lion shifters."

"Right," I said, nodding. "Like that lion that lay beside me when I was in the grass. Was that you?"

"Yes," he said. "Before, I was a lion while in our world, and a man when in the spirit world. Now that you brought me back, I have changed. I am a ghost in both worlds, but I can be both lion and human in our world. This is very special, Itzel. Most lion shifters cannot be both in this world. I hope you know how grateful I am for what you did for me."

"Good," I said. "I gave up my mother for that."

"I'm so thankful," Kwame said, cupping my cheek in one hand and leaning in to kiss me gently. "I know it is not an equal sacrifice, but I will give up my throne if you wish to become the ocelot queen."

"You can do that?"

"Of course," he said. "I am the eldest child. I inherit the lion throne. But if you need to fix your country, I will leave the throne to my sister. She prepared for that job for years after I was killed. She is quite capable."

"Don't you want to be king?"

"I want *you*," he said. "I am doing the right thing for my mate. Nothing could make me happier, except to know that I am leaving my people in good hands as well as serving you."

"How did I get so lucky?" I asked, leaning in to press my lips to his.

"Maybe you were due some luck," he said, taking my hand and lacing his fingers through mine.

"Let's hope it holds while we get the last amulet," I said as the helicopter began to descend. The pilot was dropping us off in the mountains, as close to one of the monasteries as we could get. Since the monasteries were mostly human, with maybe a snow leopard or two in each if we were lucky, it might take a while to find my half-brother. Most of the monasteries probably had no shifters at all. The upside was that we only had to contend with my pheromones attracting one or two snow leopards at once. We could fight them off if needed until we found Gao Jetsun.

We were pretty sure he lived somewhere around there. Luring him out would be the hard part this time. Well, that and not getting assaulted by another feline shifter on the mountain in the process. Then, all I had to do was convince Gao Jetsun that I was worthy of the amulet.

Easy enough.

Oh, and I'd also probably need to convince him that it wasn't my fault—or my mom's—that his father had been killed. Even though, really, it kinda was our fault. My mother had the affair. My father had killed him because of the affair. I was a result of the affair.

Yeah, I was definitely going to need some luck.

When we landed, I gave instructions to the pilot, a cheetah who was loyal to Sir Kenosi and now apparently to me. He left to bring my mates to a base camp that wasn't too close to me but wasn't in another country altogether. Once he left us, it was just me and Kwame on the mountain.

I looked around at the alien world, the furthest thing from the warm, sub-tropical Ocelot Nation as I could imagine. The air around us felt thin and dry, nearly glittering with ice crystals. The mountainsides were steep and smooth, with snow still on top and extending down the sides. Small patches of tan, dry grass peeked out from the sandstone that surrounded us as we started up the side. Brown boulders with white and red lichen made for handholds, but also made good hiding places for anyone out to ambush us.

Which was no one, I reminded myself. There was no one here to attack us, no one who wanted to. When the magic kicked in, though...

"We will set up camp for the night," Kwame said, scrambling up the mountain in front of me despite wearing the heavier of our packs. "Let's find a good spot. In the morning, you should open the tiger amulet, and we can start searching."

Everything about this place reminded me that we were in a foreign land, about to navigate something even further from my past experiences than the other kingdoms. How the fuck was I going to convince a *monk* that I was worthy of a sacred mating amulet? My brother was some sort of celibate holy man, while I was... Weak.

I felt weak compared to that. I wasn't even sure I had moral convictions. My bargains for the amulets had been entirely sexual, not cerebral or philosophical, and definitely not spiritual. Aside from the Lion Amulet, I'd traded all of them for sex. I'd never really had to convince someone I was worthy, and I wasn't sure that I could. I didn't know if I was worthy of something sacred.

I'd fucked a stranger to forget a lover. I'd ripped his clothes off and thrown myself at him. I'd drugged a man and driven him to insanity, and when he'd come for me, I'd been scared, but I'd gone willingly. And if I was brutally honest with myself, some dark part of me had awakened that night, a part of me that liked being handcuffed to that bed and fucked so wildly that his mattress was shredded in the morning.

At Sir Kenosi's, I'd fought him at first, but by the end, I was lying face down in half eaten food, begging helplessly for him to degrade me if it meant I'd get his beautiful cock. And while I hadn't enjoyed Tadeu's treatment of me, I hadn't asked him to stop. I hadn't begged the shah for mercy. I had been willing to be violated roughly, publicly, even violently. Maybe a part of me had believed I deserved it after what I'd done to Camila. The least I could do was take the wrath of my lover for her.

Only Kwame had made me sacrifice more than my body for him. He'd fucked me, too, but he said it was only to gain the mark, so he'd know for sure I was his mate. Gao Jetsun wouldn't want even that much. If I could lure him out, he might still prove the hardest to convince. After all I'd done to get the others, was I still worthy of something precious? Or was I ruined and dirty, a wrecked and worthless whore like Camila said?

I had to admit, now that I was here, that Camila might have been the better choice to convince my brother to turn over the snow leopard amulet. She was still pure, undamaged by what she'd gone through to get the amulets. And what did I mean to do with the amulets when I had them all? I'd been blinded by my anger at Camila, unwilling to turn them over. But I couldn't even touch the ocelot amulet. It too was cursed, so that only an ocelot could place it into the puzzle with the others. If anyone else touched it, we'd die. Which meant I was going to have to give it back to her or get her blessing, and even I wasn't blind enough to think she'd give me that.

And in truth, I had no right to the amulets or the throne. Camila was a worthy contender, not just for the amulets but for the throne. Was I really ready to fight her for that, though I had no claim and hadn't really earned it? Not the way she had. She was right. She'd studied and trained for it since the day she was born while I made a game of escaping the boring tutors and playing with other human children in the streets. She was a shifter who knew shifter politics while I only knew my own passions and fancies. Camila wanted the throne so much she'd do *anything* to get there.

I wasn't sure that I did. I didn't deserve to take it from her. She'd betrayed her own sister, played us all, even Tadeu. Maybe even our father. What Tadeu said had hurt, but part of that was because it hit so close to home. I had always been jealous of the shifters, but it was more than that. I'd ached to be one with some deep and primal part of me. The injustice of it had been a raw sore that never healed inside me. And since I couldn't be one, I'd found the next best thing on this tour. I'd spread my legs for whatever important man wanted to bury his cock in me, as if that brought me closer to being a shifter myself.

I guess it had worked. I was now a cheetah shifter. But that didn't give me a right to the Ocelot Throne. That didn't mean I'd done something noble or brave or worthy. It just made me a power-hungry whore who traded her body for high-value artifacts instead of coin.

Was that why Kwame had never tried to have sex with me after being marked as my True Mate? He'd been the nicest of all my men, and I'd never doubted his loyalty. I didn't think he'd lured me up here to betray me, or that he'd wanted to separate me from the other men so he could have me to himself. He hadn't tried to fuck me since I'd brought him back to life. Was he disgusted by me, by the things I'd done? Aside from a few sweet, chaste kisses, he had done nothing to indicate he wanted more than my companionship.

Noticing that his long stride had taken him far ahead, I hurried to catch up. Kwame had crested a smaller mountain and was examining a small ledge of grey stone under which one of us could comfortably sleep.

"This might be a good spot to stay the night," he said. "We can see down the sides of the mountain in case anyone is coming. We can also see anyone descending the slopes of the mountains on either side of us, and they protect us from the wind enough that we can have a small fire and probably a good night's sleep."

"How do you know so much about this?" I asked, stopping to catch my breath when I reached him.

Kwame smiled and shrugged out of his heavy pack. "I don't have much experience with mountains, but camping in the bush... That was a big part of growing up in the Lion Kingdom. The passage to manhood was filled with challenges to our strength, stamina, and courage."

My eyes wandered to the scarification on his forehead, the series of ritual scars that his father bore as well. "For royals, or for everyone?"

"Both," he said with obvious pride. "Mine might have been more rigorous, but every boy in our nation knows how to camp under the stars. Come, my queen. I'll show you how to make a good fire."

I set down my pack and joined him, marveling at his skill in an area I knew nothing of. Though there was wilderness in the Ocelot Nation, it was outside the palace gates, far from the city where we lived. I'd rarely been outside the confines of the property, let alone outside our city. Kwame knew things I'd never even imagined learning. Watching him, I was reminded that we were literally a world apart. Despite our long talks over the past few weeks and the time we'd spent together, I still didn't know my men all that well. We'd been through a lot together, though, and I knew it bound us just as strongly as the True Mate bond. We'd learn each other in time.

For now, I could marvel in the discoveries of their skill. I watched Kwame, taking direction as he showed me how to build up and stoke the fire to get it going and keep it burning. Once we finished eating and settled down next to the fire, I turned to my mate.

"So, tell me about this heat," I said. "I know a little bit, but I want to be prepared for anything that could happen."

Nineteen

"Once you're in heat, you'll be irresistible to men, and insatiable in your appetites for about three days," Kwame said. "For a few days leading up to that it will increase, and then for a few days after it will be decreasing, but you may still feel some of the effects."

"Will it affect you, too?" I asked, feeling strangely vulnerable suddenly. I'd never been interested in sex with a man who didn't want it back. All men seemed to want sex, and the fact that he was supposed to be my mate made it even more frustrating. I couldn't just shrug it off as incompatibility.

"I don't know," Kwame said, shifting on the log where he sat. "I am here in physical form again, so I think it might. And yet, I'm still a ghost, so I don't know if the pheromones will affect me as they do a living animal. As I have said, this is a rare circumstance. I have done some research, and I'm not sure that we will be able to have children, either. I'm very sorry. We can certainly try. I haven't found a clear answer one way or another."

I nodded, swallowing hard. "So you're just not interested in sex at all?"

Kwame drew back, surprise flashing across his face. "Of course I am."

"Then why don't you want to have sex with me?" I blurted. "Is it because of what I've done to get the amulets?"

Kwame stared at me a long minute, his eyes burning with such intensity that I had to drop my gaze to the fire. I poked at it with a stick, sending sparks spiraling up into the sky with the smoke. Kwame scooted over and wrapped an arm around me, reaching to tilt my chin up to face him again. "Itzel, you have done what a feline heir must do," he said. "You have sacrificed yourself, doing everything that was asked of you to gain the amulets. That is what every ruler does before taking the throne. It's how you show you are willing to do what must be done when you're on the throne, that you will sacrifice for your people."

"But I'm not the heir," I whispered.

"You will be a great queen," he said. "I admit that it was difficult to see you in pain, but I certainly don't think any less of you because you put yourself through that. I respect you even more, that you were so determined to get the amulet. And though I don't admire your sister the way you do, I admire you for what you are willing to do for her. Loyalty is a virtue many people are lacking. But you, my queen, are not."

He leaned in and brushed his full lips against mine, sending a shiver of longing through me. I clutched his shirt, pulling him closer, not able to put into words how relieved I was to hear him say those things.

"You don't think I'm stupid for still loving her?" I asked, searching his gaze.

"Of course not," he said with a smile. "I have sisters. I would do anything to keep them from being hurt, just as you would your sister. But love is not rational."

"You hate her, too, don't you?"

"I can't hate someone you love," Kwame said, smoothing my hair away from my face. "But I think you have proved yourself worthy of the throne while she has hidden behind you, knowing you are stronger than she is. One day, I think that will come back to haunt her. But you must do what you feel is right—and you have. That's what will make you a great queen. You listen to our opinions, but you have always followed your own compass, Itzel. You have behaved most honorably—most regally—on this trip."

I snorted at that. "Your people must have a different idea of honor than ours."

My thoughts were drawn back to the man I'd left behind—not my mates, but Gabor. The man who always followed his compass, who did what he thought was right. He'd seen me take the amulets. He'd seen me go out the window with Kwame. He might have even distracted Camila so she stood with her back to us, yelling at him, while we escaped. I wished I could go back to that moment, run to him and beg him to come with us. I wished I could make him lose control the way I had. I hadn't acted with honor. I'd been a mess. He was the honorable one.

I pushed the thoughts away. Gabor had nothing to do with this. He was simply a guard, one who remained loyal to Camila because he had vowed to serve the throne, and she was the next to take it. Kwame was here, loyal to me.

He raised his hands to either side of my face, turning me to him. "Itzel," he said. "I see you as nothing but admirable. Determined, loyal, brave beyond measure. It pains me to think that you see yourself any differently. If I haven't shown an interest in being intimate, it was only because I didn't think *I* had proven myself worthy of *you*."

I covered his hands with mine, staring back at him with equal intensity. "You're the most noble, worthy man I've ever met," I said, my throat tight with emotion. "You've always put me first, since the moment we met."

"Not the moment we met," he said, shaking his head sadly. "I took what I needed to make sure that you were my True Mate, though I already felt in my heart that something life-changing was happening. Asking for your trust after I took without asking, it seemed disrespectful. And since then, you haven't been in a place where that was an option."

"We're in a place where it's an option right now," I said. "I don't hold it against you that you did that to me before I knew you. I understand that you wanted to know if I was your True Mate. Of all the things that have happened to me on this tour, that was the least objectionable."

Yes, I had felt violated by the ghost sex, but it wasn't painful like Tadeu's turn or degrading like Sir Kenosi's. My encounter with Kwame had been brief and strange, and I was ready for another experience between us. I was ready for the man, not just his ghost.

I turned to him, pressing my lips to his soft, full ones. Warmth curled through me, and I pressed deeper, sliding my hands behind his head, feeling the wooly nubs of the knots in his hair between my fingers. I moaned softly, opening my lips for him. His tongue slid between my teeth, tracing along the edge before dipping deeper to caress mine. He sighed, his hands tightening on my waist and pulling my body against him.

"Itzel," he whispered, drawing his lips from mine. "If you're on the edge of a heat, this can push you there faster."

I smiled, the corners of my lips pulling up against his. "A man who's always strategizing," I said. "I like it."

I reached into my pack, rooting around until I found the velvet bag containing the amulets. As I held it, I felt a slight buzz of electricity up my arm, like the barest whisper of what I'd felt when I opened the panther amulet. I realized as I held the bag containing the mating rituals of five cat clans that I was feeling their combined magic.

Holy fuck. The weight of their importance sank into me as I untied the gold cord around the bag. I had joked about these once, but now I knew. I knew the cost of these. The sacrifices shifters had made throughout the centuries to procure these. Their significance was sobering. Joking about them seemed inconceivable, a sacrilege.

One by one, I took out the amulets. I knelt on the ground beside the fire, and with great care set them on the ground around my knees, studying the curves and edges of each, pondering how they'd fit together. Curiosity urged me to piece them all together, leaving space for the last two, but that would be a violation. They weren't my amulets, and the puzzle wasn't complete. I didn't want to activate any magic by accident. I'd already done that once, and I was dancing with fire now.

So far, each amulet I'd opened had worked on me as it should a shifter, not a human. But that didn't mean they all would. That didn't mean one wouldn't have catastrophic consequences. I couldn't play with them like a child's toy puzzle. If I fit them together now, who knew what would happen. Sir Kenosi had used his to end his life, and I had no illusion that one couldn't do the same to me. I had to be careful, not tempt fate more than I already was by opening the tiger amulet.

I found it and slid it out of its velvet bag, cupping the circular, polished tiger-eye stone in my palm. The swirls of gold in the black flowed with a faint shimmer of magic as I held it.

"Whoa," I whispered, raising my gaze to Kwame. "Can you see that?"

"You can see the magic," he murmured. He slid his fingertips across the inky black and shimmering gold, his touch as reverent as his gaze.

"Yeah," I breathed. "That's a lot of magic."

"A human shouldn't be able to see magic," he said quietly.

I swallowed. "I'm not... Entirely... Human."

I hadn't told the others about Gao Jetsun, about my father being a demigod. I wasn't sure what I was, if there was even a name for it. It wasn't as simple as saying I was the human-born child of two shifters. I was that, but I was also the daughter of an ocelot, a snow leopard, a demi-god, and a rare priestess whose powers I didn't exactly know.

"I know," Kwame said in his low, deep voice.

"You do?"

"A human can't travel in the spirit world like you did," he said. "They definitely aren't strong enough to bring someone back. Not the way you did."

"What other way is there?"

"You didn't just bring me here to visit for a moment as a ghost," he said. "You brought me back to life. You literally raised me from the dead, Itzel."

"But as a ghost," I said, feeling suddenly frightened. I'd done something that defied the laws of nature, of possibility.

Seeming to sense my discomfort, Kwame turned his attention to the stone. "If this puts you into heat, you will start emitting pheromones soon," he said. "Maybe as soon as tomorrow. They will get stronger, as will your desire, for a few days. After it peaks on the middle day, you will have a few days of decreasing libido, and then you will be back to your natural state."

I took a deep breath and nodded. The jaguar amulet had done something similar, though it happened suddenly and intensely, and only inside my body. This time, I knew what I was getting, so I was a bit more prepared. I would bring Gao Jetsun out of hiding with the pheromones, but he wouldn't want me to do anything too sexual in exchange for the amulet, since we were related. Maybe I could take him to the spirit world to see his father. Since I'd be horny as fuck during the high heat, Kwame would take care of my sexual needs until it wore off.

I slid my fingers around the amulet, searching for a seam. A hot tingle of magic buzzed through my hands and up my arms. The True Mate marks on my arm began to burn and glow, especially the last one—Tadeu's. Suddenly, my fingers sank into the stone as if it were made of oil instead of stone. I gasped and drew back, feeling a cold, greasy residue on my fingers.

"Rub it on your throat and neck," Kwame said. "That's what the maharajas said to do."

Lifting my hand to my throat, I rubbed in the salve before I could touch anything else. I didn't want to leave anything on the ground that would make someone else go into heat. The last thing I wanted was for someone else to get caught unaware of an altered cycle. Plus, it would kinda make the whole thing pointless if the monk was drawn out by the wrong woman.

For a second, nothing happened. Then, the same shimmering gold that had been coiling through the swirling patterns in the stone began to rise from it. The air sparkled with fine gold particles, so beautiful I wanted to sit and marvel at them. Instead, I cupped the amulet in one hand and covered it with the other. The tingling that had spread along my arm now rose from my neck, racing across my skin like a burn. I gasped as it hit my nose, clearing my sinuses and making me nearly choke. The magic invaded me like a hot, dry wind, filling me with images of wild storms tearing at the mountain, howling through every stone crevice and ripping out brown grasses, toppling trees, and breaking bushes. Snow piling in sparkling white drifts so pure my eyes ached at the sight, blinded by the stark beauty and crystalline cold.

I fell back, gasping for breath. Kwame rushed to me, helping me back onto the log and brushing me off. "Are you okay?"

"I don't know," I whispered, gripping his hands as he crouched in front of me. "I saw something. Am I supposed to see something?"

"What did you see?"

"Nothing," I said, throwing my hands up in frustration. "I just saw some snow. But that's not the point."

"My queen, what is wrong?" Kwame asked, resuming his seat

beside me. His brow furrowed in concern, and he rubbed comforting circles on my back with his palm.

"I don't know what's happening to me," I blurted. "I don't know how I brought you back to life, and I don't know how I kept Kenosi's cheetah and turned into a shifter. Supposedly I have some magic that made it happen, but I don't even know how to tell if that's true or not. There's no one like me, so I can't ask anyone what's supposed to happen."

"I don't have all the answers," Kwame said. "I have only the wisdom of the lion people. We would say that what happens is supposed to happen. Just as you're content to let fate take its course with your sister, you might have to show yourself the same kindness."

"I'm scared," I admitted. It was one thing to let my sister take a throne she'd been born to ascend, one she had earned every day for the last twenty years, not just a few months. It was another to sit back and relax while things happened to me that I had no control over, things I didn't understand.

To my shame, I wanted my sister, even after all she'd done. My whole life, she had been there for me. When I looked back on it with clearer vision, I knew that I was the stronger one. I'd held her up when she couldn't stand on her own, comforted her when she cried, pieced her back together when she fell apart. I had been her crutch and her strength. I'd made her strong.

Now I was falling apart, and some emotional, instinctual urge inside me reached for her, wanting her to do the same for me. But the rational side of me knew she wouldn't. She'd taken my strength like a vampire, sucked it from me until I had nothing left for myself.

"Let me help you," Kwame whispered, lifting my hair off my neck and bending to kiss my shoulder. "Whatever you need, let me give it to you."

Tears burned behind my eyes, and I leaned in and pressed my lips to his lush, full ones. When Mom died, I'd slept in Camila's room for months, as if a mere human could somehow protect her better than the half dozen armed shifters outside her window and her door. But she had wanted me. She had needed me, so I'd been there. Through every diplomatic meeting that gave her a migraine, every dinner and ball that left her exhausted and pale, I'd been there to jump in and flirt, distract skeptical royals so they didn't notice her weakness. I'd never known it was bleeding away my own strength until I had none left to give, and she wasn't here to return the favor.

But someone was. Kwame's strong arms were around me. His strong body was pressed against mine, solid as the life I'd given back to him. He would give me the oblivion I'd craved after Tadeu's death, when I had used Lord Balam without even knowing that's what I was doing. When I had taken from him because the sister I needed wasn't there for me.

"I can't," I blurted, breaking Kwame's kiss. "I can't use you like this. I did it before, and it hurt someone I love. Maybe two someones." I thought of Tadeu's hatred, of his anger, and also of Lord Balam's lack of possessiveness when other men wanted me. I hadn't understood it, but now I did.

Despite him saying he was fine with the way I'd treated him, he'd been protecting his heart—from me. That broke my heart more than knowing I'd broken Tadeu's.

Kwame stroked my hair back and gazed at me in the flickering firelight. "Itzel, you're not using me," he said. "I'm offering. You're allowed to take as well as give."

"What if I hurt you?" I whispered.

A smile teased the corner of Kwame's mouth, and he slid a hand behind my head, cradling it in his long fingers. "I'm strong," he said. "I won't break."

TWENTY

I LEANED IN TO KISS THE LION PRINCE AGAIN. HIS arms slid around me, warm and comforting and as strong as he promised.

"Thank you," I whispered.

"You don't have to thank me for giving you what you've always deserved."

"I want to," I whispered. "Thank you for letting me have this. For being so good to me."

"Anyone who's hurt you deserves worse than death," he said. "You're a queen. You should be treated as such."

I kissed him, and this time, I didn't pull away. I tasted his mouth, diving into him and letting myself fall, trusting that he would catch. His long fingers caressed my sides, tickling and teasing, until I had to smile into his kiss. It felt like freedom, that smile. It had been a long time since I'd had fun with a man in a sexual way.

I pressed deeper into the kiss, moaning at the sensation of his tongue sliding rhythmically against mine. Kwame's hands moved down my back, tightening on my waist. In one swift motion, he lifted me and brought me into his lap. I straddled his hips, rising up and cupping his face between my hands as I knelt over him. I devoured his mouth, hungrier now as a tingling sensation spread through my body and settled between my thighs. I hovered above him, not sinking down yet. The cold air snaked between us, teasing our hot bodies, urging us to move closer.

Kwame's hands tugged gently, but I resisted, letting the tension build between us instead. I'd never been in control like this, and I found myself relishing the groan that left Kwame's lips when I didn't yield to the pressure of his hands. He lifted his hips, but I drew back, not letting our bodies connect fully.

After so many experiences where I'd had no control, kneeling over Kwame like this felt like victory. Like power.

It shimmered along my limbs like magic, sinking into my blood like an addiction. I had the power, and I loved it. I wanted to make him moan and beg the way Sir Kenosi had made me.

I slid my hands up the back of his neck, feeling the corded muscles, the soft knots of his hair, the angles of his cheeks, the cool shell of his ear. My lips found their way along his jawline to his throat, and he moaned softly, letting his head fall back. I moved down, tugging up his shirt until he let me pull it off over his head. His dark skin gleamed like black satin in the firelight, and I sat back to marvel at his beauty. My nails raked down his flat chest to his abs, which tensed under my fingers as a shiver went through his body. More ritual scars marked his chest and shoulders, awakening a pride in me I hadn't known I felt. He had endured, had proven himself a man to his people.

Now he would prove his manhood to me.

I undid the button on his pants, tugged down the zipper, and slid my hand inside. Kwame groaned softly as my fingers circled his cock for the first time. Like the rest of him, it was long and hard. My mouth watered at the picture it put into my mind.

Kwame reached for my clothes, gently sliding my jacket off my arms before tugging my shirt over my head. He sat back and gazed at me as if I were the world's rarest gem, more precious than every amulet combined. His eyes heated my body, making it come to life with desire in a way it hadn't in weeks. I wanted more. More of his gaze caressing my skin, more of the sensation of power and worthiness that I felt when he looked at me as if I were a goddess and he were a mere mortal. I reached behind me to unhook my bra, sliding it from my arms and relishing his sharp intake of breath. I sat back, my top half bared to him and the firelight dancing off my caramel skin.

"You are perfection itself," Kwame breathed, his hands reaching for me before pausing.

"Touch me," I whispered, and heat shimmered through me when his cold hands began to move slowly down my back, caressing my soft skin. He stopped when they reached my jeans, and he drew another breath.

I stood, watching as he undid the button and gulped before slowly circling the top of my jeans with his thumbs. Slowly, he drew them down over my thighs. As the cold air hit my hot skin, excitement rushed through me. Kwame and I had slept in the same bed, but we'd never undressed each other, never seen each other like this. He'd never looked at me with desire burning in those eyes that had seen death itself and come back from it. He'd never leaned in and drew a deep breath of my scent as he slid my jeans lower, his eyes fixed on the spot where my thighs met.

When he had my jeans at my feet, I kicked them off and stood for a moment in the firelight, letting him drink me in with his eyes, the way the firelight skimmed along my curves, the hardness of my nipples in the cold, the chill bumps running over my skin. I felt like a goddess standing there, full and whole and charged with power.

I reached for Kwame's pants, drawing them off as well. But when he stepped closer, I nudged him back to the log. He sank onto it, his eyes still fixed on me as if in some kind of trance. Straddling his knees, I relished his reaction—the shuddering breath he took, the way his lids dropped halfway and the soft groan of torment that caught in his throat. I leaned in, pressing my lips to his collar bone before whispering against his neck. "Can I?"

"I give myself to you," Kwame murmured, his voice thick with desire. "Take what you need, my love. It's all for you."

I slid from the log, kneeling between his feet and pumping his cock with one hand while working my lips down over the smooth plane of his chest to his nipple. I flicked my tongue out against it, a shiver of desire piercing through me when he growled in pleasure. I sucked harder, nibbling at the bud of his nipple until he growled again, his hands rougher as they seized my arms.

"I'm not done," I protested, and Kwame's hands relaxed instantly. I let my lips trail down his abs, tasting his cool skin. Gripping his cock, I sank lower. It was smooth and dark like the rest of his skin, but as I gripped it and drew back the skin, the tip emerged dusky pink as if I'd unwrapped a piece of the most exotic candy. My clit throbbed at the sight of his bare cock aching for me. Saliva pooled in my mouth as wetness pooled between my thighs. Again, the sensation of power swelled in my chest, filling me with a heady rush.

I scooted back further, my knees wide on the ground and my ass toward the fire. I could feel the heat of it across the space, the cold air licking my skin and the flames heating my sex, and an erotic thrill went through me. Lowering my lips to Kwame's cock, I kissed the straining head. He shuddered, and I opened my lips, running my tongue around the glorious tip. Lust shot through me, and my lids dropped closed as I began to lick in earnest, spreading my tongue over the cool head and then swiping around it like an ice cream cone.

Kwame moaned, his fingers tangling in my hair and his breath coming faster as I lowered my mouth over him, pumping up and down. A drop of saltiness spread over my tongue, and triumph swelled within me.

"You're driving me crazy," Kwame rumbled. "I want to be inside you, my love."

"Not yet," I murmured, my voice garbled around his cock. I drew back, running my tongue along his full length as it glimmered wetly in the firelight. The tip was shiny and straining from its skin, gloriously ready. I popped my lips back over it, and he tightened his fingers and raised his hips, pushing his cock to the back of my throat.

"My god, I can smell your sex," he gasped, gripping my hair tighter. "Let me taste your sweetness."

I popped off his cock and stood, sliding over his lap again. This time, I slid all the way in, so our hips locked together. "Not this time," I said. "This time, I lead."

I rose up, reaching down to grasp his shaft and guide it to my entrance. Inside me, Sir Kenosi's cheetah growled like a wild animal, prowling under my skin and longing to break free, to fuck wild and animalistic. I hadn't been with anyone since his cheetah had come out of my body, since I'd been a shifter. I could feel a difference in my body, too, a slickness and heat between my pussy lips that was beyond my human wetness.

Kwame felt it, too. With a groan, he sank his teeth into his bottom lip, his body trembling with the effort of holding back. I smiled and pressed my lips to his for a second before sitting back, not holding back my triumphant grin as I watched his face while I sank onto him. Pleasure shuddered through my whole body at the sensation of his cold cock burying itself in my hot flesh.

"Oh," I gasped, a shiver racing across my skin. He was cold as his ghost had been in the grass that first night. I hadn't fucked him since he'd been human again, and I had forgotten the coldness of the undead.

My slick coated him, and pleasure gripped my body as his cock glided in effortlessly. I pressed down, spreading my knees and watching his dark black cock disappear inside me until he reached my depths and our hips locked together. Gripping my hip and bracing one hand beside him on the log, he lifted his hips to push his cock in to the hilt, his pelvic bone grinding against my clit. I gasped in pleasure and a dart of pain as the bare head of his cock hit just a bit too deep for comfort. Kwame growled low in his throat, and I let him guide my hips to find their pace as I began rising and sinking onto him in a slow, sultry rhythm.

"My god, you're so beautiful," Kwame murmured, watching me pump my pussy over his straining, hard cock. I looked down, too, captivated by the sight of his long, black length sinking into me over and over. I began to move faster, riding him harder. Our bodies moved in rhythm, our hips slamming together and drawing a gasp of both pleasure and pain from me each time he hit my depths and my clit at the same moment. The pleasure spiraled higher, fueled by the pain that darted into me. I had learned to love pain, to crave it, to need it. And now it was mine.

I fucked Prince Kwame harder, relishing the pain, using it to fan the flames of my pleasure until I reached the crest of what my body could contain. I cried out, my walls clenching around him as my climax gripped me. I raked my nails down his arms, throwing my head back and crying out my pleasure, my pain, my power to the stars in the inky cold night.

My calm, gentle mate threw back his head and roared like a lion as he thrust his hips upwards, gripping my body and holding me pinned as he expanded further still. Pain clenched my walls tighter, and he roared again as he pumped a burst of icy cum into my depths. The cold of it shocked me, and I cried out again as another orgasm crested just as the last one subsided.

Still, my entire body throbbed with energy, so much I felt like I was vibrating, about to burst into the sky and streak across the Milky Way in a shimmering band of gold like I'd seen swirling in the amulet.

"Itzel," Kwame whispered, gripping my hips.

I couldn't answer, though. I was still coming, my body still gripped in the throes of climax. I slid a hand over his mouth, blocking out any protest as my body writhed against his, my toes digging into the dirt, the stones, the cold earth. My pussy gripped him, milking the seed from his throbbing cock until every drop was gone. I cried out again and again, wordlessly, feeling the perfection of our bodies together as his cock stayed hard and driven deep into my center, filling me and completing me, joining with me in some sacred, primal way.

"Itzel," he said again, this time more urgently, turning his face away from my silencing hand. "Look."

I couldn't find words, but Kwame nudged my shoulder with his palm, and I turned, my brain still dizzy with the aftershock of our union. A gasp escaped my lips as a shock hit me like icy water thrown in my face. Surrounding us on every side, emerging from behind stones and bushes like spectral spirits drawn by some siren's song, were at least a dozen snow leopards.

Twenty-One

Tadeu
Shifter, Tiger Nation

"We have two very simple goals on this mission," Princess Camila said, standing in the center of the circle of tigers and other guides and guards she'd brought to her base camp in the Himalayas. You'd think we were climbing Everest from the number of people she'd paid to join her entourage, but we were currently in a small, barren valley with only a bit of snow on the northern slopes around us.

In addition to her team, Camila had allowed the cheetah reality show host and her cameraman to accompany us. Sir Kenosi himself would have been proud to land a role on this reality show. Even an idiot like me knew it would be ratings gold. Especially since Camila was sure to come unhinged when something didn't go her way. I'd known the ditzy princess for most of my life, and I'd never seen her so close to the edge. I couldn't wait to see her go off it. Maybe I'd be lucky enough to give her a little nudge.

"First of all," Princess Ocelot continued, "We're here to obtain the snow leopard amulet. Shah Tiger says a monk named Gao Jetsun has it, which means we need to hit all the monasteries in snow leopard territory in search of him. Everyone understand?"

A few people nodded or murmured agreement, including our guide, a snow leopard named Li.

"I have programmed my name and number into each of these phones. You are to keep them on you at all times."

She began handing out small phones. When I got mine, I saw that it had only one number. Well, at least I had a phone now. The shah hadn't done much beyond letting me crash in his giant palace, most of which was used for visitors only. He hadn't shown me around, or gotten someone to teach me the language, or done shit for me, really. Besides having me arrested for killing the princess, he didn't seem to know I existed.

And why would he? There were thousands of tiger shifters. I was just one more of them, some asshole who'd been shipped here when his home country didn't want him anymore. They'd gotten rid of a convict, shoved me off on the shah. He didn't want a convict. He'd only let me stay because King Ocelot had already flown me to his empire, and he didn't want to spare the expense of shipping me back.

Camila went on as she handed out the cheap phones. "Once we find Mr. Jetsun, you are to notify me immediately. I'll come and negotiate for the amulet."

"It's Mr. Gao," Gabor murmured. "Your Grace." He kept his voice low, glancing sideways at the cameras with a fierce scowl. He obviously didn't want them to hear, and from the eager expression on Ebele's face, it was clear she'd heard and was hoping the mic had picked up his words. I'd already heard Gabor trying to talk Camila out of letting the camera crew tag along, but she'd stomped all over his objections the way she always did when someone contradicted her. She had to have her way, and she wouldn't even look at someone else's idea, even if it was better. Eventually, Gabor had given up, but not before she'd used her favorite persuasive technique— the threat of execution.

Like father like daughter.

Camila narrowed her eyes and glared at Gabor. I couldn't figure them out. Was she in love with him, but she couldn't get the stick out of her ass long enough to admit it? Was he in love with her, but he couldn't tell her because she was his master? One thing was for damn sure. He wasn't afraid of her. He had corrected her in front of her entire new guard, and it was bound to go viral and turn into a GIF on top of it.

From the look on her face, Camila sure as fuck hadn't missed the disrespect. Was this their little power play that they'd hash out in the bedroom later? Or was he really challenging her?

It wasn't any of my business. My business was staying alive, and Gabor was an ocelot guard, which meant I slept with one eye open. The only reason he wasn't a convict like me was because the king hired him to kill all those people. He had a hell of a lot more blood on his hands than I ever would, that was for damn sure.

He hadn't been the one who dragged me out to be killed, so I didn't have anything against him personally. He'd watched me walk into Itzel's room the night I'd been murdered, the night I'd seen her fucking that other asshole, but I didn't blame him for any of that shit. He was a pawn just like the rest of King Ocelot's servants. He'd been busy eating the king's shriveled old ass that night just like every other night. I knew I'd had it good just shoveling horse shit all those years. I liked horses. There was no fucking way I could have done Gabor's job. I would have slit the king's throat a long time ago.

And even though I would have rather the king died, I grudgingly admired all the palace guards. They either believed in what they were doing and stuck by that conviction, or they had a hell of a lot more restraint than I ever would. I respected that in a man. I might have been a criminal, but I had morals. An eye for an eye.

A life for a life.

"When you find *Mr. Gao*," Camila gritted out, still glaring at her one remaining ocelot loyalist. "You are to notify me immediately so I can come and get the amulet from him."

"And the second order of business, Your Majesty?" asked a vampire she'd picked up back in the shah's empire.

"Secondly, there is an ocelot traitor here," she said, turning to the group.

A muscle in Gabor's jaw tensed, but otherwise, he showed no reaction. The rest of the group shuffled their feet uncomfortably, and the ones who knew he was the only ocelot in the party shifted away from him, as if her venom might spread to them if they stood close enough. Ebele's cameraman pointed the camera right at Gabor, and Ebele gave a giddy grin, obviously loving the drama. I could already see the clip making the show. A second of dead silence followed by some dramatic music would accompany the princess's words.

"Not him," Camila said with a dismissive flick of her fingers toward her guard, as if he couldn't possibly be a traitor, and if he were, it wouldn't matter because he was so powerless. She gave a tittering little laugh that made me want to slap the shit out of her.

I'd been watching her for weeks, since Camila had claimed me as her guard. I still couldn't figure her out. She was too fucking unpredictable. One minute she was as ruthless as her father, and the next, she was trembling like a leaf at the thought of meeting the tiger maharajas.

I didn't know how to feel about her. On the one hand, I knew she was a conniving snake. On the other, she'd eagerly grabbed me when the shah offered me to Itzel. It was nice to be wanted, to be valuable enough to snatch up, even if I knew she was using me like she used everyone. At least I had work to do, a job at last. She'd treated me well enough, too, not threatening to behead me every time I grumbled about something. The sad truth of it was, I missed home, fucked up as it was. It was comforting to see a familiar face, to be around someone who knew not just the language and customs I'd grown up with, but the world we'd lived in. She and Gabor were the only comfort I'd known in months. And to be gainfully employed again, not to feel like a useless burden, was worth far more than she was paying me.

"I'm talking about my sister," Camila said. "Chances are, we'll find her wherever the amulet is, so it won't be any extra work. But if she's not there, we'll hunt her down."

"And then what?" I asked. The camera swung my way.

Camila raised her chin and arched an eyebrow as if daring me to challenge her. Then she turned to the camera and spoke right into it. "And then we'll kill her."

TWENTY-TWO

Itzel
Princess, Ocelot Nation

FEAR JOLTED THROUGH ME AT THE SIGHT OF A dozen snow leopards stalking toward us. No, not us. *Me.*

They prowled like hunters, hunger in their eyes that made my thighs quake and my heart explode in my chest.

"Fuck," I whispered, leaping up from Kwame. "How long have they been there?"

"I don't know," he said, rising beside me in all his naked, dark glory. I wanted to gaze upon my lover forever, but the brief encounter was all we'd get. One time. One night, interrupted.

"I thought the heat took days to go into effect."

"It—it does," Kwame said, crouching slightly when a snow leopard moved into the firelight. It stared at us across the fire, a white mane surrounding its head that was shorter than

Kwame's but almost as thick. Balam was beautiful in feline form, and Shadow was deadly and breathtaking. But this... This was the most beautiful creature I'd ever seen. Its ice-colored eyes burned with intensity as it stepped closer on large, silent white feet, never blinking or wavering in its attention to me. The spots on its snowy silver coat shifted with each step. For a moment, I was transfixed, awestruck by the majestic, otherworldly divinity of the beast.

Kwame's strong, cold fingers wrapped around mine. "Shift. It's the only way to fight."

There was obviously not going to be much of a fight, but I obeyed nonetheless, reaching for Sir Kenosi's cheetah. I hadn't known how to shift, but when I called for it, it sprang to life with such force that it nearly ripped out of my skin. I lost my balance, lurching forward to all fours. A blinding pain shot through my limbs, and terror swallowed me whole as blackness swept over my vision, leaving me in this vulnerable position.

Seconds later, my vision cleared, and I lifted my head and snarled, baring my cheetah fangs at a snow leopard. Beside me, Kwame had shifted into a lion. He threw back his head and roared, the immense sound filling the night, echoing down the mountain and into the valleys below. My heart swelled with pride at the sight of my gentle lover staking his claim to the death like the ferocious beast he was inside.

I had no time to dwell on it, though. A snow leopard leapt at me, and I snarled and swiped my claws across his face, leaping aside. Fear charged my limbs, and I shot forward, sinking my teeth into another leopard. My fangs sank through his skin, and the sweet tang of blood exploded across my tongue. He roared and ripped free of me just as Kwame dove in and clamped his enormous jaws around the leopard's neck.

Another one charged, but I darted aside, my smaller size and speed giving me an advantage. Kwame hurled my attacker across the clearing, and he landed with a sickening crunch against a sandstone ledge. Another leopard leapt at Kwame, slamming him to the ground. They rolled away in a blur of fangs and claws, roaring and growling and biting. I darted away from another attack, only to find myself cornered by two more. I turned, and someone fell onto my back, his teeth sinking into the back of my neck as he mounted me.

I squeezed my eyes closed and screamed. I could feel him trying to penetrate me. Suddenly, I felt a rush of air. Opening my eyes, I saw an enormous snow leopard drop to the ground in a crouch in front of me. He opened his jaws and roared, slamming a giant paw against my attacker's head. The leopard on my back flew backwards, thudding to the ground next to the fire. I scrambled to my feet, but the leopard who had just freed me clamped his jaws around the back of my neck, lifting me by my skin.

He latched on and turned, slamming his shoulder into another one. I lost sight of Kwame under a blur of more snow leopards. I screamed, but my lover couldn't hear me, and my attacker didn't release me. Charging forward, he swung me at another leopard's legs. My body took his feet from under him, and then we were charging up the mountain. I screamed again, hoping my mate would hear me, that

Lord Balam and Shadow would hear me, that someone, anyone, would hear me and know where I'd been taken.

But no one came to rescue me this time. Darkness swallowed us, only the starlight to illuminate our path and bear witness.

I scratched and fought, crying and hissing, but the leopard didn't release his grip as he bounded along the rocky crags of the mountain, from one boulder to another, down into a quiet hamlet and up another mountainside. Twisting my body, I swiped at his legs, but I only succeeded in making his teeth tear through the skin on the back of my neck. The sharp tang of blood filled the air, and I twisted harder, forcing his teeth through the skin until I felt blood trickling down my pelt and falling to the ground. I prayed that it would lead my mates to me when this was over.

At last, I heard a sound that cut through my panic. I twisted my head around, trying to see who had made the sound I'd heard—footfalls bounding behind us. My heart leapt as I made out a blurry form charging our way. And then I saw another and another. Not my mates. More snow leopards chasing down their prey, ready to fight for my body.

My captor ran faster, his breath coming hard against my neck and his saliva mixing with my blood as it soaked into my fur. At last, he scrambled up a vertical cliff face and onto a ledge. He dropped me in front of a towering wedge of stone, its face roughly the size and shape of an enormous sail on a boat. Turning at the sound of claws raking down sandstone, he snarled ferociously, his bloody lips drawing back from gore-streaked teeth. A white snow leopard's head appeared over the edge of the ledge, and my captor slashed its face with his paw, hurling the predator back down the way he'd climbed.

I scrambled to my feet, my gaze flying from one side of the ledge to the other. My captor roared at another attacker, bashing him off the ledge as he tried to ascend. Turning, he raced along the ledge to the corner of the stone and pressed his face into the crevice between it and the cliff face. A grinding creak sounded, and to my horror, the towering rock began to slide sideways along the ledge. Behind it, I could see a dark entrance gaping like the mouth to hell.

I turned and streaked in the other direction, but suddenly, another snow leopard dropped down from above, landing in front of me. He pounced, pinning me to the stone under-foot. I snarled and ripped myself free, slashing with my claws. His giant paw slammed against me, and I went rolling straight toward the edge. My bloody captor dove for me, snatching me and dragging me into the entrance to his dark den. The other leopard on the ledge charged.

My captor ripped me from his reach, tossing me behind him and slamming into his attacker. The invading leopard tumbled backward and over the ledge. I cried out, leaping to my feet and diving for the light. The huge stone made a grinding sound as it began to close. An anguished snarl tore from my throat as my captor clamped his jaws around the back of my neck, flinging me deeper into his lair. My last hope disappeared with the last sliver of light as the stone sealed over the entrance, plunging us into utter, blinding darkness.

TWENTY-THREE

Kwame
Prince, Lion Nation

I woke to the chill of wet blood freezing in my fur. With a jolt, I sat up. The sky was lightening with the promise of the new day, but one look around told me that the sun would not shine for me on this day.

Itzel was gone.

When I leapt to my feet, the searing pain of my injuries made me stagger drunkenly. Blood soaked the ground where I had fought one snow leopard after another until I collapsed under my injuries. Around me, coals that had been scattered from the fire lay black and dead. A snow leopard's body lay motionless a few feet away, but there was no sign of another living soul.

My queen was gone. I'd only had one night with my mate, one night that had ended before the moon crossed the sky, before it was complete. My lion cried like a lost cub inside me. I knew I should lay down and heal, but I couldn't waste any time. I had to find her. I had to save my mate. One mating would not be enough to last my lifetime.

No. I wouldn't think like that. Itzel wasn't dead. I had heard her crying as they stole her away. I'd fought to follow, but I'd been piled under more and more attackers. They'd left me alive, though, no doubt following her trail once they knew she was gone. They had no interest in killing. They only wanted me out of the way because I'd tried to keep her from them. When they realized she was gone, they must have abandoned my broken body and run after her in a mating frenzy.

How had it happened so fast? It was all wrong. The tiger maharajas had explained exactly how their amulet worked— just like a regular heat. It should have taken days, not an hour. It should have been gradual, not instantly strong enough to draw out that many snow leopards. Had they deceived me? Or were Itzel's pheromones infinitely stronger than they should have been?

All I knew was that making love to her was unlike anything I'd ever done before. And I knew that I had to find her before they destroyed her. True, they didn't want to kill her. That didn't mean that they wouldn't. If they all got hold of her at once... Not just a handful of them, like might be attracted to a typical female in heat. There had been dozens. Knowing how far apart snow leopards lived made that even stranger. They must have come from miles around. If they all mated her at once, they could hurt her. Or worse.

My mate was not weak. She'd already been through so much, things that would have destroyed a weaker queen. She'd grown stronger with each one. And I knew that she was proud of her strength, just as I was. But this was something different. She'd never experienced a heat, and this was no ordinary mating time. This was something powerful and unexplained. Something that drew snow leopards from hiding all over the mountains, something that made them fight for her and leave her mate for dead.

I had to find her before they broke her, body and spirit.

I started up the mountain, letting my lion guide me. He would take me to my mate, my queen, my love. My savior.

I called out to her, silently and aloud, wandering over stones and boulders, logs and slippery patches of snow that scalded my feet with cold. At last, I had to lie down and heal further. I considered going back to the spirit world, but I refused to entertain the possibility that she was there.

I woke around dark that evening, leaping to my feet with a renewed sense of urgency. It had been a full day since they'd taken her. I'd wasted too much time. I ran through the valley and up the next mountain, roaring for her all the way. Darkness fell, and still I hadn't found her.

I heard a scraping over the crest of a small ridge, and the scent of smoke and sizzling meat found my nostrils. I charged toward it, scrambling over stones and leaping toward the sound, my heart thudding in my chest. If someone had set up camp there, maybe it was her captor. I could smell a wild ocean, the salty brine of the sea, and damp earth and water collecting on leaves in the moonlight.

And then I was over the ridge, skidding to a halt. Lord Balam sat at a campfire, his cloak pulled over his shoulders and down his tattooed arms, the fur rippling from his skin as if he were mid-shift. The shadow of a black panther flickered in the firelight and then disappeared into the darkness.

"That better be you, Kwame," Lord Balam said, crouching by the fire, his eyes alert as he watched my every move.

With a shower of magic, I shifted back to my human form. "I lost her," I said miserably.

Lord Balam stared at me a long moment, and a dart of fear pierced my heart. I had regained my human form when Itzel brought me back, but I didn't know how immortal that form was. I wasn't keen on finding out yet. Not until I knew if my mate was in that world. If she was, it wouldn't matter. I'd give up the human form I'd fought for in an instant. Once a shifter found his True Mate, life without her was unlivable.

"How'd that happen?" Lord Balam asked, easing himself back onto the stone he'd been using for a seat.

"Yes," rasped a gravelly voice from the darkness. "Tell us."

"I fought for her," I said, sinking onto the ground beside the fire. "She opened the amulet, and instead of taking a few days, her heat was instant. We were not prepared. I'm sorry."

To my surprise, neither of the men attacked. Lord Balam poked at the meat cooking over the fire, his brow knit with concentration. Shadow, who had slunk out of the darkness as I spoke, only watched me with those eerie green eyes.

"I should have known that would happen," Lord Balam said. "Itzel may be human, but there's nothing common about her."

"You know I would die to protect her," I said.

To my surprise, Shadow nodded. "Yeah. We all would."

"You don't blame me," I marveled. "How do you not hate me?"

"We know you're her mate," Lord Balam said. "There's no use pointing fingers. That won't get her back. We're all on the same team here."

"Yes," I said, letting down my guard for the first time since I'd found them. Despite the things that had happened to me in the past, these men were restoring my faith. Friendship could be true. People could be trusted. There was more in the world than betrayal and grief. There was good. There were people, even strangers, who showed kindness, who shared a fire and their food and their mate, without complaint or competition.

Not everyone was as transparent as I was, but it hit me then that they wanted her back as badly as I did. They ached for her in their bones, just as I did. They would do anything for her, just as I would.

"What do we do?" I asked, anguish lacing my voice. I'd failed her. My first chance at protecting my mate, at beginning to repay her for what she'd given up for me, and I'd failed beyond the worst I could have imagined.

"The only thing we can do," Lord Balam said. "We keep searching until we find her."

Twenty-Four

Itzel
Princess, Ocelot Nation

I woke with a jolt, panic ripping through me. Scrambling to my feet, I looked around. A glass wall surrounded me on two sides, with stone making up the last two walls, ceiling, and floor. I'd been lying on a thin pallet on the floor with a blanket. Though the room was chilly, heat trembled inside me like a mirage, and my skin was slicked with sweat. Between my legs, my sex throbbed like a hungry animal.

"Oh, fuck," I whispered, sinking back to my knees on the mat. It came back to me then—fucking Kwame, the intensity of our bond and the rush of power that had come over me. The way the snow leopards came out of the mountains around us like ghosts to watch the holy spectacle. The fight they'd had to get to me. The one who had stolen me, hauled me up here, and dragged me into the dark. I'd fought, changing into a human so he might not want to fuck me.

But he'd simply become a man, thrown me over his shoulder, and carried me through the dark, tossing me into this enclosure and leaving me here. I'd fallen asleep on the only soft spot in the room, in complete blackness. Now, I'd woken to find the room lit dimly by candles. Beyond my glass cell, I could make out more of the man's lair.

It didn't look very lair-like. It looked like some kind of expensive experimental lab, with metal equipment on long tables, something that looked suspiciously like an upright hospital bed with restraints on the arms and legs, microscopes, and other shiny silver instruments reflecting the soft, flickering glow of candles placed around the room. It was all so incongruous, so unexpected. I'd thought he'd dragged me away into a cave, not a hidden spy operation. And if he had such high-tech gear, why the primitive candles for lighting?

I jumped up and approached the side of the cage. I was still naked, as he'd found me, but I didn't feel any grogginess, so I could only assume he hadn't drugged me or done anything to me while I slept. I pounded on the glass, yelling to be let out. A minute later, a man appeared from a side door off the lab area. My cage was comfortably sized, at least ten feet across in either direction, like a small bedroom with nothing but a mat to sleep on.

The lab was much bigger, easily the size of a house with an open floor plan. I couldn't even see into the shadowy recesses off to my right. To the left, it opened up, with higher ceilings, a large empty area, and the door through which my captor had just appeared. The door was my goal.

"Let me out," I called, banging on the glass.

The man approached slowly, giving me plenty of time to take him in. And I took in every inch of him, drinking the sight of him with incredulous hunger. He was the most beautiful man I'd ever seen in my life, and I didn't think it was just the lust pulsing under my skin like something alive.

He was a tall, lean Asian man who looked to be in his mid-thirties. He wore dusty-orange trousers and a matching tunic that reached the top of his thighs, along with a coarse wool robe over it. If that was supposed to make him look unappealing, plain, or asexual as a monk, it failed. His tall frame only hinted at his strength, the muscles I'd felt when he carried me in here the day before. Or... Whenever it was. We were underground, so I had no idea whether it was day or night.

My captor paused about ten feet from the glass and stood watching me. His eyes in human form were the same color as they'd been in feline form, a pale seafoam color that was equally blue and green and reminded me of an icy glacier. But he didn't look cruel. Only watchful. The rest of his face was alert, too, the candlelight highlighting his beautiful bone structure, his high cheekbones, sculpted jawline, and full lips. His lashes were dark and thick, as were his brows, giving him a brooding, edgy look despite his pale eyes.

He spoke to me in a language I didn't recognize, but when I shook my head and told him as much, he nodded and tried again. This time, I recognized the language as the one we used to communicate with the Lion Clan.

"Let me go," I said, fumbling my way through the foreign words.

One corner of the man's mouth twitched in the slightest smile before he spoke, this time in my language. "What are you?" he asked, the words flowing off his tongue more slowly than a native speaker, but fluent and precise.

"I'm trapped, that's what," I said, pressing my palm to the glass.

"Get dressed," he said, nodding to something behind me. "Then we talk."

I turned and scanned my dim enclosure, finding a pile of folded clothes next to my bedroll, along with a box and a bucket in the corner that I could only hope wasn't for what I suspected it was.

I pulled on the clothes, which were obviously his. They were clean but worn, and I found myself hoping I looked half as good as him in a pair of oversized orange pants and a shapeless orange tunic. Then I scolded myself, because I shouldn't want to look good for my kidnapper. I yanked the shirt over my head, then gasped aloud at the erotic charge that shot through me when the garment brushed my nipples. I had not been prepared for the way the shirt touched me, the way my body reacted.

Fuck. This was not good. Clenching my teeth, I drew the pants on, ignoring the thrill of sensuality when the fabric caressed my thighs. I had to suppress a moan as I slid them over my mound, which was... Swollen. It was bigger than it should be, than it had ever been, and aching to be touched. I could feel the heat and slickness between my folds, throbbing in my pussy lips, singing in my clit. Had he seen that when I stood talking to him? Shit. He must have. He must know exactly how horny I was right now.

Gingerly, I let the waistband of the pants settle into place, nearly moaning again when the seam at the front brushed my swelling. I took a moment to compose myself before returning to my captor. He stood watching me as if transfixed, his eyes a shade darker than they had been, a burning lust in them that I could read from ten feet and a wall of glass away. The fabric on the front of his pants was pulled tight, straining against his erection.

A hot tremor shimmered through my entire body, nearly making me swoon in place. My mouth watered, and my juices flowed thickly along my slit, wetting me for his entry.

He wanted me, and I was just about panting for someone—anyone—to touch me. God, I needed to be touched. I wanted to rub myself all over everything in the room. Kwame had warned me this would happen, and though it had been a bit more sudden than expected, I could make the best of it. It was one guy. I could have been begging the entire Snow Leopard Nation to fuck me.

Oh, god. The thought filled me with a thrill that made slick fill my swollen lips. I wished he'd let them all pile on me, one after another plundering me with their cocks. I had enough slick for all of them. I was so wet I could feel it soaking the pants already.

I shook my head to clear it. I had been in this situation before. Sir Kenosi had taught me well. I would please this guy, and he'd let me go, hopefully before the heat wore off. I could still get the amulet. I just had to play my cards right, wear him out before he wore me out. From the fire raging inside me and the wetness coating my thighs, I didn't think that would be a problem.

"Are you sure you want me to keep this on?" I asked, toying with the hem of the shirt as I stepped to the glass wall separating us.

The man swallowed before nodding. "What are you?" he asked again. "Why are you here?"

"I'm here because you brought me here," I said with a coy smile. "Which I assume means you want to have me to yourself."

Honestly, the thought wasn't as abhorrent as it should have been. I was dying to touch him, my fingers twitching with the urge. He was so beautiful. It could have been worse. I could have bene lusting after some crusty old man in my desperation. If I was going to ride out the heat with someone, this guy didn't look like a bad choice. Of course, for all I knew he was some sick murderous freak like King Ocelot, one who might eat me alive in my heat. Why else had he locked me up in his dungeon, which was complete with a lot of equipment that clearly had torture potential?

"I brought you here because it was unsafe for you there," he said. "You were calling my entire clan to you. You would have been gang raped." He swallowed again, his eyes widening as if he'd just realized what he said. His cheeks pinkened, and heat swelled between my thighs. God, he was adorable. And if the mention of a woman's heat could make him blush, I sincerely doubted he was some kind of serial killer. Well, at least not a serial rapist. Maybe he hadn't brought me here for torturous purposes after all.

I stared at him through the glass, my palm pressed to the smooth, cool surface. His pale eyes stared back into mine, unblinking and intent. My heart stammered in my chest, and this time, the thing happening to my body was north of what I'd felt before. A fluttering in my belly that made me dizzy and giddy at once.

"Am I safe here?" I whispered.

The man swallowed and looked away. "I want to promise you are," he said slowly. "But I've never... Your scent is... Unusually alluring."

He choked out the last word, color rising to his cheeks again. He was still hard. He was also a monk. A celibate monk in an isolated area in an isolationist clan. Which meant he might even be a virgin.

The thought was strangely erotic, and more slick oozed into my swollen pussy. I clamped my knees together so hard my thighs trembled, pressing my forehead to the cool glass to relieve some of the heat raging in my own cheeks.

"Are you a virgin?" I whispered, my eyes still closed. "Because if that's why you brought me here... I can show you things. I don't mind. I... I want to."

"No," he said sharply. I yanked my head back from the glass, my eyes flying wide. Fuck. This heat was clouding my mind, making me do things, say things.

"I'm sorry," I said. "I've never been in heat before. It's... More intense than expected." I squeezed my eyes shut, willing away the yearning inside me.

The monk stepped closer to the glass, his eyes bright with curiosity. "How is this your first one? You must be well past... The usual age."

"Yeah," I said. "I just became a shifter."

"You *became* a shifter?"

"Long story," I said with a sigh, my shoulders slumping at the memory of what my mate had given to make me a shifter.

The monk swallowed again, watching me with those intense, alert eyes. "We have days," he said at last. "If we don't talk, we might be tempted to do something more."

I snorted with laughter. I was already tempted. I'd given in to the temptation without even fighting. Camila's cruel words came back to me, cutting deeper each time I remembered them. She'd called me a whore, and maybe that's what I'd become. I'd started this tour as a virgin, and now I was thinking it wasn't that bad to be captured by a guy to be used as a sex slave for a week because at least he was good looking.

"You'd better start talking," he said. "How did a cheetah end up in the mountains of Snow Leopard Territory? How did you become a shifter? Why are you here?"

I sighed. "I'm here because my sister is the heir to the Ocelot Throne, and I'm collecting the mating amulets. We didn't know how to lure out the snow leopard who has the amulet, Gao Jetsun. So, we thought if I went into a heat, it might draw him out. Which means you have to let me out of here so I can find him before the heat wears off."

He looked at me for a long moment. "I can't let you out," he said. "Every snow leopard in our nation is outside the door of this place. The moment you walked out, they'd attack you."

"If he's one of them, then at least I'll be able to get the amulet."

"He's not," the man said sharply, turning away. He bowed his head and took a breath.

My heart thudded in my ears, and my breath shook as I whispered my realization aloud. "Because you're Gao Jetsun."

He didn't say anything.

Fuck. I waited to be disgusted by him, to feel revulsion that I'd been lusting after him. But I only felt disgusted by myself. When I looked at him, my breath still caught in my throat at his beauty. When I let my eyes roam over his broad shoulders, his lean build, his long legs, and the very obvious erection straining against his pants, a throb clenched between my thighs again.

What the fuck was wrong with me? This was bad. This was really fucking bad.

Or maybe not. He wasn't in heat. He had morals. He was a monk, for fuck's sake.

He doesn't have to know, a sultry voice whispered inside me. You can pretend you don't know that's your brother. He didn't say he was Jetsun.

"I'm your sister," I blurted out, desperate to have him look at me with the disgust I couldn't feel for him. "I... Wow. That was the shittiest way I could have done that. Oh my god. I can't believe I said that."

He looked up, his eyes wary now, his face blanched of color.

"I'm sorry," I said. "Let me start over. Can we? Can we start over?"

"I shouldn't be here," he whispered, staring at me with a stricken expression. "There's something unholy about you."

"That's an understatement," I muttered.

Jetsun backed away a step. "I'll go. This cage is for the purpose of protecting our females when they are in your situation. There's medicine to suppress your heat in the trunk behind you. No one can get in without a key."

"Don't leave me," I blurted, suddenly terrified. More terrified to be alone in the dark with this fire raging inside me than to be trapped looking at a man who looked like sex itself, but whom I could never even touch. More terrified to be alone than to be thrown outside for all the men in the clan to take turns with. There was something inside me, raging and clawing and writhing to get out. It wasn't Sir Kenosi's cheetah. It was something that had always been there, though I'd never dared to look too closely at it.

Lord Balam had known. He'd told me from the start I wasn't human, but I hadn't pressed him for answers. Maybe I'd always known, but I'd been too scared to find out. I'd laughed it off, denied it, ignored it. I hadn't wanted anyone to know, not even my sister and best friend. Because some part of me had always known there was something trapped in there, something more terrifying than a man-eating ocelot. I knew without taking a single drop of medicine that it couldn't put out this fire.

I flattened my hands against the glass as if I could grasp the surface somehow, pull it to me, reach through it and grasp him and beg him to stay. "I—I can't be alone," I said. "Please stay. Just talk to me. Talk me through this. It might be safe, like you say, but I can't do this. I don't know how. Those girls you're talking about, they've done this. They've prepared, Jetsun. Up until a month ago, I was human. I lived my whole life as a human. Don't leave me with this feeling. I'm not lying, not trying to get you to let me out. I'll stay right here, where you can't get to me. Because I really am your sister. Nothing can happen between us. I just... I don't want to be alone. The things inside my head—I can't be alone with them."

"I can't be alone with you," Jetsun said, his voice so low I could barely hear it.

"We'll be okay," I said. "We'll talk each other through it. We'll talk about... About family! I'll tell you about your dad. My dad. You can tell me about him. Safe things. We have this wall between us."

Jetsun swallowed and stared back at me with those beautiful, somber eyes. "I have the key."

The ache inside me, the heat, flared with longing. It whispered in my ears, in my mind, telling me I could lure the key from him later. I could get him talking, and turn the subject, convince him to open the door. He was innocent, good. I was not. I was the temptress. I would lure him to the door, lure the key into the keyhole.

No. What was I thinking? Jetsun was my brother. My half-brother, at least.

Oh, god. I couldn't stop.

"Okay," I whispered, closing my eyes and resting my forehead against the glass. "Go."

After a pause, I heard the soft pad of his footsteps across the room. I opened my eyes to see him cross the large space until he reached the tall stone wall at the far left side of the room. He pressed his hand to a circle in the stone without looking back. Anguish gripped my blazing body, holding me frozen with horror and loss over a man I'd never known and would never know.

The scraping, grinding sound I'd heard when the giant stone moved the day before now echoed through the huge chamber. A slice of light cut through the room, making me stumble back, blinking against the brightness. Beyond the stone, I heard the clamor of a dozen voices shouting at my captor. They wanted in. They wanted me out.

And even though I'd imagined it in some sexy way, now that the reality hit me, I shrank back, terror gripping me. He was going out there with the key. If they attacked him, they could get it. They'd come back for me, the entire mate-thirsty mob.

Jetsun reared back, drawing his arm behind him. For one second, I didn't understand. And then a cry tore from my throat as he hurled the key through the crack into the blood-thirsty mob outside.

TWENTY-FIVE

Tadeu
Shifter, Tiger Nation

THE CROWN PRINCESS OF THE OCELOT NATION was losing her shit, and I was loving it. Sure, I'd joined her posse, but that didn't mean there was any love between us. I'd needed a job, it was nice to be in demand, and yeah, I'd wanted to see Itzel's face. But Camila had always been a frosty bitch, not to mention manipulative as fuck, and I had zero shits to give about the shifter princess. She'd been yanking her sister's strings for as long as I'd known her, and even if I didn't love Itzel anymore, I hadn't forgotten what kind of person our princess was. Gabor wasn't the only reason I slept with one eye open nowadays.

"Who took my comb?" Camila screamed, standing outside her tent with her hair in a frizzled mess. This alone was worth being her lackey. Watching the princess fall to pieces on camera, looking like shit and sounding like the unhinged psycho she was.

"Your Grace," Gabor said, stepping between her and the camera and laying gentle hands on her shoulders.

Ebele deftly stepped to one side behind Gabor's back, aiming her cameraman at the scene.

"I'm sure the comb is in your tent," Gabor murmured, giving Camila a meaningful look before cutting his eyes sideways in the direction the camera had moved. "Let me find it for you. That's not a job for a princess."

"No," she said. "It's not. It's her job." She pointed one trembling finger at the human concubine she'd chosen from the shah's harem to serve as her maidservant on the journey.

"Why would I take your comb?" the concubine protested, giving Camila some serious stink-eye.

"You're jealous," Camila hissed. "I'm a princess, and you're just a whore."

"Your Grace," Gabor said, his voice harder now.

Camila jerked away from his hands, shoving them off her shoulders. "You're going to take her side?"

"Let me look for the comb before you make accusations."

"She took it," Camila shrieked, tossing her matted hair. I'd seen Camila in her natural state only recently, when she'd run out of her room to make sure I was still guarding Itzel's door, ranting her suspicions that I was going to run off with Itzel and betray her. Her hair had always been thin and straight, colorless and lifeless. But I'd never imagined she made it that way on purpose. Apparently before her ladies fixed it each day, it was a frizzy mane that tried to be as wild as Itzel's but lacked the volume to do so. Basically, it looked like shit, and she'd gone to great lengths to hide it her entire life. Which made it even funnier to see her freak out about it in front of the entire world.

"I had it yesterday, and now it's gone," she was screeching. "I'll have her executed!"

"You can't," the concubine shot back with a sassy tilt of her head. "I belong to the shah, and the only reason I came along is because I'm being paid to escort you. But this? This isn't worth it. I'm out. Wipe your own ass from now on."

I busted up laughing, along with a few others who knew they were beyond the reach of Camila's wrath. Gabor glared at me. He was stuck with her. I wasn't. I'd been hired to escort her, too. The best payment had always been the satisfaction of knowing it pissed off Itzel, though, and that had begun to wear off now that I couldn't see Itzel's face every time she saw me with her sister.

I had wanted to hurt her the way she hurt me. To betray her the way she'd betrayed me, to let her feel it the way I did each time she walked by with one of her lovers, especially the one she'd given her virginity to. That had been mine to take, not his. He hadn't believed hot-whispered promises in hay lofts, hadn't learned her body so well he could make her moan in minutes, memorized her every curve and angle like a beloved photograph, hadn't listened to her gasp I-love-you's as her sweet cum drenched his tongue or dripped from his fingers. I had waited years for her to be ready, patiently coaxing her into comfort and confidence with her body, helping her shed her inhibitions and inferiority complex about being human in a shifter family.

I had done everything for her, and he'd gotten all the benefit. But it mattered less every day. She hadn't just thrown her virginity away on some meaningless fuck. She loved the asshole. Anyone could see it. She'd forgotten me, moved on. I couldn't hurt her because she simply didn't give a fuck where I was or who I was with.

It pissed me off that she could care so little when I still cared so much.

"Fine," Camila said after glaring at the concubine with murderous hatred. "I can't order your execution. You're dismissed. You are no longer a part of this party. Take only your personal possessions, and leave."

The girl jumped to her feet, her eyes going wide. "You can't just leave me here. We're in the middle of nowhere. It's freezing. I'm a human. And you know perfectly well that I didn't bring anything personal on the trip. I was supposed to share your tent and supplies."

"Your actions and words have consequences," Camila said, a cold triumph lighting her eyes. "I will inform the shah that you chose to leave the hunting party and make your way home on your own."

"I'll die," the girl said, her voice beginning to tremble.

"Did you think there would be no consequence to disrespecting a queen?" Camila asked. Even in her state of disarray, she was suddenly imposing, every inch an icy ocelot.

"Please," the girl cried, dropping to her knees at Camila's feet.

"Now you're not too proud to beg," Camila said, rolling her eyes at the rest of us. "Fine. Kiss my feet."

The girl's nostrils flared, and her eyes narrowed, and I knew she was pissed as fuck to be forced to degrade herself for Camila's ego. I felt for her. If I could have told her we'd all been there, I would have.

"Yes, Your Highness," she girl gritted out, bending to kiss Camila's feet. The display made me sick to my stomach. I'd been ordered to do the same before. It was why I'd kept my head as long as I had, why I'd only been beaten bloody instead of executed. Shame washed over me as I watched another person subjugated that way. I'd done it to save my life, and in the end, they'd killed me anyway. It was better to keep your pride, the way Gabor did. At least that way you died with honor.

As we stood there watching Camila threaten until the human girl trembled and begged, I swore to myself that I'd never let myself be debased that way again. They could kill me all over again, but I'd never again grant anyone the power to make me pathetic.

"We need to get moving," Camila said to the girl after she was sufficiently terrorized and clutching the princess's ankles. "Let me go."

"No," the girl sobbed. "Don't leave me."

"Gabor," Camila snapped, holding out an impatient hand. "The dart gun."

"Your Grace," Gabor said, glancing between Camila and the human.

"Now," Camila barked. "And your pistol."

"She's only a human."

Camila's teeth gritted together, her eyes blazing. "I am your master," she gritted. "Give me what I asked for or die."

The muscle in Gabor's jaw tightened, and he reached for his belt. He slapped the blow gun into her hand, the one he'd used to keep me from killing Itzel a second time. She snatched it from him, loaded it, and blew a dart into the human's back. It made a hollow sound as it pierced her jacket between her shoulder blades. The girl cried out, then collapsed.

Camila made a face to show her disgust, then shook her legs free of the girl's hands and stepped away. She handed back the blow gun and fixed her frostbitten gaze on Gabor. "The pistol."

Gabor's jaw clenched harder, but he handed her his gun.

"Good," Camila said, shaking back her matted hair. "Are there any more traitors among you?"

As she scanned the group, we all shook our heads. All but Gabor, who stared straight at her without moving. Camila's eyes skimmed over everyone in turn, never flickering when they met Gabor's insolence.

"Good," she said. "Does anyone else want to leave now?"

"I'll take the human back," said a tall, skinny tiger boy who had joined the party at the same time as the concubine.

"You're leaving the hunting party in favor of her?" Camila asked.

"I'll make sure she arrives back at the palace," the tiger boy said.

Camila leveled the pistol and shot him in the knee. A collective intake of breath met her action, and the boy fell to the ground, screaming and clutching his knee.

"Safe travels," Camila said. "Anyone else?"

No one moved.

"Very well," Camila said. "To ensure we don't have a repeat of this unfortunate scene, I will now require every one of you to swear an oath of loyalty to me. You will accompany and protect me with your lives until the mission is complete or you meet your death. Does anyone have a problem with that?"

No one spoke.

"Your Grace," Gabor said at last. "I have sworn my loyalty to the Ocelot Throne. I cannot have dual loyalties. I will serve the throne until my death."

"And I'll take the throne," Camila said, her eyes flashing dangerously. "Therefore, you owe me loyalty already."

Gabor shook his head almost imperceptibly. "No."

No one breathed.

Camila's eyes glowed gold as her ocelot strained to tear from her, to rip Gabor to shreds, to annihilate the threat.

Gabor cleared his throat. "Your Grace," he said quietly. "You are not the crown."

"Just do it," I muttered. "Don't be stupid."

Camila turned, fixing me with her coldblooded stare. "You go first."

"Okay," I said with a shrug. "Swear me in, Your Majesty."

I even said the words without mockery. My word meant nothing. I could lie with the best of them. I didn't know why Camila would even take the word of a disgraced human, why she'd think it meant anything. But I wasn't going to argue with her. I preferred to keep my kneecaps. My oath meant nothing, even to me. I'd break my word the second it was in my interest to do so. I had no scruples.

"I swear," I said. "I will protect you with my life until the mission is over, or I meet my death."

Camila's eyes narrowed and her nostrils flared. "Swear on your honor."

That was as big a joke as my momentary fantasy that I'd be like Gabor. I wasn't about to beg and grovel, but I'd never be like an ocelot guard no matter how much I admired them. Swearing on my honor meant nothing. I was a scoundrel through and through. I had no honor.

"I swear on my honor," I said without hesitation, without blinking or lowering my eyes. I could lie straight into her eyes with no guilt. Maybe that meant I was a sociopath.

Maybe it meant I knew she was one.

The vampire swore allegiance, as did the next two tigers, a human, a werewolf, and a fae. At last, Camila turned to the two cheetahs.

"We're just here to film, Your Grace," Ebele said with a pleasant smile.

"You are either a member of my temporary court, or your show stops here."

Gabor hadn't moved the entire time, but I was drawn to him the way I always was, as if people from our nation had their own gravity.

"They'd better do it," I muttered to him. "Even a dumbass like me can see this is reality circuit gold."

Ebele and her cameraman exchanged glances. He shrugged like it didn't matter, but I knew it wasn't that. He was letting her decide. Like a true journalist, she nodded. She'd do anything, even risk her life, to get the story. I admired her drive, something I'd lost since becoming a displaced shifter.

"I swear my life to you, Queen Ocelot," Ebele said, bowing. "I will follow and protect you until the mission is complete or death claims me."

The cameraman followed suit, and Camila smiled and gave a contented sigh, her eyes scanning the group with a proud air. Her loyal subjects had all pledged their lives to her, and she obviously thought that meant something. Maybe to some of them, it did.

"Now," she said, clasping her hands together. "My guard. My loyal escort, who has stayed true to me through it all. Will you really betray me now, at the last minute, when your very life hangs in the balance?"

"I would never betray you, Your Grace," he said. "By keeping my oath to the crown, I do not betray you. I honor you and the throne you will ascend."

"Take the fucking oath," I hissed behind him. "You can break your word. You can't do anything if you're dead."

Camila planted her hands on her hips and glared at Gabor. "How can I trust you to be loyal to me then if you won't swear loyalty to me now, when I need it most?"

"How can you trust me to be loyal to you then if I've broken my oath before?"

Camila's teeth clacked together as she snapped her jaw shut.

Gold blazed in her eyes again, and her pupils squeezed to vertical slits. "Take the oath."

Gabor didn't even flinch. "I'll take the bullet, Your Grace."

"Dumbass," I muttered. "There's no use in being a martyr for nothing."

Camila stared at him, her face turning the shade of a peeling sunburn, her lips pinched together so hard they were white in her red face. Without a word, she spun on her heel and dove into her tent. I heard her tearing through her things. For a minute, I thought she was going to start sobbing in there. I never knew when she'd cry, or scald me with frostbite, or whimper helplessly, or rage like a mad woman.

She emerged at last, her hair stuck to her face, her eyes wild. She charged over to Gabor, her teeth bared in a snarl. "Swear to me," she raged. "Or I'll open this."

She thrust her hand in front of his face. Gabor's nostril's flared, and for the first time since I'd first laid eyes on the man ten years before, I saw a flash of emotion. Not anger, but pure outrage. His jaw was clenched so tight I listened for the sound of teeth cracking. That's when I realized what it was. The ocelot's *fucking amulet*, as I'd called it with Itzel once upon a time.

We'd laughed about them back then. It had been fun. Most of our relationship was fun. I'd shared a decade with her. I'd watched her grow up, from a sad kid to a sassy teenager to a woman who could bring any man to his knees without even trying, without even knowing it.

Fuck. Why couldn't I hate her without still loving her, too?

A hiss of excited whispers went around the group as they realized what Camila was holding. But from the looks on their faces, no one else knew what the amulet did, either. They were all waiting, watching the drama unfold. The camera was still rolling.

"I will never go back on my word," Gabor said slowly, each word laced with venom and blood—the blood he'd spilled in the name of the throne. Suddenly, it all made sense. It wasn't just about him being an honorable man. It was about what he'd done in the name of that throne. If his word was meaningless, then all he'd done because of that oath was a choice. The lives he'd taken, the men he'd beaten, tortured, and killed. If he went back on his word now, he could have done it then. If this was a choice, so was everything that had come before it.

"What happens if you open it?" Ebele asked eagerly.

"He falls in love with me," Camila said, a vicious smile twisting her thin lips. "Then I'll be assured of his loyalty."

A murmur went around the group, but no one seemed to share Camila's triumph or excitement. They all looked horrified, outraged, or extremely uneasy with the lengths their sworn leader would go to.

"Take the fucking oath," I muttered, shaking my head. It was one thing to stand by your word, and another to be forced to fall in love.

"Open it," Gabor said, enunciating each word as if daring Camila to do it.

"Listen, Gabor," I said, somehow feeling it was my responsibility to talk him out of this. "You don't want to do this, man. You're giving up your free will."

"She can have it," Gabor said, never breaking eye contact with Camila. Their gazes were locked, neither of them relenting.

"You're going to lose your honor and your pride if you fall in love with her, anyway," I said. "You might as well swear the oath and keep your wits about you. If you fall in love with her, you won't be able to think for yourself."

Without looking at me, Camila swung the pistol my way and squeezed the trigger. A shot rang out, and the bullet pierced my muscle like a knife. I roared in pain, dropping to my knees.

"Another traitor leaves the party," Camila said. "What will it be, Gabor? Are you with them, or with me?"

"What will he do?" Ebele breathlessly narrated for the cameraman. "Will the guard break his oath to the throne and give it to the crown princess instead? Or will he keep his word but lose his heart?"

Gabor ignored the camera, the reporter, even my curses as I pressed my hands to my wounded thigh. He spoke only to Camila, his voice quiet and emotionless. "I have given you my answer, Your Grace."

"Fucking idiot," I muttered. "She won't just own your life. She'll own your heart."

I looked up, ignoring the sticky coldness coating my hands. If she'd hit an artery, this would be my final death. At least I'd die my own man. I couldn't say the same for Gabor.

He stood straight and tall, still as a statue while Camila twisted open the amulet and caged his heart.

Twenty-Six

Itzel
Princess, Ocelot Nation

WHEN THE KEY SAILED OUT THE CRACK IN THE stone, the shouts outside turned into roars. I imagined the frenzy as the snow leopards went after it. Before they could come back with it, Jetsun slammed his shoulder into the stone slab. It ground to a halt and then slid shut, plunging us into the dimly lit, shadowy cavern again.

"There," he said. "Now I can't get in, and you can't get out. We're safe from each other."

"No," I whispered, too horrified to make a coherent argument. I stared out at this man, this monk. My brother, who had gone to great lengths to make sure that no unbrotherly things happened between us.

"If I opened the door now, they'd storm the entrance. They'd mob me, and then you. It's the only way. I can't change my mind. I can't go out there for it."

"What about food?" I asked.

"There," he said, nodding to the little trunk in the corner. "There's a packet of pills in there that will suppress your heat, too. It should be gone by this evening."

"And the bucket?" I asked, already knowing what that was for.

It could be worse. It could. I kept telling myself that as I took one of the pills, praying it would be the miracle he promised. Maybe this was how Camila survived. Shifters who had jobs in the human world couldn't just take off a week when a heat hit. They'd need this. And yet, it was too hard to believe that this could dampen even a little of the lust roaring through my veins.

I could feel the tide rising inside me, though, a tsunami that would drive me mad if I didn't unleash it soon. I pushed the thought away. I couldn't mate during this heat, and there was no way around that. If the pills didn't work, I'd just have to get through it, the same way I'd gotten through everything else on this tour. I might beg and plead for him to let in the snow leopards, I might be pitiful and shameless, but in the end, I'd survive it.

No one ever said survival was pretty. I'd come out stronger, and that was all that mattered.

"Tell me about your family," I said, sinking to the floor on my side of the glass.

Jetsun approached warily.

"I can't get out," I said. "You already ensured that. We might as well talk about something. Distract ourselves with safe topics, remember?"

He nodded and sank gracefully onto the floor on the other side of the glass. Watching him lower himself to the ground was like watching a dancer twirl. God, why did he have to be so beautiful? It hurt to look at him.

I lowered my eyes to my orange-clad knees. I looked like I was in a prison uniform.

Good. The last thing I needed was for him to see me the way I saw him. Strong. Beautiful. Unearthly.

"So, you're a god?" I asked, keeping my eyes lowered.

"Half god," he said with a nod.

"If your dad's a half-god, doesn't that make you a quarter?"

He smiled. "All snow leopards are half god. So, when two of them make a child, it's still half god."

"Right," I said. "And you have the amulet."

Jetsun studied me for a long moment. "How do you know that?"

"Your father told me," I said, realizing that Jetsun had absolutely no clue who I was. "I'm Princess Itzel of the Ocelot Nation. My sister is the crown princess. I'm here on her behalf to get the snow leopard amulet."

"Are you supposed to do that? I'm only to give it to an heir. Are you the cheetah heir?"

"No," I admitted. "I'm not sure what I am."

Jetsun swallowed, his eyes dropping to my body and quickly jerking back up. "Me, neither."

"So, anyway," I said, clearing my throat. "What can I do to get it from you? Obviously mating things are out of the question."

Jetsun's cheeks darkened a tiny bit. "I took a vow of celibacy."

"And you're my brother."

"You keep saying that," he said slowly, shifting and tugging at the knees of his pants. "But I'm neither cheetah nor ocelot."

At his movement, my eyes dropped to his crotch, where his erection was even more obvious than before. I pressed my eyes closed, trying to force away the fluttering pulse in my throat at the sight of his cock outlined against the cotton fabric.

"I met your dad," I said, opening my eyes and keeping them steady on his face. I could just pretend we weren't here separated by a wall of glass that hadn't even trembled when I pounded on it. That my secretions weren't soaking my pants as we spoke, putting off so much scent that I'd made a monk hard for an hour straight. I'd just pretend his cock didn't look mouthwateringly temping right there not two feet away from me, that he wasn't my brother, and—

No. I wouldn't pretend he wasn't my brother. That would be a torture I couldn't bear. Our relationship was the only thing that could get me through this.

"How did you meet my father?" Jetsun asked slowly. "He's been dead for almost twenty years."

"I went to the spirit world," I said. "He told me to find you and get the amulet."

"You went to the spirit world," Jetsun said flatly, as if he didn't believe me.

"Yeah," I said. "Twice, in fact."

"Then how are you here? You don't smell like a ghost."

Ghosts had a smell? I tried to remember what Kwame smelled like. Like hay drying in the sun, baked earth, and a warm kitten. Was that the scent of a ghost? Or the scent of a lion?

"The first time I visited the spirit world, I was alive," I said, shaking my head to clear it. "I was taken there by a lion shifter. My mate, actually. My True Mate."

Good. Remind him I'm taken. Remind myself I'm taken.

Jetsun nodded and made a noncommittal sound.

"Actually, I was able to bring him back," I said. "I guess I have some kind of strength, even if it doesn't look like it to you."

Jetsun's brows drew together briefly. "I didn't say that."

"I know," I said. "I just probably don't seem strong when I'm like this."

"You brought a lion shifter back from the dead," he said.

It was my turn to nod. "Yeah. I know that's weird. He's probably the only lion shifter who can actually be a lion and a man in the human world. But he's still a ghost. I don't really understand it. I'm actually a human. Or, I was a human until recently."

I knew I was rambling, but Jetsun was being too quiet, studying me too intently, like a scientist in the middle of a dissection. I remembered all those creepy instruments and decided I better get to the part about being his sister before he decided to do a lobotomy on me. He might want to study my weird mutt brain that had allowed me to do these crazy things. Because maybe all snow leopards were half-god, but I wasn't. I was only quarter. Yet another anomaly.

"But then I got killed," I said. "And I went to the spirit world for longer. I went to my mom, and she told me that she'd had an affair with your dad, and... Here I am."

Jetsun shook his head. "Sorry. I'm lost. If your mother is an ocelot, and your father really is my father, how are you a cheetah?"

"Oh," I said with a forced laugh. "Because of the magic of the cheetah amulet, I was able to be brought back to life when my other mate put his cheetah inside me to heal me," I said. "Unfortunately, I'm also cursed, so he died."

Jetsun just stared at me, and I realized how outrageous my story sounded, but I didn't know how to tell it without sounding like I was spinning the world's tallest tale. I'd just unleashed my whole life on a stranger, but I couldn't help the feeling of frustration and helplessness that welled inside me. I'd lived with that feeling all my life—the feeling of being alone and inadequate. I'd kept busy to keep it at bay, playing hard when I was a kid and partying hard as a teenager. I wasn't a shifter, so I'd never been fully a member of my own family. But I was a princess, which set me apart from the other humans. I had spent my whole life trying to prove to both shifters and humans that I was enough, that I could belong. Now I knew the truth.

I didn't belong.

I wasn't human. I wasn't a shifter, either, not by birthright.

And now this god was staring at me like I was an alien with three heads, and I couldn't blame him.

Jetsun licked his lips like he might speak, and my core throbbed with desire at the flash of his pink tongue between his lips. God, I wanted that tongue. I wanted to suck his plump lower lip between my teeth and bite it. To taste his blood on his tongue. To feel it rasp against mine, his teeth clashing with mine as his tongue plunged into my mouth...

"You have met your True Mate?" Jetsun asked, interrupting my wildly inappropriate thoughts.

"Yes," I said. For some reason, I didn't want him to know I had more than one. I didn't want him to judge me, to think I was a whore like my sister did. I couldn't help the marks on my arm, but I could control what I did. I'd fucked all five of them before I had their marks. I wasn't ashamed of my mates, or even having five mates. But to tell a monk that I regularly fucked five guys seemed disgraceful, nonetheless.

"What about you?" I asked. "Do monks have True Mates?"

"No," Jetsun said. "No one with a True Mate would become a monk."

"How would you find out?" I asked. "To get the mark, don't you have to... Mate?"

Jetsun shook his head. "To become a monk, you have to consult a psychic. A wise woman who can see if you have a True Mate somewhere in the world. If you have one, they don't let you do this. It would be too cruel."

"You can't ever leave the monastery?"

"We could," he said. "But we've chosen to dedicate our lives to this practice. Why would we choose otherwise?"

I thought of Gabor, who had dedicated his life to a different kind of master. I didn't understand either of them. Who would choose a life of lovelessness when there was so much love in the world?

"How did you become a monk?" I asked instead, steering away from the personal. It was hard enough sitting here staring at his erection that never seemed to end. I didn't need to hear about his vow to never use it. Not when I knew how good it would feel to touch it, to slide my fingers down its hot length, to wrap my lips around it and—

"When my father died, I wasn't yet of age," Jetsun said, his words jarring me out of my daze of lust. "The monks took me in. When I turned eighteen, they gave me the choice to leave or stay and become a monk. So, I stayed."

"You never wanted to—"

Fuck me

"—experience the world?" I asked. "Fall in love? Have a family? Play with a bunch of little snow leopard cubs?"

The corner of his mouth quirked up in a genuine smile that sent tingles straight to my swollen pussy lips. Did this man have any idea how positively godlike he looked? How could he waste away sexlessly in a monastery?

"That never interested me," Jetsun said. "I was relieved when I learned I had no True Mate in this world. I never saw the point in love. It seems rather... Silly. Don't you think?"

"Um, no," I said. "It seems to me like love is the point of everything."

Jetsun held up a hand. "I'm sorry," he said quickly. "I didn't mean to offend you. I know you have a True Mate, and that love is deeper than anyone without one can comprehend. Maybe I'd feel differently if I had one. But I don't."

"I never knew True Mates existed until recently," I said. "I grew up as a human. And I still think that boring old human love is the best reason there is for anything."

He shrugged. "I guess I just don't see the purpose. It's complicated, people get hurt, and what good ever came from it?"

"How about the continuation of the species?"

He gave that crooked smile that made my heart flip and other parts of my body do other inappropriate things. Fuck. Why did he have to be my brother? And why didn't my body care?

"No other species requires love to carry on," he said. "I respect your lifestyle. It's just not for me."

I started to argue, then realized how silly that was. Why was I trying to convince this man that love was worth anything, even if it broke your heart, even if it got you killed? He couldn't know that without feeling it. For some reason, a wave of anguish twisted inside me at the thought. He was alone. He'd never know what love was. It seemed a tragedy of heartbreaking weight.

"Tell me about your family," I said, pressing my palms flat on my knees and trying to ignore the pull from between them. If I could just have Kwame here with me, even one time, to ease the chasm of longing inside me...

"I have no family," Jetsun said, shaking his head. "It was just my parents and me, and now it's just me."

"I'm sorry."

"Don't be," he said with a shrug. "It was a long time ago."

"Can I ask what happened?"

"My mother was never well. My father..." He met my eyes and then looked away. "I don't want to color your opinion of him, if you might know him for yourself."

My whole body felt inflamed. I understood the word as I never had before. My body was *in flame*. No, it was a flame. My skin was hot and flushed, misted with sweat. My pulse was racing, and the hunger inside me was tearing at me like an animal.

"Tell me," I groaned. "Make me think about something else."

Jetsun's eyes widened, and his tongue darted out to wet his lips before speaking. I closed my eyes, trying not to burst into flame, to let it consume my body and all the oxygen inside this torture cell and extinguish at last, relieving me of the unbearable panic clawing like Kenosi's cheetah, shredding me from within.

"Okay," Jetsun said quickly. "Okay. Until the suppressant works...

"Yes," I said, squeezing my eyes shut. "Talk to me."

"My father—*our father*—wasn't an evil man, Itzel. I don't want you to think that. He wasn't abusive or violent, he wasn't an addict or a criminal. He just wasn't perfect. I'm not trying to turn you against him before you know him for yourself."

I nodded vigorously, my eyes still squeezed shut. "More."

I heard Jetsun shifting his position, but I couldn't look at him. Not until this wave of heat was gone.

"Our father had a bit of a savior complex. I don't think he consciously wanted *Mai* to be ill. He certainly wasn't responsible. He didn't make her that way or sabotage her attempts to be well. But he was at his best when she was at her worst. He liked taking care of her, of us. He liked that she needed him and that he didn't need us. I think it made him feel powerful, knowing that he could walk away from us and be fine, but we couldn't do the same."

It sounded fucked up, but when I thought of my own imperfect parents, I couldn't say it sounded much worse than my childhood, or probably anyone else's.

"Were you close?" I asked.

"No," he said. "Not with *Babu*. There was always a distance between us. I don't think he meant to let us know, but through the years it became obvious that he'd sacrificed his happiness for us, and that he resented us for it. He'd married Mai because she needed him. And she couldn't care for a child alone, so I became another person who needed him."

"I thought he liked that."

"I think he did," Jetsun said. "But he also resented it. We'd taken his freedom. He was a member of the International Council of Feline Nations, and he'd always traveled to the conferences before Mai came along. She couldn't handle travel, so he stopped doing that when I was young. As I got older, he'd go to them if Mai was in a good place. But if she wasn't, he stayed to take care of us, and he never failed to let us know he was giving that up for us."

"Sounds pretty shitty."

"I've made peace with both of them," he said. "I'm just telling you how it was."

"Did he love your mother?" I asked, forcing myself to look at him and give him my full attention.

"I don't know if Babu loved her, exactly," Jetsun said after a minute of thought. "He loved providing for her. He loved that she needed him. He loved relieving her of the burden of her son for a few hours when she was sick of me."

"I'm sorry," I said, resting a hand against the glass.

This is what I had wanted when I came here. I'd wanted to hear my brother's stories, to bond with him, to know how he'd grown up. Turned out, it was no better than my childhood. If my biological dad was some kind of saint who was the exact opposite of King Ocelot, I might have felt terrible that I'd missed out. It turned out, he was just a man, as flawed and fallible as the rest of us. I liked that Jetsun hadn't lied, hadn't painted him to be the savior of his mother, though it sounded like he could have.

I wasn't exactly happy about growing up as the daughter of a murderous tyrant, but it didn't sound like I'd missed some idyllic childhood, either. King Ocelot hadn't been all bad. I believed he loved my mother in whatever capacity he could. He'd always doted on her possessively, jealously. I remembered plenty of happiness and love in our family, but it was between my mother and her children. Our father had always seemed resentful of the attention Mom showed us, the time she spent with us, and even our presence. He'd always treated us like an annoyance, and then like a commodity.

What I'd seen hadn't been healthy. But maybe that was why I wanted love so badly. I hadn't seen enough of it between my parents, so I wanted to make up for that. Or maybe I hadn't gotten enough of it from my father, so I was making up for it by glutting myself with it now. Why else would I need five men to fulfill my longing for love?

TWENTY-SEVEN

"IT'S NOT WORKING," I SAID, PRESSING MYSELF TO the glass, staring out at Jetsun as he sat cross-legged on a mat in the middle of the floor, apparently meditating. Still hard. God, his cock never quit.

"You can take another one," he said. "But don't take more. I don't know what it would do. It might hurt you."

I hoped it did. I hoped he had to come in and take me out to a doctor, and the doctor could give me what I really needed —dick. There was the truth. I needed to be fucked. Bad.

Now, the thought of some savage snow leopard stealing me off the mountain and trapping me in his lair for a week to be his sex slave sounded like my most delicious fantasy. Anything would be better than this. I swallowed two pills, then hesitated. I was going insane. I had said love was the best feeling in the world, but now I needed something else, something more primal, more simple, than love.

I swallowed another handful of pills, already knowing they wouldn't work. There was something wrong with this heat—or with me. And since I was terrified that it was really me, I had to believe it was the first option. I'd taken too much of the oil inside the tiger amulet. Maybe I was supposed to take only a single drop instead of rubbing the balm all over my throat. That had to be it.

I went back the wall, my heart crushing inside me with the need inside me.

"Do you need me?" Jetsun asked, rising and approaching the glass again. "What do you need? I'll help you any way I can."

I wanted to scream. Yes, I fucking needed him. I needed him to bend me over and fuck me like Tadeu had. That experience had scarred me, but right now, I would have given anything to have Tadeu in this cell with me, fucking me so hard I couldn't breathe, ripping my hair out and ripping me in half as he pounded his impossible cock into me.

"Talk to me," I whispered, pressing my hand to the glass. A fog surrounded my fevered fingers on the cool surface. I wished I could reach through, wrap my arms around Jetsun, who obviously hadn't found as much peace with his parents as he thought he had. I wanted to hold him, to tell him that even if we could never fuck, I still loved him. I loved him for breaking my heart this way, for being so good, for going through this with me and being stronger than I could ever be.

He nodded, swallowing so hard I could see his Adam's apple bob. "Okay."

"I'm sorry about your parents."

"It's alright," he said. "Nobody's perfect."

"You are," I whispered. So perfect it made me want to cry.

"No."

I pressed my forehead to the glass. "He met my mother at one of those conferences. Did you know that? His last one."

"Had they met before?"

He was asking if that's why his dad always went to those conferences. If he'd been a cheater. I couldn't answer the question, but I knew when he'd met my mother.

"No," I whispered, dampness coating my lashes suddenly. Jetsun stilled, but I couldn't look at his face as he put the pieces together, as he realized that his father had strayed from his mom, that my existence was proof of their adultery.

"My mother loved him," Jetsun said. "As much as she could. She needed him."

"I know," I said, a tear slipping from my lashes and down my cheek.

"When he didn't come home, when they told us there had been an accident, she couldn't handle the grief. The weight of life was too much for her. It broke her."

"I'm sorry," I whispered.

Not looking at his face meant I was looking at his body, where his cock was still as hard as my pussy was wet.

And he was my brother, telling me about my father, and about his mother's death. How could our bodies still ache for each other under these circumstances? It was wrong, and yet, I couldn't stop the pulse of lust that shot through me when I saw that his arousal remained.

This was so fucked up. So, I did the only thing I could think to make him hate me, to make him not have to endure the same shame I did for still wanting him.

"It wasn't an accident," I said. "He was my mother's True Mate. She told my father—the man I thought was my father —and he had him killed."

Jetsun didn't speak for a long moment.

"I'm so sorry," I said, pressing my palm harder against the glass, wishing I could reach through it, not because of the heat but to comfort my brother. "I know that isn't enough, but it's what I have. I wish I could change it. I wish they'd never met, that you'd never been left an orphan and raised by monks instead of parents."

"I was sixteen," he said. "They didn't raise me. And I am glad I ended up with them. I've had a good life in the monastery."

"That's a nice way to look at it," I said. "But I understand if you hate me, or at least can't look at me without seeing the product of the affair that killed your dad."

Jetsun shook his head slowly. "No. That wouldn't be fair. It's not your fault. And if they'd never met, you wouldn't exist."

"Would you really be sorry about that?" I asked, closing my eyes and letting my forehead touch the glass again.

"Of course," Jetsun said gently. "But it just reminds me again of what a destructive thing love can be."

"It can be," I admitted. "But not all love is like that. We'll just have to disagree on that. We had very different lives growing up, and that probably shapes what we want now."

Jetsun's eyes trailed up my body, and heat flashed across my skin, hardening my nipples and reminding me of the constant throb of my swollen sex. For a few minutes I'd forgotten, but the relief was short lived. Jetsun's eyes met mine, and he reached out a hand, flattening his palm against the glass. "What do you want now, Princess Itzel?"

You. I want you. My god, do I want you.

"You know what I want," I whispered, pressing my hand to the glass opposite his. We stared into each other's eyes for a long moment.

Then Jetsun turned abruptly and walked away, raking a hand through his thick black hair. He stood at one of the counters staring down at his equipment, his hands fisted on his narrow hips.

I stood alone, fire racing through my veins, pulsing with every heartbeat, aching with a maddening need that couldn't be quenched. I dropped onto my pallet, curling into a ball and pushing my hand between my thighs just to relieve the pressure.

I pressed my fingers harder, biting down on my lip so I wouldn't moan out loud. Heat thrummed through my body, making me want to writhe and scream, tear myself apart with need. I rolled onto my back, sliding my hand down my belly while my other hand slid up, palming my soft breast. My nipples were swollen and sensitive, throbbing when I touched them. I should stop. I knew I should stop, that Jetsun could turn around and see me at any moment. But I couldn't stop. The need had barreled into me, and I was caught in the runaway train of this screaming need, this incinerating heat.

Closing my eyes, I let my head fall back as I slid my hand under the waistband of my pants. The moment my fingers touched my scalding mound, my walls clenched and my swollen clit spasmed with sensitivity. I whimpered aloud and dipped deeper, sinking my fingers into my dripping slit. The sensation was almost excruciating, so intense I couldn't find the line between pleasure and pain. Slick coated my fingers, and I pushed them eagerly into my entrance, a gasping cry escaping my lips at the swell of relief that slammed into me. I pumped my fingers deeper, frantically thrusting them into my hungry opening until my walls clenched around them. I arched up, wanting—needing—something deeper inside me. Wanting a cock to tear me open, to seed my depths and make me scream.

I pictured Jetsun's cock straining inside his pants, and my clit pulsed rapidly against my fingers. I tried to push the thought away, to replace him with Kwame, or Lord Balam, or even Tadeu. But the crest began to recede, and I desperately needed this climax. I needed to release some of the pressure building inside me, as hot as lava inside my volcanic body. Squeezing my eyes tighter, I let the image of Jetsun come back, his smoldering eyes and full lips caressing mine while my fingers became his fingers pumping into me.

Tension gripped me, and waves of pleasure rocked through me. I cried out, letting the tsunami inside me crest, lifting me higher and higher. At last, it came crashing down, washing me under. When it receded, my hand was drenched, and even I could smell it now, something both sweet and salty, like salted caramel. I opened my eyes, reality coming back to me in little jolts.

Jetsun stood against the glass wall, so close his breath fogged in front of his mouth with each exhalation. He was breathing hard, his eyes glazed with lust.

"Did that help?" he asked, flattening both hands on the glass.

My eyes traveled down his body, down to the rigid length of his cock, and heat pulsed between my thighs again. "Not enough," I whispered.

"Do it again."

"What?"

"Take off your clothes first," he said. "Then do it again."

"But…"

"You're the most magnificent creature I've ever seen," he said, his hands pressing so hard against the glass that his palms were white. "I want to see you, Itzel. I want to see every inch of your beautiful body spread out before me."

"No one has to know," I whispered, searching his eyes.

He shook his head, his eyes never leaving mine. "No one."

I DID IT AGAIN, AND AGAIN, AND AGAIN. AT LAST, Jetsun turned and strode away through the dark, dropping onto his bed. He lay on his back, staring at the ceiling. Shame washed over me. I knew it was wrong, but I couldn't stop myself from needing more. Not when he'd been gazing at me with such longing, as if he'd spent his whole life starving, only to see food out of his reach. I was that food. Nothing else in this world could ever sate his thirst. His eyes on me had been agony, but I hadn't wanted to stop.

And oh god, he was my brother. I might not have known him all my life, but he was my blood brother. I wanted to cry with the shame of it, but I couldn't. I couldn't even regret it, not fully. My body didn't care what he was. It wanted him, all of him. My body wanted to do more than I'd done, to be filled with more than my own fingers. With each orgasm, I grew hotter and hotter, until I thought I'd burst into flame. It wasn't enough. Feeding the fire had only made it rage hotter, bigger, until it was consuming me from within.

I pressed my eyes closed and ground the heels of my hands against them, biting back a cry. I was bursting. I couldn't hold it in.

Behind my eyes, blackness bloomed, and I welcomed it. I prayed for it to take me away from my body, away from the ravaging need.

Suddenly, a woman was swimming through the darkness behind my eyelids. At first, I thought it was my mother, but as she emerged from the blackness, I saw a stranger. Her raven hair floated around her, her dress billowing in the swirling, inky darkness.

"Go to him," she said. "You can have him."

"Who are you?"

"I'm Lilith."

"Queen of the Underworld," I said. "Am I dead?"

"You've died and returned to this world. You're a bridge now, too," she said. "Don't forget."

"What are you doing here?" I asked. "Isn't this the human world?"

"I can't stay long in this world," she said. "But I can come across your bridge for a moment."

"Why are you here?"

"You called out to me," she said. "You asked for help. I'm the goddess of love and sex, goddess of fertility and creation. Your anguish brought me here."

"I'm sorry," I said. "I didn't mean to."

"Go to him," she said again. "If you want him enough, you can have him."

"I can't," I groaned. "There's a glass wall between us."

"Glass breaks," she said with a sly smile.

"He's a monk."

"At last he has seen the vision he's waited for his whole life," she said. "He has been in the presence of a true goddess. He will worship you as people have worshipped your kind through the ages."

"He's my brother," I groaned, pressing harder at my eyes, trying to chase away the hallucination.

"The only thing stopping you is your own mind," she said. "Let go of the notion of should and shouldn't, right and wrong, good and evil. All of this and infinitely more exists inside you, child."

"I shouldn't care that he's my brother?"

"Your body knows what it needs. Give it what it desires."

"I'm not strong enough to break the glass. I tried," I admitted.

"You are more powerful than you know," she said. "Go to him. Trust your body. Take what you need."

"I need him," I whispered. "I do."

"Whatever you desire, it is in your reach. You only have to

call it to you. Believe you are worthy. Reach out and pluck the fruit from the tree. It is ripe."

I pulled my hands away from my eyes and stared up into the darkness. There was no woman. There was only me. I was more than ripe. My body was pulsing with erotic electricity. Every heartbeat was a shock racing through my boiling blood, thudding between my thighs with a yearning so deep I could feel it in every fiber of my being. My blood was molten iron. My bones, my marrow, glowed with white-hot energy. It oozed from every pore, slicked my skin, and dripped from my fingertips.

I stood and looked across the room at where Jetsun lay, his arm flung over his eyes. There was no fog of desire. Everything was crystal clear. I no longer felt conflicted or weak. I felt immensely, dangerously powerful. The energy swirled over me in currents I could see now. Strands of shimmering, swirling golden light radiated from me. It all came from the same place and came back to the same place, turning silver and then pure white as it reached my body. The beginning and end, the origin and expiration, the need and fulfillment.

My center. My core. My sex.

It pulsed like a heartbeat, a relentless rhythm like the mouth of a suckling child. Natural. Shameless. Timeless.

I walked to the glass. I could feel my juices sliding down my legs now, pooling around me in shimmering waves of heat and light. It flowed out of me like exquisite, succulent lava, and it wasn't just my secretions. It was magic. *I* was magic. My bones were made of starlight, glowing like the sun had risen inside me. My blood was molten gold. My slick was moonlight. I swam through the starlight, floated through the sparkling sea of gold. I wasn't a river, I was the source of all rivers. I wasn't the the sun, I was the cosmos.

Magic flowed from me like life. Life flowed from me like magic.

Jetsun hadn't moved, but I saw his chest rise and fall with each breath. I saw the torment of his relentless erection. I knew what I had to do. I stepped through the glass and walked toward him.

Twenty-Eight

Gao Jetsun
Demigod, Snow Leopard Nation

I'd fallen asleep eating honey from a jar, and now I was dreaming. I knew I was dreaming because Itzel rose and walked through the wall of glass as if it were made of air. Candlelight flickered off her golden skin, caressing her every ample curve—her glorious, full breasts with their dark nipples, the slope of her waist down to her full, wide hips. My cock throbbed, aching with the strain of staying hard for hours on end.

Itzel's mound was swollen and red, too, and I could smell her wet honey scent from across the room. She walked toward me slowly, as if she, too were caught in the spell of a dream. Her dark eyes shone with desire and love as she stopped above me.

"What are you doing?" she whispered.

I slipped the spoon into my mouth, sucking at the sweet honey before smiling up at her. "I'm eating honey."

"Why?"

"Your sex smells like honey," I said, because it was a dream and I could say those things to my sister. "I'm trying to cover the scent so I don't eat that instead."

Her lips parted, letting out a tiny puff of air. "Eat it," she breathed.

My cock throbbed inside my pants, and my voice came out in a rough, strangled whisper. "Don't do this."

"Do what?" she asked, raising her hands to heft her round breasts. She lifted them, massaging them and squeezing her swollen nipples. A wave of her scent invaded my nostrils, and I plugged my mouth with the spoon again, sucking greedily as her fingers moved lower, gliding over her curves. I wanted my hands where hers were, my tongue flickering over her skin like the warm candlelight. She moaned as her fingers found her swollen mound. A drop clung like nectar to one of the swollen lips, as if she were a ripe fruit that had split, spilling its juices. Her palm kneaded the rounded softness before her fingers spread her dripping lips, revealing the pink slick within. Her knees buckled, and she sank beside me, holding herself open for me.

I sucked in a breath, my cock aching to plunge into that inviting, pink slickness, to be swallowed by the divine grip of her sweet cunt.

Itzel moaned softly as she began to sink her fingers into her sex in a slick rhythm, the soft sucking sounds of her wet flesh clutching her fingers and driving me to the brink of sanity. My mouth watered as I watched another drop of her nectar hang suspended for a quivering moment before dripping from her swollen pussy lips and trickling down her plump thigh, glistening like magic in the candlelight.

"Taste it," I commanded.

Itzel lifted her fingers to her full, pillowy lips and slid them inside. She closed her eyes, her glorious lips pursing around her fingers as she sucked her own juices from her hands. My spoon clattered to the floor, and I scooped the honey from the jar with two fingers, thrusting them into my mouth and sucking greedily.

"Let me taste," Itzel panted, her fingers fucking her forbidden entrance frantically again.

I grabbed another scoop of honey and lifted it to her mouth, sinking my fingers between her plump lips. She moaned and closed her lips around my fingers, and her rough tongue formed around my fingers like the walls of a tight, hungry pussy begging to be fucked until cum flowed from her like a river to hell.

But it was a dream, so I slid my fingers deeper into her hot, wet mouth that sucked so hard that a drop of cum squeezed from my cock. I moaned and slid them deeper, pumping them into the back of her throat and rising to my knees in front of her. I had vowed to live my life in simple worship of the divine living force of the world, and this was her. This was the only body I wanted to worship, the only goddess I would ever know.

Honey dribbled from her lips, strings of it falling over her breasts and down her belly. I moaned and leaned down to capture a drop as it trickled painfully slowly toward her erect nipple. My tongue lashed across her fevered skin, and she moaned around my fingers, plunging her own fingers harder into her cunt.

I slathered the honey across her heavy tits, sucking the sweet stickiness from her nipple, opening my mouth and taking in as much of her flesh as I could. She whimpered and buried her hands in my tangled hair, dampening it with her nectar. The scent of it invaded me again, sending my mind deeper into the fog of lust. I was lost already, too far gone to stop.

But no. I was only sucking her tits, not her pussy. I hadn't touched her sacred, flowing cunt.

"Drink me," she moaned, throwing her head back and opening her knees further as she knelt before me.

"I can't," I rasped against her slick nipple.

She snatched up the honey and dipped her hand in, scooping up a fingerful of honey and burying it in her opening, spreading her lips and smearing it until it mingled with her wetness and dribbled down her spread thighs.

"It's just honey," she whispered, lifting my chin. My eyes locked with hers, a pleading in her wild, dark gaze that tortured my soul. She lay a hand on my chest and pushed me back, and after a second's hesitation, I lay back on the bed, my fingers stealing one brush against her bare thigh.

I was already lost to this dream. I would just taste the honey, drink it as it dripped from her cunt. I didn't have to touch.

She crawled forward and climbed over me, kneeling above my parted lips. I gripped her thighs and opened my mouth, letting the first drop of her sweetness honey my tongue. I saw worlds unfolding, blossoming with one taste. Worlds of endless pleasure, of deep green grasses and flowing streams, and a little girl running with black pigtails bouncing behind her. I lifted my face, my tongue lapping the juices first one thigh and then the other.

"Please," Itzel begged. "Please fuck me. Eat me. Possess me. I'm yours, Jetsun. Body and soul. There's nothing wrong with pleasure."

"Even when it's unnatural, when it leads to madness and death?" I asked, sucking the flesh of her thigh into my mouth so I wouldn't go further, wouldn't give in to the beckoning, begging opening of my sister's hungry, willing cunt.

"Especially then," she said, spreading her knees and lowering herself until she was a breath away from my lips, until I could feel the heat shimmering from her swollen sex that needed to be licked, and sucked, and fucked, and filled with the seed that swelled my balls, aching inside my cock until I nearly cried out for release.

With a groan, I gave in, wrapping my hands around her thighs and jerking her down, burying my face in her. I sucked her, ate her, fucked her with my tongue, letting it extend to its full feline length as she writhed and screamed, riding my face as orgasm after orgasm rocked through her. I could feel her contracting around my tongue, her tight, sweet walls plundered and licked clean as more and more cum flowed from her.

At last, she slid off me, and I fell back, exhausted and ready to fall into a deep sleep, deeper than this sweet dream where I could indulge a little, even if I never fucked her. But Itzel only grabbed my robes, tearing them off in one swift motion, then stripping my pants. For one second, I felt exposed, my swollen cock giving away every secret desire I possessed.

No woman had ever seen me like this. No woman had ever made me like this. Itzel climbed onto me, straddling my face as she took my cock in her hand. Her touch sent a pulse of pure desire through me, and a cry of anguish escaped my lips before she bent forward and slid the head of my cock between her slick lips. She licked the drops of cum from my tip, moaning as I raised my mouth to her opening to drink from her cunt again.

Sucking harder, she ran her tongue around my cock, then sank her mouth onto its length, pumping with her hand as her mouth sucked me off harder and harder. I found the same rhythm with my tongue, plunging it into her as her orgasm built. At last, she came against my lips, crying out around my cock. The sound of her pleasure pushed me over the edge, and I arched up, cum spurting into her mouth. She moaned and lapped it up as it ran down the bulging veins of my cock, still throbbing as it pulsed drops of cum every few seconds.

I sank back, finally satiated even if I hadn't fucked her. Itzel smiled over her shoulder at me, then climbed off and lay down beside me. Our bodies mingled, our limbs tangling and the last flickers of the dying candles shimmering off our golden skin.

"Don't fall asleep," she whispered, running a fingernail gently along my jawline, sending a wonderful shiver of satisfaction through me. "I'm not done."

It's just a dream, I told myself as I drifted off. *It's okay. It was only a dream.*

Twenty-Nine

Itzel
Princess, Ocelot Nation

I PACED THE ROOM WHILE HE SLEPT. I COULDN'T sleep. I needed more. This was stronger even than the jaguar potion, less frantic but deeper, a need that ached in the marrow of my bones and the roots of my teeth. Yes, what Jetsun had done helped, and I knew even that much was wrong. But I needed more than fingers or a tongue inside me. I needed hard cocks and floods of cum.

I stopped pacing and looked at Jetsun sleeping there, his body long and lean and as absolutely perfect as the god he was. The dying candlelight flickered over his golden skin, the soft lines of muscle in his thighs, his chest and abdomen, and the perfect length of his delicious cock. My mouth watered, and the ache between my thighs throbbed painfully as even more wetness pooled there. I had an ocean inside me, enough to keep me wet for every man outside the doors. Maybe I could open them for just a bit, let them in. What did it matter if I knew them? I couldn't remember why it had ever mattered.

I shook my head and pressed the heels of my hands to my eyes. What was I thinking? Was I really desperate enough to open the door and let every snow leopard in the nation gang-bang me at once? With a groan, I sank to my knees on the stone floor.

How did Camila get through this?

I knew she locked herself in a room and only saw female servants. Did she take the pills to suppress the worst of it? Did they work for her? After all, her mother was the same as mine. She must have some of her magic. So how did she resist ordering her maidservant to bring her a man, or every man in the castle? Would it really be so bad to let the snow leopards have at me? It was better than fucking my own brother, even one I'd never met before, one I didn't grow up with or think of in a brotherly way. He wasn't even really a brother, just a half-brother of a dad I'd only just met. It wasn't like he was a brother I'd been raised with, the son of King Ocelot, the man I'd always known as my father.

If only I didn't know...

I pressed my palms against my temples and groaned. What was wrong with me? Was it just the heat, or were my morals really that loose?

No. No, I wouldn't fuck my own brother. There had to be a line somewhere.

I went back to the glass wall, staring at it for a moment. How had I gotten through it? I laid my hand on the thick pane, as if I'd find it all an illusion. But it wasn't an illusion. And Jetsun had thrown the key outside. So how had I walked through it?

I remembered the spirit world, and how I'd simply walked through a wall to find my mother, because that's what I wanted to find. But this was here and real and very solid when I put pressure against it. The last candle sputtered and went out, plunging me into a darkness so complete that even my cat eyes could see nothing. Unsure what to do, I lay down on the floor outside the glass room and ignored the throbbing need growing inside me every moment, growing stronger and stronger, like a wildfire raging out of control, blown onwards by hot, relentless winds.

It had to give. I would wake up, and the fever would have broken in the night.

I dreamed Sir Kenosi was back, that he was fucking me into the bed in the cheetah tower, but the mattress was too hard. I kept telling him to turn me over, but he wouldn't. I woke to the rocks grinding into my back as a stiff cock pounded into me. His honey-tinged breath was hot against my cheeks, his hand hooked under one knee as he drew it up and drove into me with deep, powerful thrusts. His cock was long and full, and each time he drove into me to the hilt, his swollen balls pressed against my ass and his pelvic bone ground against my aching clit.

I cried out in pleasure with each thrust, completely lost to the moment, to the man fucking me in the dark, in my sleep. And then a tiny flicker of consciousness found me, and I remembered. The heat. The glass. My brother.

"No," I cried out, my eyes flying wide in the blind darkness, my palm flattening against his strong chest. "Jetsun, stop. I'm your sister."

He caught my hand and pinned it beside my head, grinding deep and making my clit throb toward climax. "It's just a dream," he whispered.

He caught my other hand and held it down, pumping his cock deep inside me, moaning in pleasure as I struggled for another moment. My body tightened around him as I fought, but I was too slick to put up any resistance. My body wanted this, even if it was wrong in every possible way. Especially then.

"It's just a dream," he whispered again, lowering his beautiful lips to mine. "I'm whoever you want me to be."

His full lips caressed mine, softly at first and then harder, as his cock glided into me effortlessly. Like a dream.

If it was a dream, it wasn't real. My brother wasn't pinning me to the stone floor and fucking me so good I could feel the orgasm slowly building inside me like a tidal wave. His lips weren't caressing mine, teasing them open, his tongue tasting gently while his cock drove hard, grinding me into the ground.

If it was a dream, I could give in. I opened my lips and let his tongue in, let him taste my mouth. Our moans mingled as I arched up, rubbing my clit harder against him. I braced my feet on the floor and raised for every thrust, slamming my hips against his. He gripped my hands and pushed himself up so he had more leverage, pounding into me with bruising force as an orgasm gripped me.

It was like nothing I'd ever experienced, a tsunami instead of a wave. I screamed as he drove his bare cock deeper and deeper inside me. I slammed my body against his with helpless abandon, shredded his lip with my teeth, his hands with my claws. My cheetah was raging to come out, and I wrestled with her as Jetsun swore at my violence, meeting it with his own. He bit at my lip, and the taste of our mingled blood only fueled me. I was wild, possessed as the orgasm ravaged me, wiping out everything in its path.

It went on and on as I screamed and tore at him, and he tore back, snarling and biting and ripping at me as I did him. My claws raked through the skin on his back, and he roared in pain, arching up and driving his cock so deep into me that pain bloomed where he reached my depths, lifting my pleasure on the crest of the wave that never stopped breaking. I screamed, and he roared again, his cock jerking and swelling as hot streams of cum shot into me again and again. At last, I had his seed. His blood ran in rivulets down my hands, my arms, dripping with his sweat onto my chest. Screams of pleasure and horror wracked my body as I came again, and again, and again, until everything went black.

THIRTY

Itzel
Princess, Ocelot Nation

"COME, MY CHILD."

Sight came back to me, and I found myself standing in a room next to a pair of lovers. It was dark, but I could see them locked together in the throes of passion. Her head was thrown back, her eyes closed and her mouth open in a cry of pleasure. Blood trickled down her hands, her arms, her tumbling waves of hair. The man held her, one hand under her back and one braced on the floor. His mouth was painted with her blood.

A pressure on my hand drew my attention to the person who had spoken. It was Lilith.

"What's happening?" I asked, jerking my hand away. Had she tricked me, somehow lured me to fuck Jetsun so that I'd die again?

"It's all right," she said, taking my hand again. "Take a walk with me, child. The world will be just as you left it when you return."

"How?" I asked. "Why are we frozen? Why am I outside my body?"

"You've stopped time."

"I did?"

"Not you alone," she said. "Both of you."

That's when I saw that on the other side of her, his hand clasped in hers, stood Gao Jetsun. Somehow, he was still in the room, his cum hot inside me, and also here outside himself, too.

"This is a rare thing," Lilith said. "It takes great power to stop time. Only two of the most powerful beings in the world can do it by joining as you have."

Jetsun glanced at our entwined bodies, looking both doubtful and utterly freaked out.

"What does that mean?" I demanded. "How am I one of the most powerful beings in the world?"

"I was the first High Priestess," Lilith explained. "The power of creation came from me to every woman on earth. But when I went to the spirit world forever, I gave my power to one woman in the living world. The High Priestess. She carries more power than any other. She's the living embodiment of life, of sex and fertility. The divine feminine, the divine mother."

"My mother," I said.

Lilith shook her head. "Not your mother, Itzel. *You*."

I stared at her, not knowing how to react, how it could even be possible. "What?"

"You, my child," she said. "Each time a High Priestess dies, she passes her power to someone in the living world. Sometimes it is her child, if she has the capacity for great magic like you do. If she's childless, it's someone else with the ability to contain such magic. Your mother's magic didn't follow her to the spirit world. It passed to you."

"But... I'm human."

"And so much more."

"How?" I asked. "If I have this great power, how could I not know?"

"It was locked within you," she said. "It should have been unleashed when you matured, but it seems your caretakers didn't see to it that it was. It has been seeping from you since you discovered your sexuality. Haven't you noticed how easily men fall to their knees for you? Haven't you taken each man you mated as a True Mate? Who else would have such power?"

"I don't even really know what a High Priestess is," I protested.

"It is you," she said, stroking my cheek gently. "The bindings on your magic have been loosening since your first sexual experience. Each time you reach climax, your magic is spent, but it is also recharged even stronger than before. With each lover you've taken, it has grown stronger, and more has been released. You may not have known you had this power, but you have great instincts. You have done exactly what I would have recommended, had I been there to coach you. You have taken many lovers and let them satisfy you often."

I shook my head, backing away. "I... I don't want to be some magical sex goddess who has to drag around a bunch of fuck boys."

Lilith only smiled. "How you handle your magic is up to you. But it's there, whether you chose it or not. When you went into heat, the last of the bindings were broken. Your full power has been realized. You are now the High Priestess of this world, Princess Itzel."

My head was spinning with what she was saying. Lord Balam had said I wasn't human, but I'd never imagined I was someone... Powerful. All those years I'd yearned and ached to be a shifter. Now, that seemed such a small magic.

"But... Tsewang said the High Priestess was a baby..."

"When you died, the power cannot follow you to the underworld," she conceded. "But you were raised from the dead."

"I got the power back?"

"Yes," she said. "And... That child kept some as well. One day, she will take your place."

"What... What does that mean?" I asked. "What do I have to

do? What are my responsibilities? Will people know what I am? Am I like a queen to other priestesses?"

"No one can know who you are," Jetsun said. "It's too dangerous in our world. You'd be exploited for your magic."

I turned to him, a funny twist in my belly. "Did you know?"

"I... Yes." He nodded. "I realized it pretty quickly. The way you drew so many shifters to you so suddenly. The strength of your pheromones. Your effect on me, despite twenty years of discipline and control over my physical urges. Your allure is irresistible, Itzel."

I released Lilith's hand and reached for Jetsun. I wanted to say something meaningful, something profound, but I was too overwhelmed to express anything close to that.

"I'm sorry," was all I managed.

Jetsun hesitated a moment, then slipped his hand into mine. "I would have told you."

"I know."

"Come," Lilith said again, taking my free hand and tugging gently. "When you walk through time in this way, you may change it. What would you like to change? Would you go back and save your mother? Your father? Your True Mate?"

"What are the consequences?" I asked, though my heart swelled at the thought of bringing my mother back. Not as an undead ghost, but as she'd been.

"Does it matter?" Lilith asked. "Just a month would change if you brought back your lover."

"But everything would change," I said. "Everything that's happened since then."

"Is it really so much?" Lilith asked.

Suddenly, we weren't in the dark room anymore. We were standing in a large clearing in the jungle with a helicopter behind us. On the ground at our feet lay a body—not Sir Kenosi's but mine. Sir Kenosi stood over me, along with Shadow and Lord Balam. Sir Kenosi held a beautiful ruby cradled in his palm. A cry of protest caught in my throat. I wanted to tell him no, tell him not to do it.

"Would you save your True Mate from his fate?" Lilith asked. "What if you could have him back?"

"He gave his life to save me," I said, my breath catching.

"Would you give it back?" Lilith asked.

I'd never have met Gao Jetsun. I'd live in the spirit world, knowing that I was his sister but unable to meet him. I'd have known what kind of monster my father really was, but I'd never have the chance to do anything about it. I'd never have seen the heartbreak I'd caused Tadeu. My sister would have gotten the tiger amulet, and she'd be on her way to get the snow leopard amulet, to negotiate it from Jetsun instead of seducing it from her own blood brother.

"But then you'd trade places with him," Jetsun said quietly. "You'd never have left the spirit world."

"I can't undo that," I whispered. "I can't change what I did. I can't let Camila have endured what I did. I can't make my other mates lose me again."

"Very well," Lilith said. "And what about your other True Mate? Would you save him?"

"Who?" I asked, my heart stuttering in my chest. "Who died?"

"This one," she said. She pulled at my hand, and suddenly we were in a brightly lit arena. Sickness rose in my throat. The stands were crowded but eerily silent, the spectators frozen around us, straining forward with fists raised and bloodthirst in their eyes. A tiger stood frozen, its huge head lowered, its striped pelt thick and glowing under the spotlight aimed at the floor. I turned, my heart hammering in my chest, and saw a man halfway shadowed by the tunnel from which he was emerging. His head was held high and proud, defiant against the death he knew was his.

"No," I whispered, my whole body shaking. Tadeu's death had been the most horrific thing I'd ever witnessed. I'd lost my mother, but I hadn't seen it. I'd never been forced to watch something so monstrous, and not merely because it was a gruesome way to die. I'd loved Tadeu. Maybe I always would. He was my first love, and nothing could change that, no matter who he'd become. I could stop it from happening. I could save him, and he'd still love me. We could get married quietly, the way we'd always planned. I would give myself to him, and he would never have to see me with Lord Balam just hours after he'd been killed.

But Lord Balam.

If I saved Tadeu, I'd never have been with Lord Balam. I'd never go on Camila's Amulet Tour, never meet Shadow, never fall in love with his quiet intensity or Lord Balam's unwavering loyalty. I'd never meet Sir Kenosi or save Prince Kwame. I'd never know the true terror of my father's reign, never know he wasn't my father at all. My True Mates would live their lives without meeting the person they were supposed to meet, the companion to their souls.

"It would save him and Sir Kenosi," Lilith said. "You'd have the life you always wanted."

Tears stung my eyes, and I wanted to sink to the ground, to let sorrow overtake me. Because I knew I couldn't do it. I couldn't change this most terrible betrayal. The truth was, I no longer wanted that quiet life. It was no longer enough. And that betrayal might have hurt Tadeu worse than this one. He thought I'd betrayed him before, but he'd been wrong. Now, he was right. I hadn't ordered his execution then. But I wasn't undoing it now. Because choosing him would mean betraying all my other mates. With a sob catching in my throat, I shook my head.

"One more chance," Lilith said. "One more chance to save the ones you love, to change the past."

She tugged at my hand, and together we walked out of the arena and into the street outside the palace, one I'd known all my life. I'd played here, run with human children, kissed the boy I loved, strolled with my sister, ran ahead of my mother yelling for her to come and see something unremarkable to anyone but a child.

"Would you save your mother?" Lilith asked. "The High Priestess of the world, the woman who is the goddess of life itself? Would you give her back her life and relieve yourself of the burden of her magic at the same time?"

We'd reached the palace gardens behind the ocelot palace. Bright sunlight blazed down, and I had to shade my eyes so as not to be blinded. My eyes adjusted, and there was my mother, as beautiful as she'd always been, sitting on a stone bench. My father stood over her, looking younger and thinner, the way he had when she lived.

"How dare you disrespect me like this?" King Ocelot raged, his face red and his eyes blazing gold with his ocelot.

I startled, glancing sideways at Lilith. The world was no longer frozen. I could hear them speak, could see them move. I stumbled, barely catching my balance. I wanted to pitch forward into her arms.

"I assure you, I would do no such thing," my mother said.

"You're right," the king said, seizing her wrist. "You won't. Never again."

"No," I cried, leaping forward.

Strong arms gripped my waist, pulling me back. "If you interfere, you're altering fate," Jetsun said quietly. "Do you really want to do that?"

I choked on a sob, turning to bury my face in his chest. His strong arms circled me, cradling me against him until I got myself under control. When I lifted my face, they'd frozen as I last saw them, with my father standing over my mother, holding her wrist as she stared up at him with fear and surprise.

"Will you stop him?" Lilith asked, turning to me. "Would you bring back your mother?"

If she'd never died, we could have run away. She could have taken us and run back to Gao Tsewang, my real father. She could have raised us as his children instead of King Ocelot's.

"I could have grown up with you," I said to Jetsun. "We could have found your father."

He shook his head. "My father was already dead, Itzel. He died before you were born."

"Right," I said, shaking my head to clear it. Temptation, longing for my mother, had blinded me. There was nothing for us if we left King Ocelot. He would have hunted us down. And my mother had chosen to stay in the spirit world with her True Mate.

"If this happened because I mated with a snow leopard, because the High Priestess and a god came together, did my mother get this chance?" I asked, my throat aching with the words.

"Yes," Lilith said.

"She chose not to erase King Ocelot from her life," I whispered. "She could have gone back in time and never married him."

"Yes."

I nodded, a tear slipping down my cheek. "But she couldn't," I managed. "Because it would have undone Camila from existence."

Her choice had been even more impossible than mine. Yes, I was sacrificing lives by my choice, but not my own. My mother was stronger than I'd ever be. She'd chosen to give Camila life instead of having a life with her True Mate. She hadn't known it at the time, but that decision had cost her own life.

"Should we stop him?" Lilith asked me.

"No," I said, another tear sliding down my cheek. "I can't change the past. What's done is done. My mother chose what she did because it's what she wanted. I honor her decision."

"Then there's nothing for us to do but go back," Lilith said.

I fought back a sob, clutching Jetsun to stay upright. "Do you want to go back and save your father? Or your mom?"

He shook his head. "No. Changing fate is too dangerous."

"If I choose not to change anything, can I make one other request?" I asked.

"You have fathomless powers within you," Lilith said. "The power of life rests in your very being. You can summon life wherever you are. You must learn your magic now, Itzel. Your true powers."

"How do I remove the curse?" I asked. "Do I have that power?"

"A shifter's powers are at their highest during a heat," Lilith said. "You know how to increase it."

"Then I lift the curse," I said, feeling a surge of electricity burning in my chest. I lifted my arms, letting it race up my arms. "The curse is gone," I commanded. "It was laid by the High Priestess, and now it's removed by the same power. Let it never bind anyone's mate to a fate separate from hers."

A bolt of white light shot from both my hands, exploding into the air like a sonic blast high overhead. I gasped as the magic left me in one pulse, leaving me staggering to keep my feet.

"So it is," Lilith said.

When the surge of power left me, I felt both giddy and exhausted. I was glad to have released anyone else from the fate Sir Kenosi had met, but it didn't bring him back. He was still gone. My lover, who had given me life, who had made me a shifter. I could never repay him, even now. Jetsun and Lilith took my hands again, and together we walked out of the garden. The next moment, Lilith was gone, and the Ocelot Kingdom was far away. I was bruised and bleeding on the floor, but there was no pain. I wrapped my arms around Jetsun's strong body, clinging to him as I felt the fullness of my body. I was filled with his seed and finally, finally sated.

"Did that really happen?" I whispered against his cheek. Sweat dripped from his hair onto my face, running down his skin and onto mine, cleansing my body as his cum poured out of me and down my crevice, pooling on the floor under us with the sweat and blood of our bodies.

"It has to be a dream," Jetsun said. "It has to be. We can't have done what we just did. Because all the magic in the world can't change the fact that you're still my little sister."

"Then it's just a dream," I agreed. So I got up and walked through the wall and lay down on the bed, thinking it was odd that I could do it in this world, too, and that it was kinda pointless for Jetsun to lock me up if I could just walk through walls now. Maybe I really was dreaming. Maybe I'd never left the pallet on the floor at all.

Thirty-One

I woke with an unbearable heat pulsing through me. My body ached all over as if I were clutched in the throes of a fever. My skin was slicked with sweat, and the swelling between my thighs craved more. There would never be enough. I needed what had happened with Jetsun to be real, to happen again... Oh, and again and again.

"Jetsun," I whispered. "I need you."

A shattering crash sounded, and shards of glass rained down around me, peppering my scalding skin.

"I can't help myself," he growled, his voice nearer now.

"Come." I opened myself for him, not caring who he was, just knowing that I needed this more than I needed anything. I didn't care if it was a dream as long as it eased the sickening, drowning heat inside me.

Jetsun's hands were rough as he clasped me to him. "I'm sorry," he whispered miserably, pushing his body between my legs. A shot of overwhelming desire wracked my body, and I spread my legs, wrapping them around his hips.

"Fuck me," I breathed, arching up against him. I pushed him back, rolling over on top of him. Grabbing his cock, I positioned it against my slick opening. He groaned as I sank onto him, the relief so great I cried out. I could feel shards of glass piercing into my knees as they braced on the floor, but I relished the pain. I began to move on him, the pressure inside me mounting. I moved faster, but I was too slick, too wet. I needed more friction, more tension.

I needed him to fuck me like Sir Kenosi, my mate who was gone from this world. I needed him to punish me, to make me beg. I would beg for him.

Come to me, I prayed silently, deliriously. Come back to me, Sir Kenosi. Please. I need you to fuck me, too.

Suddenly, Jetsun's hands on my hips shifted, and I could feel them on my shoulders. No, not Jetsun's hands. His hands were still on my hips, and another pair of hands was on my shoulders.

"Kenosi," I cried, my heart clenching. I twisted around, straining to see, but there was nothing but blackness inside our cave.

"I'm here," a deep, familiar voice growled. "Give me back my cheetah."

"Then fuck me," I said, leaning forward over Jetsun. I lifted my hips, and Sir Kenosi's hand wound into my hair, pushing me forward. His body collided with mine, and I arched back against him at the thrill of contact.

"Stay still," he commanded, grabbing my hips. I heard the tinkle of his belt buckle, and then his cock swelled against my entrance where Jetsun filled me.

"Fuck me in the ass," I begged.

"No," he said. "In your cunt."

I gasped as his cock strained against my already full entrance, but he didn't relent. He pushed me down on top of Jetsun, forcing the head of his cock through my opening. I cried out at the strain, but he pushed deeper, growling as he stretched me further than I'd ever been, his cock easing through my slick and pressing tightly to Jetsun's. The sensation was like nothing I'd ever felt, filling me until I thought I'd be torn open.

"Oh god, stop," I cried. "I can't."

"You can," Sir Kenosi said, his voice gentler. "Just relax."

He reached down to wet his fingers in my juices, slathering them on the rest of his cock to slicken it. I began to relax, and he pushed deeper, his cock straining inside me until it reached my depths with Jetsun's.

"Now I fuck you," Kenosi said, tightening his grip on my hair and drawing back. He thrust into me, his cock locked against Jetsun's. I cried out with each thrust as their cocks sank into me together, stretching my walls with unbearable pleasure and pain. Jetsun sat up, wrapping an arm around my back and pressing his bare chest to mine, plunging me down onto their cocks. Kenosi held my hips, adding extra force.

"Come for me, Princess," Sir Kenosi said, reaching around to squeeze my clit. It was so sensitive I cried out, my body jerking and my walls tightening. He thrust his cock up to the hilt inside me, holding me pinned down on him and Jetsun. My walls clenched tighter, too tight for two cocks inside me at once. I screamed as pleasure crashed over me and bursts of light exploded behind my eyes.

I needed my other men, too.

As waves after wave hit me, I couldn't stop the cries tearing from my lips. I screamed for Balam, for Shadow, for Kwame. Even for Tadeu.

"Holy shit," a rasping voice growled. "Is that Itzel's scent?"

"Shadow," I gasped. I couldn't think of more words. I reached for his voice in the dark. "Fuck me."

"What the fuck is going on?" Tadeu's voice demanded.

"Come," I said. "I need you all. Now."

"She needs this," Jetsun agreed. "Do what she asks."

"Who the fuck are you?" Lord Balam asked.

"Does it really matter?" Sir Kenosi asked, sliding out of me, his cock still stiff. "Your mate's in heat and begging you to fuck her."

There was a short pause, and then I felt their hands on me, so many hands I couldn't tell which set belonged to which mate. They were stroking my breasts, pinching my sensitive nipples, smearing my juices over my thighs and belly, moaning with desire. Someone lifted me from Jetsun, and then I was standing in the middle of them, all of them touching me at once. A moment of intense vulnerability flared inside me as I stood exposed, six sets of hands on me and no way to know who each belonged to.

But a wave of lust rushed through me at the idea of being touched by strangers this way. Wetness flooded between my thighs, and one of the men growled in response. I basked in the attention, moaning in pleasure as fingers and palms found their way over every inch of my body. Fingers dipped between my thighs, and I whimpered as he drove them deep into the tenderness there. He withdrew and sucked at his fingers, moaning with pleasure at my taste.

Someone pulled me into his arms, his long hair brushing my cheek. "Shadow," I murmured, squeezing him to me.

"I'm here," he said. "What can I do?"

I wrapped my arms around his neck, and he lifted me off the ground. Twining my legs around his waist, I sank onto his stiff cock.

"Lay me down," I said. "I need them all."

Shadow lowered me to the floor, and I was reminded of the glass around us, but I didn't care if it cut into me. I needed something to relieve the pressure inside my skin, to let out some of the magic filling me until I couldn't take it.

Shadow swore quietly, and I knew he'd felt the glass in his hands and knees. Without a word, he rolled us over, so he was in the glass and I was on top, as I'd been with Jetsun.

"I need you all," I said.

A cock pressed into my hand, and I wrapped my fingers around it, sighing with pleasure as the cold, stiff shaft throbbed at my touch. I brought it to my mouth, tasting his cool skin, inhaling the dry grass and baked earth smell of him. Someone lifted my other hand, placing it on a bigger, rougher cock. Heat shot through me, and I pulled my mouth from Kwame's cock and licked Lord Balam, eliciting a rough growl from his throat. He tasted like rain in the jungle, like my first time, like trust. He kept his hand on mine, stroking it up and down his thick, veined shaft.

"I must have you, my love," Kwame said, his voice choked. "Your scent is making me lose all control."

He pulled away and stepped over me, crouching behind me, and a wave of desire rushed through me.

"Fill me," I moaned. "With Shadow."

Kwame strained against my entrance, and I gasped in pain. "You're too tight," he said. "I can't get it in."

"She can take two at once," Kenosi said. "It's so tight you'll feel like your cock's in a vice, but she can take it."

"I don't care, just do it," I said. "I need you both."

"Yes, my love," Kwame breathed, and then the head of his cock, slick with my juices, breached my entrance. I cried out and reached for Kenosi, wrapping my fingers around his slick shaft. I began to pump his cock while Kwame pushed deeper.

"Jetsun," I gasped. "You, too. Fuck me in the ass."

There was no hesitation this time. We were past that point, past anything but this need driving us all relentlessly forward toward the edge of some precipice I didn't yet understand. Jetsun climbed onto me, pressing the head of his cock to my second entrance. A tremor shimmered through my entire body, and I arched up and spread my legs wider, offering him access. His hand pressed gently on my lower back as he eased in, stretching me to fit his cock. Kwame and Shadow still stretched my pussy so full I thought I'd burst. With all three of them inside me, I could barely keep from coming again.

Kwame began to move first, pumping into my tightness with guttural grunts. Shadow and Jetsun matched his motion, all three of them plunging into me in unison. I cried out, relishing the pain, the rightness. My hands pumped up and down the shafts of my other mates. Only one person was missing.

"Tadeu," I cried. "Come and fill me. I need you, too."

"If it'll shut you up," he growled, but I could hear the tremor of desire in his voice. His tremendous, impossible cock filled my mouth, and I was full and complete at last. I stretched my lips around his enormous girth and moaned with relief at the taste of him, the one I'd always known, like hay and leather with a hint of iron. It was the taste of my sexual awakening, of afternoons in the stable when I'd escaped my tutor and instead spent the hours kneeling before my skillful older lover, taking a different kind of instruction.

He slid his big hands around my head, thrusting into me, fucking my mouth. Behind me, Jetsun's breath was hot on my neck as he leaned over me, his hips pummeling my ass as his cock sank into me while Kwame and Shadow pumped into my pussy. Balam's hand guided mine on his thick cock while his other hand slid under me, squeezing my breast and pinching my nipple until I moaned around Tadeu's cock again. Kenosi thrust into my other hand, his long arm reaching down to grab a handful of my ass, spreading my cheeks for Jetsun to sink to the hilt into my tight ass.

It was so much, too much, but I could feel the completeness of our group, all together in the most intimate way. I couldn't stop them, even when I wanted to scream that I couldn't take it anymore. Tadeu's hand twisted my hair, and he pumped harder, nearly gagging me. Tears leaked down my cheeks as I tried to stop myself from choking as his cock plunged deeper, past my gag reflex. I could feel saliva trickling down my chin, but I didn't stop sucking. Sweat broke out across my forehead, and I could feel their sweat slicking me as they drove into me harder, as if daring me to break first.

But I wouldn't break. I could take them all. I wanted to take them all. I was a vessel meant to be filled. Wetness slicked my flesh, trickling down my thighs as Shadow's hot cock hit all the right places inside me, and Kwame's cold one hit everything else. The strange smell like burnt sugar seeped into my nostrils, and I realized I could see my mates now. The swirls of golden light shimmered around us, as if our group was something holy. It bound us together, forging us into one, as if we were the amulets fitting together at last. It glowed brighter each moment, circling my mates with a kaleidoscope of color.

I felt the magic shimmering inside me, too, rising with each thrust as my mates pumped their power into me faster and faster, in a frantic, frenzied rhythm that was both agony and ecstasy. The dueling sensations overwhelmed me, carrying me higher than I'd ever been. At last, I couldn't hold it inside me. My body shuddered and tightened, clenching around the men as a convulsion of pleasure gripped my body. Roars filled the cave, and teeth clamped down on my shoulder. I screamed, and Tadeu thrust deeper. Everything in my body clenched at once, and hot spurts of cum flooded into me, over me, filling and drowning me, drenching me and cleansing me. Its salty tang flooded my mouth and throat. It flowed over both my hands and down my arms. Jetsun's grip crushed my hip as his cum erupted from his cock as it drove deep inside my ass. Shadow's claws sank into me as he thrust upwards, and Kwame gripped my thighs to hold me in place and drove himself to the hilt at the same time. Together, their cocks throbbed, shooting jets of cum deep inside me, filling my very depths and until I couldn't hold another drop.

Suddenly, bright light shot out of me, filling the entire place with a blinding burst of magic, and I screamed as I came again, and again, and again.

Thirty-Two

A FEW DAYS LATER, I WOKE AND SAT UP WITH A start. My head was clear. My body felt cold, and there was a gaping absence inside me. For the first time in days, my body felt like it was truly mine again. Mine, and sore as fuck, like I'd just run a marathon. The marathon sex for the past week must have done it.

"The heat broke," I blurted. I was lying on a mat in the middle of Jetsun's cavern, candlelight flickering around me.

"We were bound to fuck it all out of you eventually," Sir Kenosi said with a grin, straightening from one of Jetsun's microscopes.

"Don't speak to our queen that way," Kwame said, pushing past him and coming to kneel beside me. Something felt wrong in my body, as if I were forgetting something that I should remember. I looked around, searching for the others.

"Where are they?" I asked, my chest squeezing. That couldn't have been a dream. Kenosi was here, so it must have been real.

"They're all here," Kwame said. "Your heat broke in the night a few days ago, but you needed rest, so we let you sleep."

"A few nights?" I asked, jumping to my feet. Ouch. Maybe it was a good thing I'd slept through a few days of the worst pain. Looking down at myself, I saw a hundred little scratches and cuts. Black and blue bruises covering most of my skin, and I had two bandages on my shoulders. The price I paid for fucking a feline as young and temperamental as Shadow.

"Calm down," Sir Kenosi said. "What's the rush, Princess? You got somewhere important to be?"

"Where are the others?" I asked, glancing around. The room had been cleaned up. No glass or blood or other fluids were apparent, though the glass wall we'd broken was now a gaping hole.

"Gao Jetsun went off with Shadow to teach him meditation," Sir Kenosi said. "It's about time that little panther learned some chill."

"Lord Balam is consulting the oracle," Kwame said. "He's quite upset that it didn't tell him how powerful you are."

"Oh," I said with a little laugh. I searched around for some clothes but found nothing. "Jetsun told you about that, huh?"

"No," Sir Kenosi said with a scowl. "You summoned me from the dead. You summoned all of them from wherever they were. That's a fuck-load of power there, Itzel."

Kwame rubbed his chin. "What are you, exactly?"

So, Jetsun hadn't told them. I was grateful that he'd let me do that myself.

"We'll talk about that," I said. "But first, what about Tadeu? And some clothes."

"There is something we should talk to you about, too," Kwame said.

My stomach knotted, but I managed to stay on my feet. "He left?" I whispered.

"You could probably use a shower," Sir Kenosi said. "There's clothes in the bathroom."

"I'll get the others while you do that," Kwame said, turning for the door. The huge stone was ajar, and daylight streamed in.

Tadeu had left. Was that the hollowness I'd felt when I woke? As I showered, I tried to pull myself together. I still had five mates. *Five.*

I should have been overwhelmed by that. I was happy to have them and to have Sir Kenosi back. But Tadeu should be here, too. He was as much my mate as the rest of them.

When I stepped out of the bathroom dressed in the simple jeans and sweater I'd found waiting for me, I was greeted with the scent of spicy food cooking in the room Jetsun had off the side of his big cavern. I made my way there to find four of my mates sitting at a table while Jetsun stood over the stove, wearing a pair of jeans and a button-up shirt instead of his orange uniform. Tadeu was setting a stack of plates on the table.

"You're here," I said, skidding to a stop in the doorway.

"Don't cream your panties," he said, his face unsmiling and unreadable as he looked up from the table. "I'm not interested in being your mate. I'm only here because you summoned me with your magical heat."

"Oh," I said, swallowing hard. "But you could have left, and you didn't."

"I had nowhere else to go," he said with a shrug. "And I was injured. It took a few days to heal."

"I know this is simple fare," Jetsun interrupted, setting a huge pot of steaming rice and vegetables in the center of the table. "I don't usually have guests."

"It looks amazing," I said, scooting in at the table where Prince Kwame had risen to pull out a chair. "I've never been so hungry in my life."

"Fucking for a week straight will do that to you," Sir Kenosi said, heaping a giant helping onto my plate before serving himself.

"You know, you talk and act like an asshole, but I know

you're a big softie on the inside," I said. "You gave up your life for me."

That's when the ache of emptiness hit me again, and I realized what it was. It wasn't a mate's absence. It was the cheetah's. At first, it had been disconcerting to feel like I shared my body with another being. But now that she was gone—or he? I wasn't sure—the loss ached inside me.

"Maybe I just wanted to see what it was like to fuck a dead girl," Kenosi said, flashing me his movie-star smile. "I've fucked every other type."

I rolled my eyes and turned to the others, changing the subject before digging into my food. "I guess I'm not a shifter anymore."

"You raised people from the dead," Shadow said, eyeing me warily. "Are you a necromancer?" I remembered when I'd tried to catch him, how he'd called me *witchy woman*.

"I've been told I'm the High Priestess," I said. "Whatever that is."

Everyone gaped except for Jetsun and Lord Balam, who nodded. "I thought as much," he said. "I've been circling that for a while, but I didn't think it was possible until the last few days."

"Well, then," Sir Kenosi said, digging into his food. "If anyone here's intimidated by being with a woman stronger than you, now might be a good time to leave."

"If anyone here was intimidated by a woman who's stronger than them, they would have left a long time ago," Lord Balam said, frowning at Kenosi.

"No one can question Itzel's strength," Shadow said. "We just didn't know what magic she possessed."

"Why didn't you think I could be a priestess?" I asked Lord Balam, pausing from shoveling food into my mouth. I felt like I could eat forever.

"The High Priestess role is often passed down in families," he said. "Simply because oftentimes, powerful parents create a powerful child, one who has enough magic to become such a being. But since no one is supposed to know who the High Priestess is, I had no way of knowing that the last one had been your mother. And you told us you were only human, not a witch or even a shifter. I assumed you'd have shown more signs if you were her."

"Apparently my magic was bound," I said. "And it came loose when I came of age, and then completely broke out when I went into heat."

He nodded. "We must not let anyone else find out about this. Only your mates."

"Okay," I said. "I never knew before, so I don't think it'll be hard to hide it now."

"Your magic is unbound now," Sir Kenosi said. "You're pretty much the most powerful being in the entire world, and you've never been trained to control your magic. It'll be really fucking hard to hide."

I looked around at them all, realizing he was right. This wasn't just something to talk about over a meal and go on as if nothing had happened. The last week felt like a dream, but it wasn't. It was real. The life I'd lived up until this point was over. Everything would be different.

"We could stay here," Kwame said. "Until you learn to control it."

Jetsun cleared his throat. "Actually, this all belongs to the monastery. I've broken every vow that I made to them. I am no longer a part of this order."

"Oh my god," I said, dropping my fork and staring at him. But of course he'd forsaken his oaths when we were together. To say nothing of the fact that he was my brother.

Holy fuck. What had we done?

"It's alright," he said quietly. "I was ready for a change."

"So, what now?" I asked. "I'm... Dangerous somehow?"

"Maybe," Lord Balam said.

"Just don't piss her off, and you'll be fine," Sir Kenosi said.

I swallowed hard despite the joking tone in his voice. I'd always been the least dangerous person in my family—practically impotent without magic.

"Speaking of..." Tadeu shifted in his seat. I still couldn't get over what a giant he'd become.

"What?" I asked.

333

He glanced at Kwame. "I was out looking for your sister for the past few days."

I narrowed my eyes. "You're going back to her?"

"Fuck, no," he said. "She shot me in the leg and threw me out of her group."

"She's also the one who ordered your execution," I said, glaring at him. "I guess she wanted to get you out of the way. Away from me. You may not believe it, but I had nothing to do with that."

"I thought you were fucking with my head all that time," he admitted, staring down at his plate.

I pushed my plate away. "Well, I wasn't."

He nodded. "I guess that makes more sense. I was pissed. I didn't think your sister even knew who I was. I didn't see any reason she'd want me dead. She told me you had ordered it, and she showed me you and Balam..."

"I know what she did," I said, lifting a hand to cut him off. "I know she's dangerous. But she's still the heir."

"Tell her why Camila shot you," Shadow growled.

Tadeu nodded. "I objected to her opening the ocelot amulet."

"What?" I breathed, my heart stopping in my chest. Camila didn't want anyone to love her. Not like that. Not in a love potion kind of way. She wanted people to respect and fear her, to serve her. She wanted blind loyalty, and I'd given it all our lives. She'd never wanted a man to fall in love with her, to follow her around like a lovesick puppy, blinded to her faults and even the fact that his love was manufactured by magic.

Then a worse thought entered my mind, and my heart stumbled in my chest. "You're in love with her?" I asked. "Even though we're mates, and I was able to call you here?"

His lips tightened, and he shook his head. "No. She made us swear loyalty to her. Everyone in her hunting party. As if she were forming a rebel group to take out the king."

"That's not possible," I said. "She'd never go against our father."

"I'm just telling you what happened," he said. "Everyone in the group swore loyalty to her under the threat of death. I swore."

I swallowed hard. "You're bound to her?"

Tadeu snorted. "My word means nothing. I broke it five minutes after I swore when I dared to disagree with her. And if you're still worried about it, she dismissed me from her group when she shot me."

"Wait, so she threatened to open the amulet unless everyone swore loyalty? The choice was to swear an oath to be bound to her, or be bound to her as her love slave? That's sick!"

"Shut up for one fucking minute, and I'll tell you," Tadeu said.

Kwame shot up from the table, his eyes blazing. "Don't speak to our mate that way."

"Calm the fuck down, Little Prince," Tadeu said, shaking his head. "Itzel knows how I talk."

"Go on," I said.

"One person in the group refused to swear loyalty to her, and that's when she got out the amulet. He said he was already sworn to something else."

"Gabor," I breathed, gripping the edge of the table.

Tadeu nodded. "She threatened to open the amulet if he didn't swear she came before his other oath. He refused."

My head spun, and I thought I'd be sick. Gabor was in love with my sister. Not because he loved her. I could have dealt with that. But because she'd forced him to fall in love. She'd done the thing my father had done to all those girls. I'd known it was wrong when I found out he was doing that, but I hadn't known them. I knew Gabor. I knew him down to his proud, strong, immovable heart. A heart she had tampered with, tricked, seduced against his will.

That wasn't the only thing Camila had in common with my father. All this time, I'd vowed to get her to the throne so that his reign would end. But hers would be nothing but a continuation of his. She wouldn't listen to me. I wouldn't be an advisor. Father would be her advisor. Together, they would bring twice the terror and evil that he'd brought on his own.

"No," I whispered. "I can't let her take the throne."

"Then let's stop her," Shadow said. He'd pushed me more than anyone else, pushed me to open my eyes and see Camila for what she really was. But I'd refused.

Only now did I realize. She was her father's daughter through and through. She was manipulative and cruel, delighting in the pain of others if it would benefit her, not caring about anyone but herself, not just humans but other ocelots. People, all people, were just pawns to her, pieces in the game of her reign, pieces she could pit against each other the way she had me and Tadeu, playing us both for her advantage.

"It's a little more complicated than that," Kwame said, shifting in his chair.

"It was never simple," I said. "But whatever arises, we'll just have to overcome it. She can't be allowed to rule a country. Not if she'd take away someone's free will when they refuse to bow to her if doing so means betraying their own—and *her* own—country. A queen is never more important than her nation."

I looked around at the six faces around me. No one gasped at my treasonous words. No one said I was getting too big for my britches, or that I was a backstabbing usurper. They all nodded in solemn agreement. My chest tightened with emotion as I looked at my mates. I was the one with a rebel army. There may only be seven of us, but I knew how strong we were.

Shadow, my young, idealistic but volatile panther with pain in his past and conviction in his heart, who could disappear in the time it took to blink.

Lord Balam, my rock, who could read the oracle and never hesitated to do what needed to be done to protect me or seek justice. A man who was highly respected by the king of the second most powerful Feline Nation in the world.

Sir Kenosi, the dirty joker who used rude comments to hide what he truly was—a man who would give his cheetah and even his life to save mine. A man who had used the injustices he'd suffered to make himself stronger and better, who had enough income to fund any army and enough business sense to charm anyone who might oppose him.

Prince Kwame, the dreamer and lover who needed no reason to believe in me but did so with complete confidence because I had restored his life. A bridge between this world and the spirit world, a prince with strong alliances in other Feline Nations, a man who would believe in me and love me even when I couldn't love myself.

And Gao Jetsun, a god who had powers I didn't yet know and a man I barely knew at all, a monk whose beliefs were so opposed to mine. And yet, after what we'd been through, a man I knew shared a bond with me that could never be broken. Now, I just had to start seeing him as a brother, not a lover.

Last, Tadeu sat opposite me, the man I knew best out of all of them, and yet, the man I trusted least. He was a giant of a man with anger and resentment we hadn't yet worked through, who had loved me and hurt me. A man who could dwarf any other fighter, whose anger could fuel him to cause great destruction when aimed at the right target.

We were all bound by what had happened these past few days. They were a fearsome and scrappy, mismatched, broken, and perfect army. And there was one more member of that army.

Me. The High Priestess, the bearer of life-giving magic, the wielder of unknown power. Once I harnessed it, learned to control it, I would be every bit as fearsome and worthy an opponent as my lovers. If I was going to keep Camila from the throne, I'd need it.

Because she was a worthy opponent, too. For so long, I'd let her deceive me. I'd believed she was weak because she wanted me to believe it. Now I knew the truth. She was strong and determined, more cunning than I'd ever be. It might take every one of my men and all my strength to do what needed to be done. But I was ready to do it.

"Okay," I said, nodding. "Let's do it. Let's take down Camila."

Kwame cleared his throat. "There's a slight complication," he said. "When you summoned me here, I was brought with only the clothes on my back."

"We went back to the camp yesterday," Tadeu said. "All your things were gone."

Jetsun set a folded orange cloth on the table and slid it

toward me. "I know it's not much," he said. "But this is for you."

"Holy fuck," I whispered, realization dawning. "Camila has all the other amulets."

READ THE THE FINAL BOOK IN THIS SERIES HERE: https://books2read.com/felineroyals4

Free Bonus

Join the B-Team newsletter to get a bonus, deleted scene from Book 1 in Tadeu's point of view! https://www.subscribepage.com/p5b7l2

You'll also be the first to get future bonus scenes, exclusive content, and news!

www.ingramcontent.com/pod-product-compliance
Lightning Source LLC
Chambersburg PA
CBHW020531020726
47494CB00006B/1714